Use It Up

A Novel

Scott

Award-Winning Author

Wellinger

Use It Up

A Novel

by Scott Wellinger

World Wide Publishing Group

New York   Los Angeles   London   Toronto

For information, address: World Wide Publishing Group.

Jacket design by Jason Goodchild
Jacket photo by Ken Wasolinsky

Printed in the United States of America

10 9 8 7 6 5 4 3 2 1

ISBN: 978-0-9861514-0-8 (Ebook)
ISBN: 978-0-9861514-1-5 (print)

For those who continue to search for, find, and fight for their soulmate. You are inspiring and your lives are well-spent.

Epigraph

"Use it up. Use it all up. Don't save a thing for later."

~ The Tragically Hip

Part One

Past is present, present is past.

1

THEY LOOKED HAPPY.   THEY ALWAYS LOOKED HAPPY in public. Appearances were everything.   Being happy and healthy in the eyes of strangers were the rules well-played.   The façade was to remain impervious to all outside the immediate family. In restaurants. In view of neighbors. In public, full-stop.

The family of five went about business as privately as possible, work and school, all matters within the nest needn't be fodder for outside review. Judging is what they did unto others, the necessary byproduct of being Catholic.   They watched and judged and the ilk, hoping that nobody was doing the same to them.   Not that strangers would have anything in which to judge, It was sacrilege for any Devlin behavior to be the subject of reproach.

On this summer day in 1980, the frolicking about the beach of Cape Cod was a rare respite from the miasmic.   Vacations were as infrequent as the tenure held by the patriarch, Thomas Devlin. Length of employment and pay were thereby necessary to earn one. There hadn't been a reason to cancel the vacation on this particular summer.   A vacation prior to the start of school was invariably planned at the genesis of summer, and just as invariably cancelled because Dad had been fired again.   It was with joyous bewilderment that this getaway was actually going to take place.

Thomas—known as Tommy by all those who didn't refer to him as Dad—had a work history as erratic as his temperament. Tommy was a mechanic who was running out of garages in eastern Massachusetts in which he hadn't been formerly discharged from employ, without the ability to be rehired. There were always reasons for losing his position, none of them included his attitude or performance. Not by his account. The fault rested on anyone and everyone including either of his two boys. Usually his lazy coworkers or his dense bosses, though his sons would bear the repercussions for the world's ineptitude. Tommy took out his every albatross, his every umbrage, on his sons. Jimmy and Henry received the most corporal of maltreatments, often through no fault of their own.

On the occasion when they did deserve reprimand, the penance always outweighed the sin. Words weren't used to articulate the deviance in expected behavior, talk was cheap. Behavior modification was a hands-on business. The beatings drew blood, mangled bone, left both mental and physical scars.

Beatings were handed out to the Irish twins, the Devlin's middle and youngest children, with such frequency that the two boys flinched with every physical interaction. When Tommy wasn't disciplining his offspring, the nuns at Saint Ann's Catholic school filled the intervals. The boys were hit with hands and objects alike, whatever was convenient for the aggressor.

From time to time, Tommy would afford whomever was to take a beating the option to pick between convenient objects with which to be struck. To choose the instrument of their demise. Jimmy would always choose the one with the highest propensity for damage. Ruler or wrench would invariably be the wrench. Why? Because fuck him, that's why.

Women didn't receive such treatment. Women were sacrosanct. Cherubic. Angelic. Even when they weren't. Not that either Tommy's wife, Faith, nor his oldest child, Margo, ever deserved a manhandling. But a man cannot hit a woman, so the odd irritation was deemed one of the boy's fault. Sometimes both. His sons had caused the mood swing, the sarcastic retort, the error in judgement. They had caused the dereliction through one of the their misdeeds, and a correction needed to be administered. Whichever one was closest in proximity to the angered patriarch would suffice.

Margo always felt guilty when one of her deeds, either in perception or in veracity, became the impetus for the licking of wounds. She would always tape, bandage, and apply apologies when one of her younger brothers sustained injury. Which meant she communicated through apologies. She lived with guilt anyway as penance for being brought up a Catholic, but added veriscolor on her soul completed her abject diffidence.

Faith Devlin, formerly Prichard, modeled the behavior for which Margo should emulate. Or so she thought. She excelled at martyrdom. She felt guilt simply for being devout, additionally if there was any public display. Born into original sin, Catholics are always guilty and in a constant state of penance. Faith Devlin took it to another level.

But no such feelings were endured for her boy's beatings. That was how she was raised, being the youngest of thirteen. She watched all eight of her older brothers go through the same rearing. Her role now as a mere Devlin matriarch was to be as flitting as possible and to deflect any wrongdoing where possible, deferring inevitable discipline to Tommy. 'Wait 'til your father gets home' meant a virtual life on death row until the executioner arrived and was apprised of tales of wrongdoing.

Bereft of a meaningful relationship with her own father, Faith often lamented that the connection between Tommy and Margo was peculiar. Their interactions consisted of nothing torrid or prurient, but insalubrious none-the-less. Tommy doted on his daughter not like they were dating, there wasn't a sexual component, though 'daddy's little girl' had been escalated to something a bit more odd.

Onlookers would frequently comment on how well the three children were raised. How polite. How respectful. How in comparison to other children, who were allowed to run amuck in the bystander's estimation, the three Devlin children were a refreshing display. While listening to the strangers pontificate on how well they were being raised, Jimmy and Henry would unfailingly and telepathically attempt to communicate to them, *If you only knew*.

This particular summer in 1980, the weeklong vacation was a welcome interlude of happiness. The weather was as beautiful as the beach. The usual July humidity fended off by the coastal breeze. The packed sand on Cape Cod was powder-soft. The crashing waves effervesced salt into the air. All wounds were healed by briny water and sun. It seemed that all ills had been remanded to the house that they had left behind in Bridgewater, Massachusetts, just fifty miles west. Fifty miles was just out of reach, too far a journey for problems to manage.

Until vacation day number six.

Jimmy was just over ten months older than Henry, who was almost ten years of age that summer. Faith hadn't had any space between pregnancies between '70 and '71, she had no sooner delivered Jimmy when she began expecting Henry.

The two brothers were close in every way, not solely age. They shared rooms and often fate. But human nature dictates that two people can simultaneously be close yet completely different. They were competitive. There was a tinge of jealousy between them. And they would fight. Which of course they had learned how to do first-hand.

While bikini-clad, twelve year old Margo was taking in the rays of the hot sun on the beach with her parents—with lemon in her hair and baby oil on her person—the two boys were having a disagreement in the surf. Faith was also taking in the sun, enjoying the days without housework and meal-planning. Tommy took refuge under an umbrella, the beach addled by too much bikini speckled scenery to ignore. His eyes fixated on every one, shielded by his fake Ray-Bans.

The three were lost in relaxation, the tinny and distorted musical stylings of the Brothers Johnson's *Stomp!* emanated from the portable AM/FM transistor radio nestled onto the shaded blanket.

Nobody was privy to the altercation until the volume of cries from bystanders, pointing out that a boy was drowning in the Atlantic Ocean at the hand of another. The commotion rose above the level of both the volume and the low fidelity in which Quincy Jones hadn't intended.

It didn't take longer than a few breaths or a full measure of Louis Johnson's bass-line for the elder Devlins to realize that the incident and subsequent rabble was created by their offspring. Faith was embarrassed. Tommy was angered. He snapped out of his fanciful notions of pulled bikini strings and beautifully shaped female buttocks and exposed breasts, quickly ascending to his feet. He cleared the distance to the waterline and high-knee'd his way through the soft sand, over the crashing waves, toward his sons.

Jimmy hadn't noticed his own imminent danger, else he would have unhanded his younger brother. Instead, he continued to hold Henry's head under the tumultuous tide, continuing to successfully fend off the waning struggles of his younger sibling.

The one-sided fray was dismembered once Tommy covered the distance. Henry gasped for the air his lungs craved once he was released and his head rose out of the rolling tide. Jimmy just then realizing that the likelihood of his reaching eleven years of age was in peril, a thought not given prior to the confrontation. Jimmy shrunk, awaiting the blows he would receive twenty-fold.

But they didn't come. Not immediately. Not while they were in public. Shouting to be sure, but no violence. People might discern where the violent behavior from the minors had been gleaned. Alternate from what was the immediate want and usual disposition, Tommy dragged his boys from the water to the shore explaining how they always ruin everything. They ruined the vacation, they ruined his entire life.

The Devlins would placidly leave the scene, ashamed of what had occurred. Embarrassed as they packed their belongings on the beach and the walk of shame as they exited it. The day at the beach was over. The vacation was over. But not before a trip to the hospital.

Unencumbered by a calm that a cool-down period would normally afford, Jimmy was beaten within an inch of his life for nearly taking Henry's. Tommy had waited until they were in private. Off the side the road where nobody could intervene or witness.

When asked at the hospital what had caused such carnage, the youngster said what he was told. Excuses had come naturally, an expert at the ripe age of ten. He swam too close to the rocks. Rocks that nearly everyone in the emergency room knew hadn't existed.

2

MR. AND MRS. THOMAS DEVLIN FORMED THEIR family at an incipient and tender age. Not too young for nineteen-sixty-nine, but widely considered too young by today's standards. And it was quite by accident as well. Though in the white suburban sixties you didn't admit to those sorts of things, even if inquired. You just did the right thing. Your duty as bequeathed by elders and church, hoping against hope that people suck at math.

Tommy had been turning wrenches for a local garage while finishing high school, knuckles perpetually caked in grease and blood, when the need to get married presented itself. He would have married her anyway he told himself—she was pretty and good and loyal and mindful—but the plan got bumped up a bit. Plans change. He was nothing if not adaptable. Tommy's old-man had incessantly told him that the quickest way to make God laugh was to announce your plans. That was just one in a long list of nuggets from the sonofabitch that had proven out.

Faith had never been in a romantic relationship, never had a boyfriend, prior to Tommy. She'd never even been alone with a boy that wasn't a sibling. Certainly never kissed a boy on the mouth. Didn't know what second base was other than in Phys-Ed softball. The mere thought of doing any of those sinful things demanded her to kneel, bless herself and be immersed in prayer.

But she made up for lost time midway through her sophomore year of Catholic high school.

She had gone with her father to get the family wagon fixed at Bridgewater Auto Lube and Service, and within a few months she would be in need of a station wagon of her own. Eyes had locked, and the boy who confided that she was the prettiest girl he had ever seen, gave her heart palpitations.

Faith was the youngest in a long line. Her parents old and tired of rearing. The duties were acquiesced to her older siblings who took on the role in name only. They were off doing what teenagers do, too busy to deal with the most junior of the baker's dozen. Forgotten and oft ignored, she fended off naiveté as best she could. The only reason she was with her father on that fateful day was because she preferred a ride over having to walk into town for her volunteer-work at the church social.

Tommy didn't go to the same school. He didn't often go to any school. He found it better to earn a dollar than learn how to earn more of them. He reconnoitered her school which was attached to the Saint Ann's cathedral, a place he had not attended since being confirmed. He had to be sly in his investigation—with nuns and priests swarming in every nook and cranny of the school in the foiled attempt to save virtues —being exposed would prove problematic.

Margo's conception took place under the bleachers in the dark gym while Faith was supposed to be in mass. While Jesus was tee'd up behind the Monsignor who was preaching the good news, Faith was horizontally prostrate under her more immediate savior. It was painful and wonderful and sweaty and salacious and sinful. She would finally have something to offer when in confession, all prior admissions had been vapid.

Faith had accompanied Tommy on a few subsequent dates, nobody within her home had been interested in the new gentleman caller. Not a person therein so much as noticed her absence on the

16

nights she was out. Nor her morning sickness. Nor her weight gain. She didn't have to convince anyone that her hymen was intact, thankfully, as that would have added another sin. Night after night she would lie under tommy who pumped himself into her loins in the backseat of his 1976 Cadillac Sixty Special, neither party aware the job had already been accomplished. The steamy windows, the perspiration soaked Medici crushed velour, the tangled hair and clothing were facets that Faith was all too eager to accommodate. The attention quenched her desire. The sweet sound of panted breath around the words, "You're so pretty," fulfilled a previously unrecognized need.

The two had known of the other's existence for no more than six weeks when Faith's lack of monthly blood required both explanation and confession. She told no one but the man who put her into the circumstance, who seemed surprised but not shocked.

Tommy had been with other girls. He knew enough that he was Faith's first, as he had taken other's virginity as well. He knew what virgins felt like, what they acted like. Was it simply bad luck that this one got pregnant? That was the one thing he didn't know.

The archaic ritual of asking for blessing came without fetter or question of veracity. If either her mother or father had an inkling as to the swiftness of the nuptials, neither of the Prichards inquired. Faith was given away without negotiation, nothing as primitive as livestock exchanged, nor did Tommy make any promise of their daughter's life as a Devlin.

The Catholic ceremony took place within two months of the station wagon's repair. The only other soul privy to the knowledge of another life produced from the union was the Monsignor—having taken Faith's confession—who insisted upon an immediate union. The high priest wouldn't compound the sin by lying, he would prevaricate by omission. The community wouldn't be aware of the subterfuge. Catholics believe in the parting of seas, of an ark, of Adam and Eve, of water turning into wine. They would also believe in eternal love at first sight, of immediate fruits of that passion, and the impossibility that this union could end badly.

The procurement of an apartment took place in lieu of honeymoon, a dwelling that could only be described as shitty. It was one bedroom—one room period if you didn't include the bathroom—located in the same town of Bridgewater, Massachusetts. And in that bedroom is where all future offspring bearing the name Devlin were conceived. Margo too young to be sentient of the ongoings from her crib, as was Jimmy in late 1970, or Henry in mid 1971.

It wasn't until the passing of Tommy's father, the last of the elder Devlins, that they were able to move from the one room shit-hole to an actual house. The fishing cottage on nearby Carver Pond was bequeathed to Tommy, who used it as collateral on the purchase of a home just three miles from the apartment. The cottage wasn't much, its value derived from the property it sat on. Waterfront property was and is to this day a premium no matter what shack is set upon it. The bank gave them a mortgage they could hardly afford based upon the value of said shack.

Margo finally had her own room at age five, and the boys would share another. Faith had her own room as well, as Tommy was home just long enough to administer beatings then off to the camp according to his accounts.

While the boys wrestled for a corner of their shared space, Margo was able to paint hers any color she wanted. Pink of course.

When Tommy wasn't turning wrenches, he was looking for a new place to do so. Outside of those activities, he was disciplining his boys or doting on his baby girl or at the camp that was shoemakered together by his father.

Faith was yet again ignored, left to devise formulae for raising children, all the while praying to God for the strength.

THE RUSTLING AND MUFFLED CLANGS OF KITCHEN accoutrements awoke Henry. The eight year old snapped out of deep slumber, searching about his room as he blinked the sleep from his eyes, finding Jimmy snoring along the other wall in his bed. He felt around his own bedding blindly, finally realizing that his dog was missing from his usual spot on top of the covers.

Henry threw the thick blankets off of him, leaving his bed and shared room in his red, footed pajamas. He padded down the hall, the clock on the wall in the den said four-oh-three when he was able to get his eyes focused in the seemingly bright light. Darkness blanketed the outside, an absence of any light negated sight through the living room window. Though it was winter, he knew the time on the clock wasn't indicating afternoon. The fog of sleep was waning. He looked further around the small house. His dog wasn't underfoot. The winter air outside was being fought off by the fireplace, the hot coals were losing the battle. In the kitchen he found his father packing some food into a cooler and his dog, Fonzie, wagging tail by his ankles.

"What's going on Dad?"

"Takin' Fonzie ice-fishin'."

"At camp? Can I come?"

"You've got school, don'tcha?"

"I can skip. It's easy anyway. I won't miss anything. Please?"

"Quiet or you'll wake your sister."

"I'll have Jimmy or one of my friends write down the assignments, I'll do all the work when we get back."

"What did I say? Did you hear what I said? The answer is NO. Now go back to sleep or you'll wish you'd never left your bed."

"Why are you taking Fonz? You never take him fishing," Henry said.

CRACK! The back of Tommy's hand sounded like a whip and felt about the same to Henry. Tommy had turned, struck his son and spun back to the mundane task of packing sustenance before Henry knew which way was up. The blow nearly knocked him off his feet, his cheek immediately turning red. Henry knew not to cry, that would only make his father more angry and worthy of something to actually cry about.

"I'm tired of repeating myself. Get back in bed while you still have the ability to go yourself."

Henry slowly turned to do as he was told, eyes filled with tears but none dared leak.

His father commented further before he'd left the kitchen.

"Not that I have to explain myself to you, but since you don't do anything with the mutt, I guess I have to."

"What do you mean, Dad? I do stuff with him all the time."

Tommy took a step toward his son. Henry wisely ran, knowing to retreat to the safety of his room. He was fortunate that this particular time, his father didn't follow. Henry could only assume that the reason for the pardon was that an early morning beating would likely be loud and wake his prize daughter from her unneeded beauty sleep.

But Henry couldn't go back to sleep no matter the effort. Couldn't think of anything else all day. Not while he made ready for school, not on the bus ride to Saint Ann's. Not while his friends goaded him into playing tag, nor while his teachers unsuccessfully dealt instruction on the various lessons of the day. Not even during the always fun and spirited game of duck-duck-goose in Phys-Ed. All he could think about were the events of that morning.

He loved to fish, as most boys who grew up near a pond did. Of course he wanted to go to the fishing cabin that his unknown Grampa had built. Of course he was disappointed that his father had said that he couldn't go. But that wasn't what festered in his mind. Time with his father, even when they were doing something fun, inevitably meant the greater likelihood that something would cause an annoyance. That annoyance would manifest into injuries both major and minor depending on the severity of that irritant. What bothered him was that his father had taken Fonzie, and his father hated his dog.

The neighbor to the left of Devlin house on Mallor Street had needed to rid of puppies a few years prior. The litter was the result of a curbside romance, one that hadn't continued once precautions had taken place to avoid the female from getting loose again in the future. But the damage had been done, and puppies needed to be parsed out free of charge in the hopes that the price would incline quick sale. Faith had been blindsided by Henry when he first saw the black puppy with a small tuft of pure white on the chest. She relented without consultation and the dog had the name Fonzie—after Henry's favorite television show—by the time he was carried around to the other side of the fence.

Henry took the dog everywhere. Except school of course, and only because dogs weren't allowed at school, even if tied-up outside. Nor were canines allowed at church, though for Henry the two shared the same location.

Tommy made no secret of his animosity toward the mutt. Then again, the patriarch made no secret of any of his feelings so far as Henry could tell. The situation was tolerable so long as The Fonz wasn't underfoot. And for three years Henry made sure that he hadn't been.

But in late 1978 and early 79 Tommy was out of work. Again. It happened every few years, at minimum. Sometimes multiple lapses in

21

employment occurred in the same year. In this latest bout of unemployment, and while Henry was at school, the dog was a constant source of frustration. A vexation that both Henry and his dog had sustained multiple beatings for.

So why then was his father making nice? Why was he voluntarily taking the dog fishing? It confounded Henry, and even at eight years old there wasn't much common knowledge that confounded Henry. A lethally quick study at all that he experienced. A memory near eidetic. But this was different. Whatever his father's motivation, Henry could not summon or fathom.

The day took a year to unfold. On normal occasions, any excuse was a good one to stay after school, stay away from home until supper. Henry would even stay on the playground for after-school catch-and-kiss with the girls if desperate enough.

He and his brother Jimmy were always outside, even in the dead of winter. There were no video games, nor a television in every room. Neither tablets nor smartphones had been invented yet. In those days you were outside playing—in the street or yard—or at school on the church playground or playing one sport or another. Not at home. Not inside anyway. The Devlin boys had additional reasons for staying at bay.

But not on this day. Henry raced home, deciding to not wait for the bus to pick him up.

He hoped that he was worried for nothing. That the two had carried on like new best friends. Dogs have the ability to give unconditional and sometimes unrequited love, the reverse was not true with his dad. Fonzie had always tried his best to win over his father, an effort the canine was often kicked for. But maybe Fonzie's efforts had been rewarded on that day. A new leaf or something. Maybe the only questions that should be racing through his mind were how many perch had been caught and how they would be prepared that evening. Any preparation was good as long as tartar sauce was available.

But when he got home, there was no dog. No father to gingerly make inquiries to. Fonzie was still fishing with his father. His mother was home alone, as per usual, who offered nothing in purpose of solving the equation. She was too busy cleaning. Please go outside, she asked, she needn't another mess to clean. And so he waited. And waited. He did so in his room, despite his mother's request, alone.

He wasn't doing any of the three possible things to do in his room in those days. He wasn't sleeping—who could sleep at a time like this? He wasn't praying—though he thought maybe that he ought to be. He wasn't doing his homework—which he could easily accomplish on the bus ride into school in the morning once his dog was safely home.

Thirty minutes before the usual supper time, the car pulled into the driveway, the front door subsequently opened producing Henry's father. Sans Fonzie.

Caution went to the wind. Henry stood before his father, confirmation that his fears were for good reason.

"Where's Fonzie?" Tears continued to wet his cheeks, his lower lip quivering, no matter how much he tried to remain strong. He would get a beating, but it would be worth it to finally know where his best friend was.

"Gone," Tommy said as he took off his boots without looking at his son.

"Gone *where*?"

"You'll watch your tone or your day will get a damn-sight worse."

"How could it? Where's Fonzie?"

"I gave him away. You never took care of that dog, so he's in a new home. A better home on a farm. He can run and play now."

"You gave him away? To whom? Where is he? I'm going to get him," Henry said without mind to his words or tone. He went toward the front door in order to put on his snowsuit and moon boots.

23

Tommy lifted the boy up and threw him back in the direction from which he came. Henry landed on his back, continuing to slide on the hardwood away from his father. The wall on the far side of the hallway stopped him abruptly.

"You'll forget about that goddamned dog," Tommy yelled. "He's on a farm and happy. He's forgotten about you I can guarantee ya that. Now get outta my sight before I make it impossible for you to remember anything."

The knock to the back of the head, and sharp pain up Henry's spine brought back the realization that more was at stake than his dog. If he proceeded confronting his father as he had, a trip to the hospital or worse would be the icing on the cake. His determination remained strong, though the method would take restraint and tact. Henry decided to wait for his father to pass, invariably to make way to the kitchen with his cooler. Henry remained where he was on the floor, his father stopped to address him from above.

Tommy looked down at Henry and said, "I'll tell you like my old-man told me. 'The world don't end until you're dead. Until then you got plenty more punishment in store. Take it like a man.'" Then he went to the kitchen.

Henry picked himself off the floor, got dressed for the weather and went out into it.

As the door was about to close behind him, Henry heard his mother call to him.

"Don't go too far. Supper's almost ready."

Who can eat at a time like this, lady?

Henry decided he was going to go look for his dog. He would knock on doors, interrogate as many people as possible. But he would find his dog. His best friend.

Jimmy was out in front of the house with his friends playing street hockey. The play was already paused for an oncoming car when Henry showed himself.

"Sorry Henry," Jimmy offered.

"What do you know about it?" Henry's tears, in his father's absence were free-flowing and beginning to freeze on his cheeks in the cold air.

"Fonzie is gone. I know. I saw."

"You saw him give the dog to some farmer? Where is he? Why didn't you stop him? How? Weren't you at school today?"

"I skipped. Me and the guys were playin' hockey on the pond. Saw the whole thing. He didn't give Fonzie to any farmer, Henry."

The rest of Jimmy's friends—and to a much lesser extent Henry's since they were about the same age—were all leaning on their sticks taking in the conversation. It seemed to Henry that they had already been informed about the situation, or had seen it first-hand, meaning that he was the last to know about the location of his own dog.

"What do you mean? What happened?" Henry was almost too afraid to ask.

"He fuckin' drowned him Henry. Cut a couple of holes with the auger, chipped the ice between and sent Fonz down under the ice head-first. If Fonz came back up above the hole, he got poked with the chipper. Poor fucker drowned under the ice. Or froze to death. Either way ...."

"You're lying! Take it back!" Henry closed the gap between he and his brother, gave him a hard push which did little more than move him backward. "Take it back!"

"Nothin' to take back. It happened." Jimmy turned to his friends behind him. "They'll tell ya. We was all there."

"Why didn't you stop him, Jimmy? Why didn't any of you stop him? How could you just watch?"

25

"And end up in the hole behind him? Nothin' we coulda done, Henry. I'm real sorry. For real. I know I mess with ya, but I wouldn't lie about this. I know how much you liked that dog. Hell, I liked the dog. We all did. Right guys?"

They all chimed in their own versions of "Yeah" and "cool dog."

"I'm gonna kill him," Henry said. The thin layer of ice on his face from his tears cracked as he spoke. "I swear to all of you that I'm gonna kill that sonofabitch. God as my witness. And I think He'll forgive me, cause He doesn't want him either."

JIMMY WAS OLDER THAN HENRY BY THE NARROWEST OF margins, but one grade difference was a chasm the younger brother was not cool enough to hurdle. Henry was the youngest in his family and when he wasn't tormented by corporal punishment at home, or to a lesser degree at school by nuns, he was enduring all but what would kill him from his brother. The teasing and practical jokes were more or less incessant. Teenage years are tough enough without the added strain of torment.

Adolescents struggle with finding a place within a society by aligning themselves in their immediate pack, the process is a test of confidence. How can one build self-confidence when any thought or action deemed outside of acceptability is punished with the most immediate and harshest of consequences?

Henry was fifteen years of age and in the throws of the stress and strain. If adolescence was the cake, his home-life was the icing.

The fall of 1986 came with the usual struggles, the usual falling of the leaves, the usual cool days and frosty New England nights. Homecoming and school rivalries renewed. A new school year, yet the same old cliques. The same nuns and teachers, the same priests looking to persuade young boys into vocation. But something was different about that autumn. Or rather, someone was different.

Katherine Bradar had lived at the bottom of Mallor Street, less than a dozen doors away from Henry Devlin, for as long he could remember. But he had never noticed her before, had not yet been taken by her demure beauty and charm. He often wondered if the same were true for her in those days. Had she just noticed him, or was he still invisible to her? She was in his class, his neighborhood, and his mind since day one of freshman year.

Henry would often be lost in thought, staring at her in class, when invariably a nun would call upon him. Prevarication was futile, he was caught in every instance. Nuns could be cruel that way. They were vowed to celibacy and made mission to pass on their frustrations in the name of virtue. The Catholic way of teaching was always the buzzer over the bell. That which didn't kill you, made you smarter. Given his grades in school, one would think that respite from embarrassment would be granted. But it was not the case. Humiliation was sustained when he didn't come out of his Katherine-Fog in split-second timing. The pause making it obvious to everyone in the room that the Devlin kid was caught daydreaming, though he still came up with the correct answers on the spot in every instance.

Henry's daydreaming that year invariably involved Katherine's fawn-colored hair, her stark beauty, her thin and blossoming frame. He would get lost in her features every time. He had memorized every cell of her, and was awed by every one.

It wasn't his fault, he continually told himself. Henry was always distracted, even prior to noticing Katherine Bradar. Henry was smart, with a near eidetic memory, ergo learning was quite easy for him. School was boring and various distractions were welcomed. Homework was accomplished quickly on the bus-ride to or from school, along with the cheaters who were looking for correct answers.

Katherine was neither easy nor boring to him. In studying her, he was never distracted. Every subtle curve, every nuance became a fantastic journey for which he longed to explore.

The day came when he finally mustered the courage to speak to her. What came out of his mouth was likely the same exact phrase

28

uttered by the first hominid who attempted communicating a primitive thought to his fellow ape. Clubbing Katherine on the head and dragging her to his den was not an option, nor had it been acceptable for thousands of years. He nearly aborted the mission after trying to regain some sense of dignity, retreating to lick his wounds, but she was kind and saved him. She did her best to put him at ease. She told him to call her 'Kat' and suggested that maybe he could take her to a movie. He agreed and thought her not only beautiful, but brilliant as well. A movie would mean less opportunity for speaking, less chance of him reinserting his foot into his mouth.

Henry could think of nothing else for the rest of the week leading up to the Friday night date. He played out what would happen hundreds of times in his mind. Every scenario led to him making a complete ass of himself, which would then be communicated to the rest of the school. The Monday after was going to be a fresh hell.

In an effort to thwart his inevitable embarrassment, Henry made the mistake of consulting Jimmy, who taunted him rather than come to his aid. His brother played with him like a cat who would eventually kill the damned mouse whenever toying with his prey became tedious.

But Henry pressed on, seeking out advice from his mother, who was ever playing a mousy game of her own. She warned about getting too close, about being a gentleman, about 'keeping his out of hers'. That was the sum total of their discussions on the premise of sex. In other words, she was of no use.

Margo made him still more nervous, if that was possible. His older sister listed off all of the things that he shouldn't do, so many that Henry was unsure of what was possibly left that he *could* do. Though she did help him get ready for the date. She helped him dress the part, even if there was little confidence that Henry would actually pull off the occasion. If nothing else, she helped keep Jimmy at bay while Henry tied

29

up the bathroom when it became date night. Margo even walked with him to the Bradar door so she could give him some final tips.

"Are you gonna get her some popcorn?"

"Of course," he replied with a role of his eyes. The sidewalks were narrow so they walked shoulder to shoulder down Mallor Street. He made sure to bring plenty of lawn-mowing and snow-shoveling money he had saved over time. Henry wanted to make sure that if Kat wanted something, he would be able to pay for it.

Margo embraced the hugging of trees, feminism, the tie dyed Kurta, and patchouli oil since her early teens. She wasn't an activist, but she did consider herself to be a free-spirit and free-thinker.

"Does she even like popcorn?"

"Who doesn't like popcorn, Margo?"

"You shouldn't assume and just order for her. Maybe she likes Jujyfruits. The trick is to open doors and do all the things that men are supposed to do, but still give a girl respect like she's your equal."

"So I'll get her some Jujyfruits. I feel like there is more than enough pressure on me already where solving the hurdles of the feminist movement might be a little too much meat on my plate. I'm only fifteen. You do get that, right?"

"That's a solid point, sorry. Anyway, just don't act so nervous. You're sweating through your shirt," Margo pointed at his moisture stains.

"Would that I could, Sis. But I can't help it, I'm terrified."

"Duh. You're like a dog in the presence of a vacuum."

"Very helpful, thank you."

"She's probably just as nervous as you are."

"I highly doubt that, but I hope so. Do you think I can go to the door by myself?"

They had covered the twelve-door distance from Devlin to Bradar residence quickly.

"Yeah. Of course. Good luck."

"Thanks, I'm gonna need it."

"Just don't be a dick and you'll be fine."

"Sage advice, I'll keep that in mind."

Henry and Kat could have easily walked to the movie theatre. It was less than two miles away, but Kat's father insisted upon giving them a ride. Henry immediately recognized the difference between Kat's father and his own. Mr. Bradar was soft spoken, if and when he had something to say. When he did speak, he asked questions and seemed genuinely interested in the answers. It definitely didn't seem like he was going to beat on Henry if he said or did something wrong. Nevertheless, he still vowed not to take the chance.

"You can call me Stephen," Mr. Bradar said. But Henry couldn't. He was too afraid. Afraid that if he called an adult by their given name, his father would jump out of hiding and break his neck. It was always Mister or Missus or nothing at all.

When they were dropped off in front of the theatre, Mr. Bradar pointed out the payphone and instructed his daughter to call home when the movie was finished. He even offered to give Henry a few dollars for the movie and the quarter for the phone, but he didn't take it. He of course wanted to, but again if anybody were to leak the information to his parents, Henry would suffer the wrath of Tommy Devlin.

Henry paid for the tickets to The Karate Kid Part 2 and they got in the line for concessions. He really wanted to see Top Gun, but that wasn't what Kat wanted to see. He had a feeling he wasn't going to be concentrating on the movie anyway.

"Is this you're first date, Henry?"

"Yeah. Is it that obvious?"

"Kinda. But it's cute."

His face felt as though he was getting a sunburn. "Is it yours?"

31

"No," she said. "But it's only my second. I don't get around like that."

"No, of course not. So what are you gonna get?"

"Do you want to share a popcorn?"

Henry smiled. *See Margo? Popcorn.* "Extra butter okay?"

"As long as I have some soda."

It was their turn in the line, Henry ordered two Cokes and a big popcorn with enough butter to coagulate the arteries of an elephant. He paid and the burgeoning couple made way into the depths of the theatre. She picked seats nearly dead center of the middle row.

Henry loved the way she looked at him. He loved the way she daintily sipped through her straw. He loved the way she chewed. She could have been given to flatulence and he'd not thought any less of her. She was as perfect as she was timidly intimidating. He couldn't wait for the movie to start. For the theatre to go dark. He prayed that he had the nerve to kiss her when it did.

But he didn't. The previews where finished, the opening credits were running through the opening scenes of the movie, and he still hadn't so much as reached in her direction. Henry didn't even go after a handful of popcorn while Kat's hand was in the bucket.

Kat eventually took charge. She held his hand until it was too sweaty. She whispered in his right ear for him to relax. But he couldn't. Finally she leaned in and kissed him.

"See? That wasn't so bad. Nothing to be nervous about," she whispered.

Henry went in for another kiss, hoping to do better the second time. It felt amazing, as if her mouth was formed specifically to fit his.

"This isn't my first time seeing this movie either," she confessed. "I saw it at the end of summer of break."

"Did you want to go to a different movie? I thought you said—"

32

"—I wanted to see this movie because I've already seen this movie. So we could do this? I thought you were supposed to be wicked smart?"

"I'm a little lightheaded right now."

Kat laughed in a way that made Henry melt like the faux butter on his popcorn.

The two were too busy making out to notice that Jimmy and his friends had snuck into the theatre, into the seats just behind them.

Jimmy had known about the date, of course. Henry couldn't talk about anything else in the days leading up to the event. He knew about the plan to take her to a movie. And he knew it would be fun to watch. His brother's struggle would be too delicious to ignore. Involvement in adding torment was more excitement than Jimmy could forgo.

Though they were so close in age, the two brothers were entirely different. Henry was shy and polite and smart and sensitive. Jimmy sought out trouble, rejected authority, skipped school, and was brash.

Jimmy invited his friends to come along for the fun. They hadn't made a plan of what exactly they were going to do, but they knew that they were going to do something to Henry. When they saw him with the cute young girl, how awkward and nervous he was, they formulated a strategy.

When the movie started, and the two lovebirds began to kiss, Jimmy headed to the lobby to get the manager.

"Two kids are having sex in the middle of the theatre," Jimmy told him. "I'm a devout Catholic and I find that behavior offensive. I can't concentrate on the movie with that going on. I paid to enjoy the Karate Kid, not see some sex show. What kind of place are you running? Wait until my parents hear about this."

The twenty-something manager apologized and informed Jimmy that he would take care of it immediately. No need to get parents involved.

When Jimmy left his seat to get the manager, his friends gave him a few minutes before they enacted the second facet of operation humiliation.

Derek, Jimmy's best friend in the group of miscreants, waited until just the right moment to reach around Henry's left, pouring his small carton of milk from the concession stand onto Henry's lap.

Henry shot to his feet while Derek and the rest of Jimmy's friends started laughing hysterically, quickly leaving their seats and exiting the theatre.

By this time, the manager had arrived on the scene, asking the two lovebirds who were disrupting the movie to accompany him to the lobby.

Henry was completely humiliated. He was being pointed at and laughed at and yelled at simultaneously in the lobby. It was Friday night, the theatre was packed with kids of all ages, some with parents, some with dates. The white liquid on his crotch was not what it looked like, he tried to say. But the words wouldn't leave his lips. A crowd had formed. Adolescents from both Henry's school and Bridgewater Public were laughing, adding to the humiliation.

Kat couldn't take anymore.

"I'm gonna call my dad to come pick me up," she said as she walked away.

"Wait I'll come—"

"—I don't think so," she said.

34

Jimmy shouted from the group he had amassed. "Didn't you already cum?"

The lobby erupted with laughter.

"I'm gonna fucking kill you Jimmy."

Henry crossed the lobby and began to beat his brother with the strength of ten before anyone was able to intercede.

As he was being pulled off of his brother, Henry yelled, "I'm not through with you Jimmy. I know where you sleep."

5

THE DEVLIN BOYS FIGHTING IN PUBLIC WOULD normally have caused even greater discourse and violence once retreated to the confines of home on Mallor Street. But Tommy Devlin wasn't around much in those days. He hadn't since the winter of '84, two years prior. His father was only around for dinner and to administer beatings, which left a lot of room.

Henry silently assumed that his father was working odd hours or at the camp on Carver Pond, which needed a ton of work done to it, at twenty years old it was falling apart. He hadn't asked either Jimmy or Margo their take, hadn't even thought to. Tommy's absence didn't make Henry's heart grow fonder. In fact, it kept the lion's share of the bruises at bay. Temporarily. When the senior Devlin did show up for supper, he would make inquiries as to which of his shitty sons needed reprimand. Once informed, he would either make leave or make up for lost time depending on news of malfeasance.

Ignorance was bliss-like until the winter of 1984. Henry had come home from school to a house filled with yelling and screaming. It could be heard from outside even though the house was completely closed up. The house was a bear to keep warm so extra panes of windows were installed inside, known to those who owned supremely modest homes like the Devlins as 'storm-windows'. Additionally, towels and blankets and weatherstripping was plied to every conceivable crack or crevice to keep the weather out. And yet the muffled yelling could be heard from the driveway.

Henry knew something was terribly wrong. Fights were never public. He and Jimmy took their licks in silence. The Devlin women, both old and young, rarely cried or carried-on, the outpouring of emotion was done behind locked door if necessary. His mother didn't stand her ground. Not ever. She would profess her disapproval from time to time, but if his dad put the proverbial foot down—which happened all but one time so far as Henry could remember—well, that was the end of the subject.

He opened the outside screen door then the actual front door, the argument became louder than anything he had heard to date. His parents hadn't heard him enter, else they would most likely have put pause to the fray. Henry knew that as well.

After making way to the kitchen, he saw his mother's face swollen and wet. Not swollen like it had been struck, swollen like it was an overindulgent sponge. Tears were oozing from her eyes and nose, dripping down off her jawline and chin. Henry turned toward his father who was leaning against the counter on the opposite side of kitchen. They paused once they noticed their company.

"Oh, Henry. Uh," Faith said as she tried to straighten herself. "Why don't you go find your brother in the park or something."

"What's going on, Mom?"

"Nothing. Your father and I just have to talk for a while."

"Are you okay?"

"Henry! Out! You can leave under your own power or by ambulance, it's up to you." Tommy. Ever the pragmatist. Ever the enforcer.

Confused and an under-confident early teenager, he did as was suggested and sought out his brother.

Jimmy was in the park. He and his friends were often there. As they were on this day, smoking cigarettes, when Henry found them.

"Fun's over boys, here comes my brother," Jimmy said to his best friend, Derek, and the rest of the fellowship. Derek flicked away what Henry believed to be a cigarette, though it could have been a joint for all he knew.

Henry completed the remaining thirty-foot interval between them. "Hey Jimmy, can we talk for a minute?"

"What do you want?"

"Alone?"

"Me and the boys don't have secrets. Whatever you got to say, just say it."

Henry hesitated, looking at the group of faces to determine what he should say publicly. Dirty laundry was cleaned at home. But the idiots that his brother hung out with were always attached to the hip and that seemed unlikely to change no matter how much Henry pressed.

"Mom and Dad are having a huge fight. I don't think he hit her, but whatever's happening, it doesn't look good."

"So?"

"So they're screaming at each other. You can hear it from the street." Henry thought that was all that needed to be said to convey the urgency of the situation. He was wrong.

"And?"

Two in the fellowship of idiots started chuckling. Henry desired violence but knew he wouldn't be able to achieve the upper-hand on all of them for very long. Instead, he shook his head and explained further to abate sustained stupidity.

"*And,* something is really wrong this time. I don't think he got fired again. She's used to that by now. And she was really upset. I've never seen her like that."

"Thanks for letting me know. I won't go home tonight. You should think about sleeping at one of your friend's house too," Jimmy said. "If you have any."

It was more than a single-word reply but still not what Henry was looking for.

"Don't go home? That's all you have to say about it?"

"If he was yelling and she was crying, that means he's gonna want to beat on somethin'. Margo'll be safe, but you and I should stay scarce for a day or two."

"But why is the question I'm asking you. Why are they fighting?"

"Who knows? Who cares? If that's all you've got, we have some pressing business that we was in the middle of."

"Yeah. And you interrupted," Derek said.

Henry decided that the conversation was pointless and decided to walk toward the center of town. The walk might allow his brain to produce the basis for the latest bit of unrest. The root-cause was most certainly his dad, but the variables too complex for the equation to balance. Too jumbled to decipher any hidden meaning or code.

The downtown area was abustle. Kids went to the movies after school. To the arcade. To the diner. There was always something to occupy the life of a teenager in the small suburb of Boston.

Music came from the speakers outside the record store juxtaposed to the other staple businesses in downtown Bridgewater. Henry always found solace in music. Music had meaning even if his life didn't. Everyone loves music, but Henry found comfort in it. He found meaning. The melodies and beats and chord structures and lyrics made sense to him.

Henry thought of his mother. She loved music as much as he did. She would always put on records when his father wasn't around, which was more often than not. When she wasn't listening to music, she would watch it on television. *American Bandstand. Soul Train. Solid Gold.* It was music that bonded them. It was the only thing that gave Henry any confirmation that he had come from his mother. They supposedly shared blood, they definitely shared love of music. He certainly didn't have any familial tie with his father, his brother was no prize, and Margo was fifteen and off learning how to be a hippie around that time. And so it was music that he clung to.

Outside the music shop, Pop-Rocks, Henry stood thinking and listening to the speakers spill Frida's *I Know There's Something Going On.*

He opened the door and went inside the store. He sought comfort and Henry found contentment within those walls. The exploration of music new and old was a journey worthy of the effort. Inside those vinyl albums was hidden treasure. Among the cassette tapes was gold. Every emotion could be conjured or soothed in music. Music was pure. Music was always true.

The owner new him well. As did the young employees. Henry was often found hidden in the stacks, searching for truth. The young man who worked behind the counter waved Henry over. He couldn't remember the employee's name at that moment, and the owner didn't require name badges to refresh his memory. It was odd that he couldn't remember, Henry thought to himself, he remembered almost everything.

"Hey, Rusty held this for you." The employee produced an album from behind the counter. Henry and Rusty, the owner, had talked about the new Van Halen album that was coming out when last they spoke. He had obviously saved him a copy. The blue album with an angelic baby smoking a cigarette on the cover was still wrapped in the original plastic.

"He wasn't sure if you wanted it on cassette or vinyl," the employee said. "If you don't want this one, I think we have a couple of copies on tape."

"Tell him thanks and he got it right. I prefer the sound on vinyl, but records don't travel so well. If I love it I'll record it so I can hear it on my walkman. But it's not the same," Henry explained. The fact that he

40

couldn't remember the name of the clerk was beginning to drive him nuts. His brain was officially frying.

"Very true. Do you wanna hear it now?"

"Yeah. Why not?"

Rusty owned and operated a laissez-faire operation. He constantly had music playing during hours of operation, and he let his best customers choose what they wanted to listen to. Even if it was Judas Priest or Slayer. If a customer didn't like it, they could go to one of the big chain music stores.

The employee took Frida off the turntable and put on another vinyl copy of Van Halen's 1984. He gave Henry the used jacket so he could look at the liner notes while a full minute of synthesized crap filled the shop. Reading liner notes was another ritual that Henry enjoyed at Pop-Rocks, one that wasn't afforded at the chain stores.

The guy behind the counter allayed Henry's fear. "It's not all like this, don't worry."

Henry was still unimpressed when *Jump* finished but was hopeful for the rest of the album when *Panama* came on.

Halfway through the third track, someone tapped him on the shoulder while he bobbed his head to the beat laid down by Alex Van Halen over the store's speakers. He turned to see his sister and her friend, Jessica.

"Who would have thought you'd be here?"

"Margo. I'm always here."

"I know. It was sarcasm, dork."

He handed the clerk the album jacket and thanked him. The young man nodded his head as if to say, 'of course'.

Henry pulled his sister away from her friend by the elbow.

"I'm glad you're here. I just came from home. Mom and Dad are having a huge fight. He was screaming, she was screaming. It was a real mess."

"I know."

"You know? What's going on?"

She pulled him further into an unoccupied corner of the small store.

"Look, you're a man now. Well, almost. At thirteen you're more mature than the other men in our family, so by that standard you're the *only* man in our family. I'm gonna give it to you plain. Our dad is not a good guy."

"Really Margo? How many beatings have you taken? I mean ever? He ever take anything from you? Kill anything you loved? No? Not his pride and joy Margo, hell no. She can do no wrong. I'm well aware that he has some severe character flaws. How ever did you figure it out?"

Margo crossed her arms over her woven Baja hoodie with a look of annoyance. "Feel better? Do you want to hear this or not?"

"Sorry. Yes. Well, no, but yes."

"Not only can't the sonofabitch keep a job, he can't keep his dick in his pants either. I think it's been going on for a while, but I don't know for how long or with whom. Mom must have proof, once and for all."

Henry looked down at his winter boots, the brown, winter slush melted on the battered hardwood floor around them. He was surprised but not shocked. "So now what?"

"Who knows? She won't divorce him, you know that. Mom stick up for herself? Never happen. Plus you know what the church says about divorce. Ever the martyr our mom."

"So what do I do is essentially what I'm asking?"

"If I were you I would ignore it. Mom won't talk about it with you, and Dad will beat you for disrespecting him. Just pretend like you don't know anything like the rest of us. Hasn't mom taught you anything? Appearances are everything."

SIX MONTHS BEFORE HIS BROTHER PLAYED WHAT became the infamous 'Cum-quickly Kid' prank in the movie theatre, Henry was celebrating the achievement of making the Saint Ann's Varsity Baseball Team. At fifteen years old, nobody made the varsity squad. Some seniors at Saint Ann's didn't. The coach fancied himself a retired professional because he played in a sub Triple-A, Cape Cod league, once upon a time. Coach Lou had dedicated himself to vicariously reliving those days through the Catholic youth.

The Saint Ann Crusaders had made it to the Massachusetts State Playoff game every year since Coach Lou took over the team. They won three out of four, and had gone to the New England Regional game once. They were New England champs their first crack at it.

The town of Bridgewater took baseball seriously, the school took it seriously, and therefore so did the church. You had to be a member of the congregation in order for your children to attend, which brought in more donations in the weekly offering at mass. A winning program meant college scouts attended with regularity, and that meant more people in the community wanted to send their boy to Saint Ann's Catholic school. More students meant higher revenues in the form of tuitions, uniforms, and the like. With Coach Lou, business was good.

The 1985-86 school year brought a new Athletic Director to Saint Ann's, but not without a lot of fuss and bother. The Director had been a former administrator for the National Collegiate Athletic Association, which made Saint Ann's desirable for all those parents who had children involved in sports. The Board of Directors set the application aside and made the hire sight unseen, a former NCAA was a shoo-in and they were lucky to get him.

Dana Corning turned out to be a woman.

If the only community nightmare was that the new director was a woman, it would have eventually faded away with an elbow and chuckle. A funny footnote. But she also had a head on her shoulders. And an Agenda. She had seen too many athletes make it to the collegiate level for their skill alone, the student would either fail out or was pushed along without the required learning to graduate. She had seen some athletes graduate with a college degree yet couldn't read at a junior-high school level. This was a blight she could not abide. A pandemic which needed remedy at the root.

Director Corning mandated that all student athletes at Saint Ann's maintain a three-point-oh minimum grade-point average in order to make any roster. All teachers had to fill out weekly performance evaluations on every student athlete while in season. Any student falling below a solid B in any of their subjects would be at a minimum benched, a C or below almost certainly meant being cut from the squad. All coaches were required to maintain an elaborate metric for the athletes on their squad, minimum average grade-point as a whole just one facet of the elaborate metric. The coaches obviously loathed it and revolted. Teachers were already overworked and underpaid and protested the additional workload required for both themselves and of their students who also happened to play a sport, or heaven forbid, multiple sports. The priests and nuns saw that potentially more seats would go unfilled in church as parents would take their kids to another, less demanding school. The uproar grew.

But Director Corning won.

She had a contract and threatened a lawsuit, one that the diocese wished to avoid.   Corning additionally threatened to go to the press. Bishops and Cardinals were summoned and, ultimately, Athletic Director Dana Corning stayed.

That is why Henry Devlin made the Varsity Baseball team at fifteen.   He was smart.   He had a perfect grade-point average, which brought several numbers in Coach Lou's metric well above passing. Had the reasons for Henry making the team remained a secret, it may have proven to boost Henry's low confidence.

But they didn't.

Coach Lou told him regularly that he was hated by everyone on the team and that he was simply a necessary evil. Henry could feel the disdain with every look from his coach, which of course trickled down to every starter on the roster.

And so Henry warmed the bench that entire year.

They made it to the State Regionals—one game away from the State Championship Game—like they did every year, with Henry technically being a right-fielder. He sat on the bench listening to Coach Lou's big pre-game speech in the dugout wondering if the spring 1986 version was the same as it had been every year prior.

"…. And so I say to you all, especially seniors, you need to lay it all out on the field today. There might not be a tomorrow for you. Use it up.   Don't look back at this game and wish that you had done more. Nothing gets left in the tank. Now is your time. Today is your day."

It was all that Henry could take. He was sick of being meek. The bible they taught in school and preached about at mass said that the meek inherit the earth.   In his estimation, the meek didn't inherit shit. The meek get walked on. He had quietly sat and hoped and still he sat. Henry didn't want a gift. He worked for it and he wanted a chance. He was done with the shadows.

"Can I leave it all out on the bench, Coach?"

"Who said that?" Coach Lou looked left and right, up and down both tiers on the bench in the dugout.

"Me," Henry said. "I'll be here on the bench like I am in every other game, I'm not sure how much more bench-warming I can muster. I mean I'm giving it my all, Coach."

"Fuckin' wise-ass, huh? You're more annoying than kudzu. Just shut your cock-holster, Devlin. You know why you're here, and playin' ball ain't it."

"I'm just speaking the truth. You don't even know if I suck because you never let me play," Henry said.

"I've seen you practice. You're here to bring up the GPA of the team. If I had my way, you'd be off my team and kneelin' in front of one of the priests. Ya know, the thing you're good at. But obviously I don't get my way."

"Is that how you got your job? By giving one?" Henry had never said anything like that to an adult in his entire life. He had watched his brother Jimmy mouth-off a bunch of times, and was always getting a beating for it. Henry was going to get one for this, he was sure of it, but anger took over.

"You want a piece of me, Devlin?" Coach Lou grabbed an aluminum bat from the rack to his right in the dugout. "I'll knock your fuckin' teeth out."

"That'd be good in front of all the parents, Coach. You'd *blow* another big day."

The coach was seething but realized the boy was right. He couldn't kick his ass right then and there. He would have a chat with his parents after the game, a game he was damn sure not going to let Devlin play.

The team captain whispered something to his coach in an attempt to calm him down, then addressed Henry above the team grumbling.

"You're wasting your breath, Devlin. Everybody just needs to focus on the game. Forget this distraction."

"You don't want to be here, and nobody wants you here. You take up space on the bus and my roster," Coach finally said after regaining his composure.

"Glad I can help the team."

They lost the regionals that year. They lost by one run, sent home by a fly ball missed by the kid playing right field. It would have been a third out for the opposing team, which would have meant a Crusader win. Instead, two runs came in and ended Saint Ann's playoff run

Coach Lou blamed the bench-warmer for distracting the team prior to the first pitch. Would Henry have made the catch that moved Saint Ann's to the State Final? Nobody will ever know. What is known is that Henry would never play baseball again, the coach didn't want him back and Henry didn't want to take the added abuse. Baseball was a sport that he loved. A sport that may have gained him a college scholarship.

But that was just the first disappointment that year. Kat running out on their first date in humiliation was the second and much more devastating to him.

JIMMY ATTEMPTED TO MEND AN ALL BUT DESTROYED fence with his brother in the fall of 1987. The bible instructed Henry to turn the other cheek—at least that is what Father Donovan pontificated about during his homily every Sunday—demanding that those who had tormented him be given another opportunity to do so in order to perfect their craft. Henry never once actually thought about those words, forgiveness was part of his nature. To a point.

Henry nearly fell from his chair when Jimmy invited him to a party he was attending. The two went back and forth for several hours at various intervals, volleying invitation and inquiry as to what the scam was, before Henry finally said that he would go. In the back of his mind he knew that he was being had. But he hoped against hope that this would be a hurdle worthy of the attempt. That this would be the breaking of bread, the metaphorical meal that would finally form a solid foundation on which to build upon. Henry hoped for the best but prepared for the worst.

The house where the party was located was only a few miles from Mallor Street, but it might as well have been on the moon. It was big and posh and overflowing with people Henry didn't know. He didn't know who the house belonged to either, but with the amount of damage being done the owner was not likely to be present. What Henry did know was that he was almost sixteen years old in a house dripping with alcohol and drugs, with juniors and seniors from both Saint Ann's and Bridgewater High. Cautious optimism was waning.

"Jimmy if you leave me stranded here, I will kill you in your sleep," Henry promised.

"Don't worry. Just be cool. I'll take care of you. By the end of tonight you're gonna be feeling great. You'll be a new man."

The reassurance placated him for the moment. The music was loud and fantastic. The women weren't dressed like the girls from his school. Saint Ann's had uniforms which were by no means flattering, the obvious point in mandating them. At the party, the women—and to Henry they most certainly looked like women—dressed like Madonna circa *Like A Virgin*. Lace barely covered breasts, hands, and legs.

The majority of the people milling about were making out. Males were aggressively kissing and heavily petting willing females. What hands weren't used to hold cups of alcohol were used to cup young breasts. Henry had never seen anything like it.

He followed his brother closely to where the host was partying. Henry was introduced, but with all of the noise and loud music he never caught the name.

The accommodating host then escorted them to a keg and a huge block of ice where people were drinking alcohol that was being poured through it. The host told him and his brother that it was each of their turns on the ice contraption, Henry very content to let Jimmy go first. When it was his turn he squatted down at one end of the block of ice, like he had just witnessed his brother do, the amber liquor was poured from the other end and the biting liquid flowed into his mouth and down his throat. When finished, Henry was tossed a Pabst Blue Ribbon, which despite his baseball skills, he nearly missed because he was so dizzy.

Henry didn't like the taste of the beer, but he liked it better than the burning in his throat from whatever was just poured into it. They made him shotgun it, opening it for him then poking a hole from which he was to chug down the entire can. When he was finished with the PBR, the next phase of the gauntlet of inebriation came in the form of a Sweetheart cup full of beer from the keg.

Within fifteen minutes of being at the party, Henry was half in the bag. The rest of night was just icing.

The room spun as Henry followed his brother through the house, stopping to mingle when Jimmy recognized someone. They made several stops, Henry was introduced in every instance. Again the loud yet fantastic music was too loud for him to hear the names of those he was meeting. Even the women who kissed him on the cheek, grabbed at him, or nibbled on his ear after saying something into it, remained anonymous.

They then went into a room that looked like an enormous living room slash library. A group of people were huddled around a glass coffee table. After another round of introductions, Henry watched Jimmy cut up cocaine on a mirror in the center of the table, snorting it with the newly formed friends.

Now it was Henry's turn. After his three bumps of cocaine at various intervals, he coughed his way through intermittent passes of marijuana. The joints made him thirsty, which necessitated more beer. More ice-luge shots were mandated before more beer was pumped from the keg.

The music consumed him. He wondered how it was possible to hear music in any other way. Led Zeppelin's *Achilles Last Stand* echoed throughout the house over the volume of the crowd. The galloping bass-line of John-Paul Jones reverberated deep into Henry's soul. John Bonham's pounding-fast drum beat. Jimmy Page's Gibson EDS-1275 made impossibly delicious sounds. Robert Plant's voice was like honey. He had heard the song many times before, he owned the album *Presence*. But he had never heard it like this. He closed his eyes and felt the song. And it felt fantastic.

"…. With all the fun to have,
To live the dreams we always had ….
Oh, the songs to sing,
When we at last return again …. "

Opening his eyes was a mistake, one that he immediately regretted. The room began to close in on him. People were too close, staring at him. He spun. The house spun. Paranoia set in. Panic. His heart began to beat irregularly and felt like it would explode from his chest. *Where is Jimmy?* Henry turned with room as it spun, trying to find his brother.

Jimmy was off in a corner getting on well with a girl from Bridgewater High. She let him touch her. Kiss her. His hands were moving south from her chest and she was giving him the green light for more when he noticed Henry sweating and circling with a look of panic. Jimmy's initial instinct was to get pissed off about being cock-blocked by his brother. His second was to ignore him and proceed to third base with the frisky girl. But he did neither of those things. Instead, he bid her adieu and corralled his brother.

"Are you okay?"

"I don't know Jimmy. I don't feel so good."

"We should go outside and get some cool air. Whatever you do, just stay calm and don't puke."

Which is exactly what Henry wanted to do, but didn't.

Henry was led out the back door, off the deck and down onto the lawn. There was a small fire in the backyard where a few people were gathered. Jimmy and Henry found a spot to sit off to the side of it in relative privacy. They could still hear the music playing.

"…. If one bell should ring,

In celebration for a king ….

So fast the heart should beat,

As proud the head with heavy feet …."

"Better?"

Henry took a few deep, cleansing breaths. "Maybe. I think I'm fucked up."

"You're definitely fucked up. But that's the point, right? The trick is go out of your mind but still maintain."

"How are you?"

"Wasted. But I've done this before. You haven't right? What am I saying? Of course you haven't." Jimmy took out two cigarettes, lit them both, then handed Henry one of the Marb Reds.

Henry didn't smoke, but up until that night he didn't do a lot of things. He took it and a drag which made him cough again. "I took a puff of a joint once. Before tonight. I've had a sip of beer too."

"We just broke your cherry there, ya party animal," Jimmy said. "Listen, you and me gotta stick together. We live in the same house. Shit, the same room, and we never speak."

"We never speak because you're never home, Jimmy."

"Why should I go home? I can't stand that place. That's why Margo's off doing her own thing. One of us should move into her room, give us some more space."

"Yeah, right. Mom thinks she's going to walk through the front door any day now," Henry said.

"Oh, okay. Whatever. Listen, the point is, it's just you and me now."

"Why all of a sudden? You've made it your mission in life to make me miserable, Jimmy. Why now? Why are we now on the same team?"

"Look I could make a million excuses, but all of the finger-pointing ain't gonna change nothin'."

"No. But you could apologize. That Kat thing at the movies really messed me up."

Jimmy started to laugh. "Cum-quickly kid."

"Fuck you. I really liked her. I still do. She won't even talk to me anymore. Not that I've ever really had the nerve to try again."

"You're right, that was a dick move. I'm sorry. But I can't go back in time. No *Back To The Future* DeLorean. If I could, I would. I'm tryin' to give you an olive tree here," Jimmy said.

"Branch."

"What?"

"It's an olive branch, dummy."

"Whatever. You're polluted and you're giving me shit?" Jimmy tousled Henry's dirty-blond hair.

"I've probably killed a million brain cells tonight," Henry said.

"And you're still smarter than me. It's hard to believe we're related sometimes," Jimmy said as he stood up. He held his hand out to help his brother to his feet. "We should probably walk it off. Mom sees you like this, she might decide to try her hand at giving beatings."

They headed in the direction of their house. The conversation was light and funny and needed. It was the first real yet inconsequential dialogue they'd ever had. Henry wondered if it was all a dream. Everything was still hazy and dream-like. Certainly at a tilt.

When they reached the end of Mallor Street, Jimmy stopped, letting Henry continue on for another ten yards.

"What's the problem, Jimmy?"

"Nothin'. Just go home. You're good right?"

53

"You're not coming home again?"

"Nah. Figured I'd go back to the party, see if that girl is still there. You had fun though, right?"

"Yeah but come on—"

"—Hey …. Wait. Speakin' of girls, isn't this your sweetie's house?"

"Huh?"

"That girl you like. The one you were talkin' about before. Kat. This is her house right?"

They were standing in front of the Bradar house at the end of Mallor Street.

"Yes. Why?"

"You should go see what she's up to," Jimmy suggested.

"No way. I am in no shape. I might be able to fool Mom if she's still up, but I can't talk to Kat right now."

"Who said talk to her? Just take a peak."

"You mean spy on her. I thought I was wasted."

"You are wasted, Henry."

"And if I get caught?"

"Then don't get caught. Do you need help? I'll go with you."

"No. No way, Jimmy."

But Jimmy was already sneaking along the arborvitae hedges toward the Bradar backyard. The wise choice would have been for Henry to just go home. Jimmy would have given up on the drug and alcohol addled idea once he realized he was in it alone.

But that isn't what Henry did.

He followed his brother to the rear of the raised ranch-style house. One of the lights on the second floor was on. The illuminated window indicated that it was either a bedroom or a bathroom. They would find out which once they reached a perch in a nearby tree. They had to be careful not to jostle the branches of the large tree that touched the house, else they would be heard. Jimmy pointed out that fact as they ascended the acer, which still had leaves for cover but the arrival of fall mandated that they were no longer green.

They reached their perch in the backyard but saw no person. The room that had a light on was a bedroom, that much they could tell. There was a dresser with a large mirror and part of a closet in plain view.

"There's nothing to see. This is crazy," Henry whispered.

"Be quiet or we'll get busted."

"What if she's naked?"

"Then lucky you."

"What about you?"

"Then lucky me too. But what are the chances? She's probably just reading or something."

"How do you know? You don't even know this girl," Henry said.

"And neither do you. That's the point. You see what she's reading or doing or whatever so you have something to talk about when you see her. Now shut up or she'll hear us."

Just then shadows rolled across the wall. They were from more than one person. A thought ran through Henry's mind that she might not be alone. That she might be with somebody else from school. If he saw her with another boy it would kill him, especially if he knew the guy. He was about to insist on aborting all reconnoitering when he saw a familiar face.

Jimmy saw him too. He turned to Henry to see if he had seen the same thing. That the drugs and alcohol from earlier hadn't been playing tricks. They looked at each other in horrified confirmation.

"I think I'm gonna be sick, " Henry said without whisper.

"Oh shit. This was a bad idea," Jimmy concurred.

Henry couldn't look, but Jimmy did.

His father passed the window, turned and looked back to the other person.

The female came into view and embraced Tommy. They began to kiss, exchanging tongues. He held her head in his hands, gently pulling her hair away from her face and neck. Tommy then kissed her neck as he moved his hands down to her breasts. She was wearing a blouse that buttoned in the front, Tommy unfastened them in order as he moved toward her waist.

"Wait. That's not Kat, Henry. Look."

"I can't. I don't wanna know anymore."

"It's not Kat. Isn't that good?"

"Is it Mom?"

"Don't be stupid. I think it's Kat's mom."

"Then how is that good?"

8

MARGO HAD BEEN GONE FOR OVER SEVEN MONTHS when Jimmy and Henry made the discovery of their father and Mrs. Bradar. There was nothing to keep their sister at the house on Mallor Street. Life had become intolerable in Bridgewater, not that there was anything holding her to the Boston suburb anyway. She was graduating soon, and plans to leave were escalated.

In the spring of 1987, before the discovery of the adulterous relations between Tommy Devlin and Trish Bradar—though there had been two years of general common knowledge of their father's infidelity — Margo was a senior at Saint Ann's High School. The environmentally conscious girl was seventeen and smart and beautiful and virtually left to her own devices once Tommy ceased paying her the attention that she had become accustom to. Daddy's little girl had grown up to be a self-sufficient, liberal, feminist with advanced ideas. Too advanced for the likes of her father, who was a known adulterer, a misogynist, and wasn't around to persuade her out of hippiedom in any case.

While Tommy Devlin was off doing whatever he did, Faith was trying to keep the family together. She put on a happy face and pretended that everybody was fine, a duty she was well versed at. She might have even convinced herself that she was fine, and that her family was normal. Faith was determined to live a Catholic life, a life which didn't include divorce. That determination was the driving force behind her belief that all would be okay. That her husband would come back to her. That her children wouldn't suffer the same consequences as those from a broken home. The matriarch refused to accept that she was losing the battle and the war.

Margo was sick of hearing her mom say, "That which does not kill you, makes you stronger." If that were true, she thought, the Devlins were a brawny bunch.

So she kept herself occupied outside the home. She went out with friends and went on trips and things of that ilk. Margo became a free-spirit and did as she pleased under the radar. She was never in trouble with the law or any other authority; no fuss no muss, out of sight out of mind.

Until the spring of her senior year.

There was a big hoopla that year, specifically in the spring, because the English Lit teacher slash Drama coach, Andrew Benning, had chosen an ill-advised movie to adapt. Mr. Benning was in his late thirties and thought himself very avant-garde. He decided to write an adaptation of the 1980 movie *Cruising*. The diocese didn't object in theory to the basic premise of the movie which was that homosexuality leads to being murdered. The true objection was that the story following a police investigation of a self-loathing serial killer was too much for young, impressionable minds.

The Catholic religion has had a long history of vilifying homosexuals despite the number of them within their ranks. The AIDS epidemic was in the daily news and was supposedly the wrath of God upon the sinful lifestyle, according to the church.

The adaptation replaced the gay serial killer with an Archangel. Gabriel would descend like written about in 1: Thessalonians in the New Testament; only in this version he came to smite those who prefer the same sex, and a police detective would try to sort out the murders.

Because of the ongoing commotion regarding Athletic Director Corning, and the continual schemes to oust her from her contract without a devastating lawsuit, the Board was too busy to take full notice of the drama teacher's production, which was already underway and a mere two weeks before opening curtain. Money had already been spent from the church coffers on scenery, costumes and the like. The controversial play and its large budget was the reason that Mr. Benning was under increasingly watchful eyes as the spring production neared.

Margo Devlin wasn't in Drama Club, nor was she involved in the production of *Cruising* in any way, to Sister Ruth's knowledge. That is why she found it odd that Mr. Benning and Margo were headed backstage of the theatre.

The nun followed them into the main entrance of the theatre, but kept a healthy distance. The teacher and student then went down the aisle to the front, up the stairs, and onto the stage. The two conversed as they went behind the curtain, Sister Ruth slowly made way down the aisle to the front of the theatre behind them.

Once she was behind the curtain, she lost track of them. She continued on backstage, walking past the woodworking slash carpentry shop, which was dual purposed for those who were getting vocational training and the building of the necessary staging for performances. The teacher and student weren't in the wood-shop.

Nor were they in the Home Economics sewing department. Again the large room backstage was dual purposed.

The final gymnasium-sized room, as the nun walked to the rear of the building behind the stage, was used for storage. All props and costumes and sets in both current and past performances were stored there.

And that is where she eventually found both teacher and student.

In a far and concealed corner was a plush, blue couch that had been used as a set prop in a production once upon a time. The two were speaking in whispers.   Benning's back was to Sister Ruth, Margo temporarily hidden from view.

Sister Ruth moved to a different vantage point to reconnoiter, only to see that the student was without her blouse. Sans bra as well.

The nun was about to say something, about to bring the entire sinful episode to a screeching halt, but something inside her prevented it. Was it her own sexual frustration? Was it her curiosity about what would happen next?   Or was it because the acts seemed consensual?   For whatever reason, she froze. And watched.

Sister Ruth watched as Benning's belt was unfastened, his pants and boxers lowered. She watched as Margo slowly sat on the couch, taking the teacher in her mouth. Benning's head rolled back as he put his hand behind the girl's head, which pulsed slowly up and down. Margo Devlin's hands were on his buttocks, pulling him towards her. She looked up at him as she fellated.

Benning whispered to the girl, but what he said the nun couldn't hear. Ruth was getting short of breath herself. A bit dizzy. But she didn't turn away. Nor did she say anything or stop it. She continued to take it all in, stunned into inactivity.

She surveilled further as the teacher stood the young student up. He kissed her, putting his tongue where his appendage had just been. They kissed long at length. The girl sat back down, Benning lowered her white panties from under her school uniform skirt. One leg was pulled through while the other ankle held onto the undergarment.

Margo slid back on the couch, Benning slowly got on top of her. She gasped when he entered her. Her breathing became louder. More wanton.   Benning looked into her eyes as he slowly withdrew and entered. His breathing became more frequent yet shallow.

Sister Ruth couldn't take any more. She was flustered and flushed and amidst Satan Himself. She didn't know what to do but retreat. And so she did.

The following morning Margo was summoned to the main office at the school. The office was centrally located between the elementary, junior, and high schools as all were administered from the same space. She was quickly ushered into an office and surprised to see Bishop McCaffrey, Father Donovan, and Sister Ruth waiting for her.

The Bishop was rarely at the school. He had an entire diocese in which he was responsible for. The children were the least of his worries.

As Margo entered the office, her look of surprise registered with Bishop McCaffrey.

"No need to fret, young lady. You've done nothing wrong. Please have a seat." The Bishop pointed toward an empty seat opposite the desk, which Margo sat in. Father Donovan was also seated in a corner while the Bishop and the nun remained standing, which did nothing to allay Margo's fears.

"As I was saying, you've done nothing wrong. In fact, on behalf of the school I would like to apologize for even putting you in such a position. Having someone such as that on our staff puts children at risk, which is the last thing that we want to take place."

"I'm sorry to interrupt, Your Excellency, but I'm not following what you're speaking about," Margo said with clear trepidation. Her voice was quiet and shaky.

"There is no need to cover for him, Margo. No need to parlay deceit on top of gross and abject misuse of his position. A full investigation is underway and he has already confessed. Mr. Benning has been dismissed and the authorities were notified, after your mother was apprised of course. The important thing is that, so far, none of this is has been your fault."

"My Mom? But he didn't do anything wrong. I—"

"—You are confused, young lady.   And who can blame you? Father Donovan and I are going to let you and Sister Ruth chat for a bit. For as long as you like, in fact. It's important that you move on from this, that you understand that you are now safe.   That nothing like this will ever happen to you again at Saint Ann."

Margo was at a loss.

As Bishop McCaffrey made his way toward the office door, Margo stood.

"Please just let it go.   There is no need to get anyone else involved. I love him. We love each other. He didn't rape me. I wanted to."

"I've heard quite enough," McCaffrey said. "The sin is his. You've been taken advantage of by a monster, by evil, young lady.   No more harm will come to you my dear, that I promise, as God as my witness. You are now inviolate from the works of Satan.   Your mother is on her way here and is very upset, as one might imagine.   She has already indicated that she will pursue this legally. It is now beyond your control. What happens to him from this point is what he deserves and is the wrath of God upon him. He will need to beg for forgiveness both secularly and with his maker." The Bishop gently eased Margo back into her seat.

"What the two of you did …. Suffice to say that Andrew Benning is a wolf in sheep's clothing.   The Lord protects his flock from such wolves," he continued.

His Excellency picked a piece of lint from his Chimere and sighed for added effect. "Anything further can be discussed with Sister Ruth. Be well Margo."

Bishop McCaffrey left the office.   Father Donovan was behind him but paused in the entryway just before leaving the room.

"I'll see you soon, Margo, " the priest said. "Though you've done nothing wrong, if you would like to unburden yourself, I'll be hearing confessions this afternoon." Then he left the office on the heels of the Bishop.

Sister Ruth took a seat behind the desk.

Margo slumped in her seat as tears filled her eyes.

"What is going to happen to him?"

"That is not for me to say," the nun said. "But he did commit Statutory Rape in terms of the law, and of course you weren't married so that—"

"—I'm seventeen years old."

"And the Commonwealth of Massachusetts has ruled the age of consent to be eighteen. You are a child, and you are unmarried."

"Sixteen. Everyone knows the age of consent is sixteen."

"Despite popular belief, or what 'everybody knows', you are not an adult until the age of eighteen. Period. Your teacher, as Your Excellency just explained, is a predator. A vile sinner doing the work of Lucifer. He will be punished accordingly in this life, and suffer eternal hellfire in the next. God will have his vengeance young lady, never you fear."

Margo put her face in her hands and began to weep.

"Why are you doing this? That poor man. You have no right."

"But I do. 1: Peter 5:2 *'Keep watch over the flock of God which is in your care, using your authority, not as forced to do so, but gladly; and not for unclean profit but with a ready mind.'* I watched you, and I have prayed about it, young lady. And I will continue to pray for your soul."

Margo looked up from her wet hands, eyes blazing into the nun's.

"You're the one who should rot in hell."

FIVE MONTHS AFTER THOMAS DEVLIN WAS INITIALLY outed as a philanderer, school was out and summer was in full swing. It was 1984 and none of the other Devlins yet knew exactly who was sweating up the sheets with their patriarch, but the sibling conversation had taken place at the music store, Pop-Rocks, earlier that year.

The knowledge was irksome—to some more than others in the family—but overall Tommy's adultery wasn't as terrible as originally perceived. He was around less, his negatively infectious attitude truant along with him. Beatings were rare, not that progeny hijinks had waned. It was more the idea that their mother suffered in silent plight while her supposed better half was injecting his seed into other willing parties. Nobody in the children's social circles let on that they were privy to such impropriety; certainly none of them were vexed by his absence, so the kids were indignant solely for the sake of their mother.

It was a period of relative peace.

The rest of that winter came and went. Likewise with spring. Summer began, school was out, and the kids spent their dog days at will. They would hang out with their respective friends or find an odd job for a pittance to afford such leisure. They would go to their cottage on Carver Pond to spend the day swimming. Suppers were spent at home, then back out again. Occasionally Henry would stay home with Faith to help out with a chore or listen to records with her.

Tommy's nightly attendance to the evening meal was spotty at best. When he did attend, the feeding was done in silence or with his grumblings about it being the same old sustenance. The metaphor not lost on Henry.

Until his attendance suspended all together.

A week went by. Then two. His failure to attend supper never lasted such an interval. Nobody mentioned it out load, but all three of the children knew something was afoot.

One evening in late July, Henry and his siblings came home to a veritable buffet. Faith had made everyone's favorite. Shepherd's pie. Stuffed peppers. Vegetarian lasagna.

Henry knew a bomb was about to be dropped. It wasn't anyone's birthday and they didn't have any company. Maybe Tommy was out of work again. Maybe he was dead, which would certainly explain the latest and most lengthy disappearance.

But the truth wasn't as easy as death.

Tommy was supposedly alive and well but he wouldn't be coming home. He found a new garage which offered him work, one with a small apartment attached. The owner and his new boss was going to let him stay there as part of his wages until he could sort out a more permanent living situation.

Faith explained over the bevy of meals that they were not getting a divorce, only that they wouldn't be living together any longer.

The three children looked at one another in silent confusion. Thomas and Faith Devlin hadn't been living together for some time, not truly. A short time passed before the silence gave way.

Margo asked why they didn't just get a divorce given the current state of their union, but Faith said that they all knew better. Divorce was against the church and the will of God, she added. Margo asked about her mother's happiness but knew better than to expect an answer, for none would be forthcoming.

Instead, their mother went on to further explain that things were going to be financially tight on Mallor Street. The cottage on Carver Pond had been paid for since Tommy's father had built it, however it was used as collateral to buy their home on Mallor. The cottage was unsuitable for permanent residence until it could be converted into a proper home. That conversion would require funds that were nonexistent, and there was no budget to save for one. The house held a mortgage that Faith couldn't afford alone, Tommy told her that he wouldn't be contributing since he would no longer be living there.

Faith was going to have to find work—hopefully her extensive experience as a homemaker would count as work history—and she was going to have to find work immediately.

And of course the anything-but-annual summer vacation wasn't going to happen. No time. No money. No joy in it. That piece didn't shock Henry, nor his siblings. The trip to the Cape was an occasional hit or the customary miss. The only thing consistent about the Devlin summer getaway was that it was inconsistent.

The Cold War had finally come to a head, nuclear fission occurred in Bridgewater Massachusetts. Only it was their nuclear family being split, not the atom. There is nothing like comfort food to take your mind off the fact that your entire world is about to change. Of course nobody ate.

Faith then explained that she didn't want them talking about the situation or the arrangement with others. Not with their teachers, not with their friends. This was a private matter and would be handled privately.

Things like this went without saying, but she made the statement nevertheless. This time it was a major problem in the home, not the usual and comparably frivolous secret. The statement should have gone without further discourse, but Margo didn't let it go.

"So what are we supposed to say?" Margo pushed herself away from the kitchen table but remained in her usual seat. Henry would never forget it as long as he lived.

"Tell whoever is asking about him that he is out of town or busy with work. I will take care of anything that should come up at school," his mom said.

"Like anyone is going to buy that bullshit? He's a sometimes mechanic, Mom. The man sleeps with everything that sits down to pee and his car is never in the yard. Who do you think we're going to fool?"

"Watch your mouth young lady! Do you think that this is easy for me? That I chose this? I'm going to put on my happy face and make like nothing is wrong for you. I'm doing the best I can and this is the thanks I get?"

"Easy on the guilt," Margo said. "You say you're doing this for us, but you're doing this for you. Keep up appearances, come what may. Make nice and pretend heaven is on earth. You may have not asked for this, Mom, but you're not helping yourself out of it either."

Henry and Jimmy sat in silence watching the argument unfold. They were both mesmerized. It was the first opposing opinion ever expressed in their home, even from Margo. The one person who Tommy had treated well—doted on in point of fact—the one person in the family that Tommy would actually defend, was getting uppity with Faith. If either of the boys expressed a contradiction, they were beaten until logic resurfaced. If Margo conveyed a minority thought, she was told to act like a lady and whichever boy was closest to Tommy was beaten until logic resurfaced. Margo had always abstained from verbalizing an opinion as a protective measure. Ironically, Tommy wasn't present for the impending altercation.

"I didn't get married to get a divorce," Faith said.

"No. You got married because you were knocked up. What am I stupid?"

"I think that's quite enough out of you. I'm doing the best I can with what I've got."

"What you've got is a wasted life, Mom. A life that is living you. And it looks like that isn't about to change."

"So you've got it all figured out? I wish I was as smart as you when I was fifteen."

"I don't want to say anything more to you," Margo said. "I'm only going to hurt your feelings and that isn't going to make you understand what I'm trying to say. You're going to do what you're going to do. Just don't expect me to like it or lie about it. You send us to a Catholic school to learn that lying is a sin, then you ask us to do that very thing."

Margo got up from the table having not eaten. She left the dining room and the home. Her favorite dish would be wasted as was the effort put forth in making it.

Once the public display was over, Jimmy devoured his food. It was cold by then, but by the way he was shoveling it in, it was unlikely that he noticed or even tasted it. He inhaled two helpings and then he too left the table and the house.

Henry sat at the table with his mom who refused to cry in front of him. She was trying to be the rock, when the reality was that she needed one.

The two of them sat in silence for a long time. Food and dirty dishes scattered about the table, kitchen counters, and sink. The detritus could wait. The cleanup was going to take an enormous effort. All of it.

Henry finally broke the silence.

"Wanna listen to some records Mom?"

Faith snapped out of her deep thought. Looked to her left at her youngest son, touching his hand with hers.

"What was that honey?"

"Do want to put on some records? Bob Dylan? Joni Mitchell?"

"Oh …. Yeah …. " She nodded her head, tears holding strong. A thin attempt at a smile hardly raised her dry cheeks. She patted his hand which was still under hers on the table.

"That's exactly what I want."

10

AFTER TOMMY ABANDONED HIS FAMILY, EVERYTHING changed. People came and went on Mallor Street. Margo, Jimmy, and Henry saw each other more often at school that at home. They passed each other in the halls or on the fields when attending a school sports event. They came and they went and they fended for themselves.

Faith was forced into working two jobs, one full-time for virtually no money but had benefits, and one part-time at night for minimum wage and no benefits. She scrimped and saved and somehow made ends meet. It was a study in new math—a new economic paradigm—because on paper nothing should have added up. She paid the full mortgage on a house that was worth less than what she would get if she sold it, especially after the fifty-fifty split with Tommy. She paid all the bills associated with said house, and heat alone was killing her.

The kid's school tuition at Saint Ann's was henceforth on scholarship, the church quietly picked up the tab as a token for doing the right thing in terms of Faith's non-divorce.

Use It Up

She drove a jalopy that was best suited for the scrapyard, but she was forced to keep putting money into it since her mechanic-husband wouldn't fix it. One of Tommy's former employers took pity on her and gave her a break on the repairs, which helped, but the car broke down so often that it was virtually a monthly expense.

Not only was there no alimony, Tommy wasn't giving her money for child support either. She did it alone.

The two jobs she worked to pay for all of said expenses meant that she too was never around.

Faith used to attend all of Henry's baseball games. A luxury she could no longer afford as of 1984. Henry's last season playing the sport was 1986, a development his mother didn't learn until much later.

Suppers were no longer nightly or at a specific hour. Each Devlin was on their own, left to concoct what they could from the provisions in the cupboards and fridge. A craft never before learned by either of the boys as it was previously unnecessary.

There was no an allowance, but there'd never been one. If any of the kids needed something, Faith would find a way to get money from the small household budget. She would only ask for simple chores in return for her benevolence. Now, the household chores increased while the kid's standard of living fell. There'd never been much to trickle down, but now there was nothing. So money, too, became Darwinistic.

Henry got a job at the local package and convenience store once baseball was no longer an occupation. In Massachusetts, the ABC didn't allow just any grocer to sell even beer and wine. The Commonwealth State left each town or city within it to determine their own regulations for sale of alcohol. Some towns were dry. Some had rules about Sundays. Still other towns limited the number of licenses to entities looking to own a package store, or *packie*. But all alcohol sales, if a town chose to allow it, was either sold at a restaurant, bar, or from a licensed state liquor store.

71

Bridgewater was a town that had decided to cease the issue of any new licenses. Meaning that those that were already in the retail booze business had the corner on the market. Stewart's was one of two packies still in operation.

When Henry first got his job at Stewart's, he wasn't old enough to handle either money or alcohol. He was allowed to count recycled bottles and cans that were returned by customers who had paid a deposit for the bottles and cans when they originally purchased their beverages. So he counted and sorted the sticky containers, adding up a nickel for each one and totaling the dollar amount for the customer who drove up to the receiving dock with his or her bottles. He then handed the ticket with the total to the customer to bring into the store for credit or cash refund for their deposit. For this job he received minimum wage.

Henry was excited that the minimum wage went up to $3.75 in 1988, his senior year. He had worked at Stewart's for three years and had not received a raise until the state mandated that the owner do so. At twenty or thirty hours, his take-home did little to fill his wallet.

With an entrepreneurial spirit, he decided that additional monies could be gathered without having to attain an additional job.

Customers returning large quantities of liquor bottles, soda, beer bottles and cans, rarely knew the exact number of returns or the exact dollar amount they were owed. Skimming a few bottles here and there, Henry was able to set aside a few dollars. This was no way to get rich, but those few dollars could then be invested in commodities for future sale. Those commodities were in high demand, especially by those who were not old enough to purchase them.

The commodities were various flavors of alcohol.

He partnered with a cashier inside the store, who was also under the drinking age but old enough to ring in the alcohol on the cash register. Once enough money was amassed from skimming deposits, alcohol could be rung into the register. Alcohol that was being taken off the same loading dock that Henry worked in.

Henry would take the booze off the receiving dock and put it in the dumpster in the rear of the store, which could then be picked up later after the store was closed.

It wasn't stealing, he justified, because it was being paid for. The owner wouldn't figure it out because his stock wasn't shrinking, it was being sold.

The alcohol that Henry dealt was sold at three hundred percent of market value, the amount split down the middle with the cashier he partnered with inside the store. All of the money was pure profit because they hadn't actually purchased the alcohol with their own money in the first place.

And the orders came in. Everyone in the school needed booze, and there were only two stores in town to get it. Neither legally. They could wait outside one of the stores and talk an adult of legal age into going in to buy it for them, or they could get it through Henry.

The owner asked Henry when he turned eighteen if he wanted to get out of the sticky, fly-infested back room and work the cash register, but of course that would ruin his gig. Of course he declined, making more money in his twenty hours per week than his mother did at her full-time job if you didn't account for her benefits.

Because he was supplying all of the events, he was asked to attend all of the local parties. Most of the time he refused to go. He would only make an appearance if there was a chance that Kat would be there.

The big party on the Cape in the fall of his senior year was the biggest party he had ever seen with the exception of the one his brother had taken him to two years prior. The party after which he spied his father with Kat's mom. An event he would never forget no matter how hard he tried. The bonfires on Falmouth Heights Beach were many, the alcohol free-flowing, as were drugs. Mating rituals abound.

Henry was happily mingling from clique to clique when he noticed her. Kat was in her own small group of girls around a small fire. They had their own boom-box turned low which was playing *She Drives Me Crazy by* The Fine Young Cannibals.

They made eye contact as Henry slowly made his way across the sand to her group.

"Hey Kat."

"Hey back."

"I never see you at these things," Henry said. He approached out of impulse, without a plan. He immediately regretted not having one. Smooth had washed away with tide as the tension was getting awkward, Kat hadn't responded right away.

She just looked to her girlfriends and giggled. Henry was unaware of their inside joke, but he was sure it had something to do with him. The faint crashing of waves could be heard mixed with other boom-boxes in the background of the slightly louder Fine Young Cannibals. The interval was brutal and he almost walked away.

"You must come to all of these things," she finally said.

"No, not really. Why do you say that?"

"Aren't you the one who supplies them?"

It was common knowledge for those who planned parties, or popular attendees, but Henry didn't know that Kat was aware of his enterprise.

"Well .... Yeah. But I don't really hang out with many people. Once they get their beer or whatever, they are kinda finished with me until the next time."

"Oh. I hear your name come up a lot, so I figured you did." Kat said.

"I hear your name a lot too. You're Henry Devlin, right?" One of the other girls in the clique from the other side of the fire pit made her way toward the male arrival.

"That's me."

"I'm Nicky," she said. "You're pretty popular."

"I don't know about that. I get them what they want. If I didn't they wouldn't know my name."

Nicky leaned in and whispered in his ear. "Can you get us some coke?" As she leaned in she brushed her breast against his arm.

Henry tried to be cool but pulled his arm away. "No. I don't supply that stuff. Just booze."

Another one of the girls in the small group chimed in.

"Hey, aren't you like a shoo-in for our class valedictorian? I heard you have, like, perfect grades."

Henry shrugged his shoulders but didn't vocalize a response.

More silence.

"Hey Kat, you wanna take a walk with me down the beach."

"I don't want to leave my fr—"

"—Oh, go ahead," Nicky said. "I'm not getting anywhere."

All the girls laughed and took swigs of their respective adult beverages.

"Sure. Okay."

The two walked and talked as they made way down the beach. Time stood still. They came to a large rock far away from the festivities. They could vaguely make out the various fires, but could no longer hear the music or the laughter. Just the crashing of the waves.

They sat in the sand by the rock, talking about everything yet nothing. The enormous pink whale on the beach was not spoken of. Their parents weren't remotely thought of. No mention was made of previous embarrassments or opportunities missed. Certainly nothing about climbing trees in her backyard. They spoke about each other. About music. About where they were going to go and what they were going to do. Dreams. They connected for the first time, their energy was electric.

And they kissed.

For Henry is was a kiss by which all others would be judged. No brother to ruin the moment. No other living soul could spoil what was meant to be. Just the two of them. He felt it. She felt it. They touched and kissed and were lost in each other. Finally all of the songs truly made sense.

It was magic.

Two hours passed before Kat started to feel bad about leaving her friends.

"We can all hang out together. If that's okay," Kat said.

"Sure."

"There are just so many people, I don't want to get separated too much," she elaborated.

"No girl stranded. I get it."

But they never should have gone back.

For Henry, the night seemed almost too good to be true. Because it was.

They arrived back at the party just in time for the police to break it up. There was underage drinking, sex and drugs. Handcuffs were donned and paddy wagons filled. And the suspects were all trying to save their own asses. Which is why they gave them the supplier. The name everyone knew.

Henry Devlin.

11

THE FALMOUTH POLICE MOVED SWIFTLY IN SCOOPING up all of the minors fueled with drugs and alcohol on their beach. They didn't need a SWAT team or need to bring in the National Guard. They backed the police vans up in the parking lot on Grand Avenue and loaded them with sniveling pseudo-adults.

Teenagers often act tough and fearless, but in reality most aren't hardened and are filled with one great fear. A fear of losing the very freedom that they have just acquired. Fear of dreams falling apart because of an indiscretion. And they are willing to do or say most anything to keep their freedoms intact.

The police knew exactly how to handle the situation. Kids drinking, drugging, and having sex on the beach weren't anomalies. This particular event, however, was on a much larger scale than the norm. The police found the kids with the widest and wettest eyes and put the hammer to them. The result was the same in every interrogation, without fail, and every minor questioned cried the same name. If the kids were lying, the police concluded, then it was the most well-rehearsed conspiracy they had ever encountered.

It took the cops longer to ascertain which of the miscreants being corralled was Henry Devlin than it took to sort out who had provided all of the party favors.

Use It Up

Once they found him, he was put into the back of a separate patrol car and brought to the station for questioning. His interrogation at the precinct was far more thorough and took substantially longer than the dozens of adolescents who were questioned on the beach.

Henry didn't panic. He was more upset that his night with Kat was cut short. Again. That he was finally enjoying some happiness, finally making some progress with Kat, only to be thwarted by circumstance. By the God who supposedly loved him. The entity that controls all things was yet again preventing him from any joy. Henry was yet again the brunt of the puppet master's sick sense of humor.

The police questioned him for over an hour but gleaned no information. Henry invoked his right to remain silent, other than repeating a single word—*Lawyer*—thereby invoking another of his rights, an attorney. A right that was ignored.

Henry believed that the truth about what was being pinned on him would ferret out. He wasn't responsible for any of the drugs seized on Falmouth Heights Beach. Nor was he responsible for supplying all of the alcohol the minors were consuming, though he did sell the lion's share of it. There was no way to prove that he had actually supplied any of it, just the word of an indeterminate number of chicken-shit rats that had sold him out. He hadn't, in fact, purchased any alcohol for resale since there was no record of his purchase, and likewise, there was no record of a theft. Even if the police figured out where the alcohol had come from, which they were very likely to do, no sale or theft from Stewart's could be linked to Henry. He hadn't been caught buying it or stealing it. The allegations that he obtained it and sold it was hearsay. Henry had watched the police show up at the front door for his brother Jimmy enough times to know how this would play out. Heard enough advice from his brother about what to do, and what not to do in case of arrest.

Jimmy had just pulled one over on the Bridgewater police a few months prior, in point of fact. Henry resolved to keep his mouth shut and wait it out.

Another virtue of the young is the belief that the system works. That any injustice will be dealt with fairly or they could activate their masses to affect change. Later in life comes the callous realization that the lady with the scales is actually an overweight, slow-moving, judgmental bitch who's ever-peeking through the blindfold. Virtue is eventually lost with the submission that the system is too big to change. Henry was still young and could still be counted as one of the virtuous.

But the slow gears of the legal system turned.

Henry didn't have a lawyer, nor did he know the name of one who would take his call. He didn't have a phone number, nor did he know if a public defender would even take the case. The police weren't going to provide him with a lawyer, quite obviously, since they refused to even acknowledge that he had asked for one. He was afforded a single phone call, and was told when handed the receiver that he would only get the one, so make it count. His brother wouldn't be available. Nor was Margo, though both for varying reasons at the time. He hoped against all hope that his mother was home.

She was.

And when she finally arrived in Falmouth, driving for over an hour to the police station from Bridgewater, she was none too happy.

She spouted off things like:

"I would have expected this from your brother, but now you?"
"This is exactly what I need right now."
"You were the one I didn't think I had to worry about."
"I trusted you and this is the thanks I get."

Like that.

It didn't matter how much he tried to explain, how many words he tried to interject, she went on with the verbal gleeting.

The police held Henry the remainder of the weekend for a Monday arraignment, despite not having any actual, physical evidence.

And on that Monday, the prosecutor wasn't able to sustain an indictment. Normally an arraignment hearing is for the purpose of attaining a plea from the accused, guilty or not-guilty, and to determine if bail will be afforded. In Henry's case, however, there was more going on. Henry's public defender wanted to try the case right there and then.

All testimony was self-serving hearsay without a shred of actual proof, his court-appointed attorney said. Henry wasn't responsible for any of the eleven charges he faced, he also said. The accused's rights were violated and an evidentiary hearing was eventually denied once the judge presiding over the case was apprised. The judge also had stern words for the prosecution and police when learning from the court appointed attorney—that was assigned only ten minutes before going in front of said judge—that his client was denied counsel when he requested it during questioning.

The case was dismissed without prejudice, meaning that when and if the prosecutor came up with any actual proof against Henry, more than the self-serving accusations of minors, he or she could refile the charges against Henry Devlin.

In the meantime, the defendant was free to go.

Henry left Falmouth to find Kat.

12

FAITH DEVLIN HADN'T EVER SEEN THE INSIDE OF A courtroom other than Perry Mason on the television, and was more than content to never see one in person. Faith spent her entire life adhering to laws both church and secular. Had it not been for her children, that streak may have stood the test of time. Unfortunately, she had grown accustom to courtrooms of late. Henry appeared before a judge in the fall of '88. Jimmy had been in court during the summer the following year. Margo was the first to have her run-in with the law, paving the way as first-born of the Devlin trio, in 1987.

The Commonwealth had prosecuted Andrew Benning for the statutory rape of Margo Devlin that year. A crime that he didn't deny, only that what took place between the accused and the minor wasn't a crime.

Benning and his attorney claimed that what the state was calling a crime was an act of love between two consensual people. They weren't claiming that Margo was a legal adult, only that she had the requisite mental capacity to form an opinion over her wants and desires. That she was a willing participant at seventeen years old, only a few months shy of her eighteenth birthday.

They would further argue that Andrew Benning was unaware of the age of consent statute, though they weren't holding too much hope that this argument would fly, since all teachers in Massachusetts are well aware of the law.

Benning and his attorney were putting most of their hope in one basket. They were counting on the prosecution's star witness, Margo. The accused was hoping that his former lover would hold up in court, if she was to testify at all.

The strategies being made by the defense were not overly worrisome to the prosecution since criminals don't get to choose which laws apply to them. Seventeen is seventeen no matter how one chooses to look at it. Whether the victim knew the requisite age of consent or not, Benning was informed of it when gaining his teaching certificate. What was troubling for the Commonwealth was that Margo Devlin, the alleged victim, refused to testify.

When a victim refuses to press charges, which happens frequently in domestic abuse and rape cases, the state can still move forward in prosecuting the alleged criminal. The cases become much more difficult to prosecute, which is often why the charges are dropped. Without a person to testify that a wrong was done to them, a jury will be left with reasonable doubt. Reasonable doubt is the wet-dream of every defense attorney. Reasonable doubt equates to an acquittal. Prosecutors know this and are therefore very choosy about which cases they move forward with when a victim refuses to testify. Prosecutors tend to move forward with landmark cases, high profile cases, or ones where they can flip the victim. It was all about winning. Whether a full-blown prosecution or cutting a deal, it was the responsibility of the District Attorney's office to bolster the win column.

A female Assistant District Attorney was chosen for the case. The elected District Attorney felt that a female prosecutor would do much better in swaying a jury as well as promote a higher degree of cooperation from the alleged victim. Only a female could possibly know what it was like to endure such a violation, he thought, and only a female could evoke the requisite sympathy that would be needed to convict the sonofabitch Benning. If he was going to move forward with the case, he wanted a conviction. Period.

The ADA in the Commonwealth versus Benning did everything within her power—and things outside of it—to persuade Margo to take the stand. She needed to flip her star witness, the victim, in order to bring the case to the correct conclusion. To no avail.

The Assistant District Attorney spoke to the school, asking for support and guidance as to how to persuade Margo Devlin to testify against her abuser. Saint Ann's gave it, but the same couldn't be said for the majority of students there. They sided with Margo. The bulk of the student body felt that if she wasn't calling it rape, then it wasn't rape. Should Mr. Benning be fired, sure. Imprisoned, no.

Margo was a good student. Not the best, but she had good enough grades and enough credit to be waved from the remainder of her senior year. She would graduate high school without having to go back to the school ever again. The ADA aided in achieving this waver, feeling that if Margo was separated from the rest of the student body, her support system, she could be persuaded to testify.

But that didn't work.

Next came pressure on Faith. The ADA insisted that this had happened under her watch, or lack thereof. Because Faith was working multiple jobs and wasn't home as much as was obviously necessary, Margo had gotten into trouble she wouldn't normally have gotten into. The minor had not been in trouble before, therefore it was a lack of supervision that had caused her current mess. Without supervision, all of her children were at risk of running amok. If Faith couldn't persuade her daughter to help the state make their case, the ADA said that she might not be able to convince the Department of Child Services that her children weren't better served in someone else's care, specifically the

Foster Care system. The Assistant District Attorney was very forthcoming about the horrors of that system.

Faith was mortified by public knowledge of her family troubles and pleaded with Margo. Faith just wanted all of this to go away, to be swept under the rug so she could show her face in public. But this too failed. Margo had dug her heels in. Fortunately, taking Faith's kids away from her turned out to be a veiled threat, or DCS was too busy to care. In either case, nothing happened.

Finally the ADA held Margo's feet to the fire. She was hindering prosecution, which was a felony. She would be incarcerated until she agreed to testify under oath that the accused had sexual knowledge of her, and that she was under the legal age of consent at the time.

Margo found the entire charade ironic. They were going to charge her for a crime as an adult in order to prosecute someone for an alleged crime because she was a minor. She also thought they were again bluffing.

She thought wrong.

Margo was arrested and sent to jail pending her own hearing. Faith tried to get her out, but they wouldn't even contemplate it without Margo's cooperation.

Faith again tried to convince her daughter, but she again refused.

For three weeks.

Margo finally relented after getting into a vicious fight while in custody. She left the fray far worse off than her aggressor. Margo was badly bruised from her beating, though luckily there would be no permanent physical damage. The ADA had made her point and she was tired of fighting, literally, both physically and against a system that was stacked against her. The prosecutor was happy that the victim had come around, the charges were temporarily suspended and she was released as long as she played ball. Margo was also informed that if she lied on the stand, they would reinstate the hindering charge and add perjury and contempt charges as side dishes.

Margo was trapped. She was being forced to help send the man she loved to prison or face going back behind lock-and-key herself. She felt defeated in her attempts to completely save Andy, but Margo was desperate to find a way out of dragging him further into the muck and mire of the legal system. Her testimony would destroy him. She sought his advice, through calls and visits, but contact with Andrew Benning was forbade.

There was only one way out that she could see, and she took it.

Margo ran.

Part Two

No more teachers, no more books.

13

JIMMY'S EXPERIMENTS WITH DRUGS AND ALCOHOL were well into beta by the summer of 1988. Faith was at wit's end. Margo had fought both her mother and the legal system a year ago, trying to protect the man who abused her. Her middle child had unofficially dropped out of school three years prior and was abusing himself with God knows how many chemicals. Faith tried to tell herself that it was a phase, that Jimmy would grow out of it. He was rebelling, probably due to the lack of a strong male role-model. Excuses, however, were nearing exhaustion.

Faith was ashamed to be seen in public, other than church, and things were getting worse. She could only take so much.

Jimmy would stumble into the house at the unholiest of hours, reeking of sin. He would get a part-time job instead of going to school and hold onto it just long enough to get a paycheck. Faith wanted him to finish school, a private school that was given to him on scholarship because of her efforts, but if Jimmy wanted to work she could certainly use the help with bills. Instead of helping her with household bills, he would blow it on chemicals. Jimmy would go on a bender for as long as the money lasted, having to find another job once it did.

Time went by. Months turned to a year. A year turned into three. Jimmy hadn't ever been a prize student, but at least school kept him sober some of the time. He eventually got his GED, only because the jobs he applied for required it, and hadn't been sober longer than one week at a time since.

It all came to a head in the summer of '88. Faith was still weary from Faith's incarceration and her disappearance, still clinging to the hope that Margo would walk through the door at any moment. Her daughter's unwillingness to do what Faith felt was the correct and honorable thing, given the circumstances, was a terrible burden and constant source of embarrassment. Margo refused to do what the law agreed was the appropriate set of steps to deal with her abuser. What the church was advocating. The moral path. But all would be forgiven if and when Margo came home.

But she didn't and likely wouldn't. Instead, Margo was on the run. A bench warrant was issued for her arrest, not that any officer would devote much time in searching for Margo Devlin.

Faith was further drained by Jimmy's lifestyle over the course of time. Her middle son had been going through his supposed phase for years, and enough was enough. She hadn't raised her children to throw their lives away. Jimmy was getting worse and Faith was afraid of losing another one of her children.

One night that summer, Jimmy tried to get inside the house at three o'clock in the morning, only he couldn't manage the key in the lock. He banged and yelled and woke not only Faith, but neighboring house lights were being turned on as well in order to ascertain the commotion.

Faith couldn't believe the state her child was in when she arrived at the door. The person on the other side of the peephole was ghastly. Completely unrecognizable. Pale. Emaciated. Unfocused eyes were sunk deep into the stranger's skull.

And it was the final nail.

She refused to let him inside the house. Faith told him from the other side of the door that she wanted him to go sleep it off. Go wherever he went and sober up. Come back home when he could talk sensibly. And rest assured, they would talk about this.

Jimmy went quiet. Faith waited a few minutes inside the front door, listening to see if her son had ventured on or if he would return, then went to bed thinking that her son had taken her advice.

She thought wrong.

Instead, Jimmy passed out on her front lawn, half of his body laying on the sidewalk. He was unconscious, urine-soaked, and couldn't be roused.

Less than two hours after Faith had stood her ground, the pounding at the front door recommenced. She refused to get out of bed. But Henry did.

It was the Bridgewater Police.

The officers responding to a noise complaint originally were going to bring Jimmy in for public intoxication. When they couldn't get him to regain consciousness, they decided to call an ambulance. While waiting for the paramedics to arrive, they searched his person for some form of identification and found enough narcotics to kill Keith Richards.

Cocaine. Heroine. Marijuana.

The trifecta.

Jimmy still went to the hospital, but he went there handcuffed to a gurney.

The gavel fell on the base, the sound echoed through the courtroom.

"Next," the man said. The man who donned the black robe and had used the gavel was Judge Schpicer. He was in his early sixties, the hair that used to be on his head was now plentiful on his upper lip. The thick, white mustache was very Sam Elliott.

"Commonwealth versus James Thomas Devlin your Honor," the clerk said.

"And why is this case here? Isn't this set for trial?"

The prosecutor spoke up. He was a low-level underling in the District Attorney's office. He was new to his position and he was there to agree to court diversion. "We have reached an agreement with this case, Judge. Before you, is a motion to set aside a disposition pending the completion of a rehabilitation program. If the defendant completes the program without reoffending or lapse, we would recommend two years probation with random screening."

"You want to defer this case for two years?" The judge knew he meant court diversion, which the young prosecutor could have said to save some time. But the jurist wanted to break his balls a bit.

"No, your Honor. Pardon me for not being clear. We would postpone moving forward on this case until Mister Devlin completes a thirty day program. If that goes well, we would plea out and sentence him to two years of probation."

"Sentencing is my job, isn't it?"

"Yes. I meant that the Commonwealth would recommend and agree to the two years."

"Very well," Schpicer said. He then turned to the public defender and Jimmy. Faith was seated in the pew behind her son in the gallery with Father Donovan. Their pastor was present in case a character witness was needed.

"And this is agreed to by the defense?"

"My client agrees your Honor."

The Judge then addressed Jimmy directly.

"Mr. Devlin. Do you understand the agreement that your lawyer is ready to sign off at your behest?"

Jimmy looked terrible. The oversized jumpsuit was falling off of him. He was cold sweating from the detoxification, the itching and pain was overtaking him.

The court appointed lawyer nudged him to respond to the judge as there were a few seconds of silence.

"Yes."

"You realize that if you fail to complete the program within the thirty-day allotment, this agreement is null and void?"

"Yes."

"And nobody is forcing you to enter this agreement?"

"No."

"You understand that you have the right to a trial by jury, and to confront your accusers and any witnesses who might testify against you?"

"Yes."

"And furthermore, you understand that in a trial, the prosecutor has to prove beyond a reasonable doubt the charges against you to a jury of your peers?"

"Yes."

"And you agree to give up those rights?"

"Yes."

"Once completing the program, you would plead guilty to your felonies without a trial and be sentenced to two years of probation. In addition to supervision, you will be subject to random testing for drugs and/or alcohol. If you fail any of those tests or fail to meet the obligations set forth by your probation officer, you would be subject to the full penalties of the crimes that you are pleading guilty to. You understand all of this?"

"Yes."

"Very well. Mr. Devlin, before I adjourn this hearing, I would like to offer you a bit of advice. Look at me Son."

Jimmy looked up at the mustache.

"You are far too young to throw your life away on drugs. You've got a second chance here. I see too many of these cases, each time the person before me tells me that they are going to behave like a productive member of society. Every time. And then they end up right back here, or worse, and the penalties get more severe. And each time they use up more of their potential. More of their freedom.

"I sincerely hope that you beat the odds, Son. I sincerely hope that you use this time to get clean, get your priorities straight, and redeem yourself."

Judge Schpicer looked at the pale skeleton, hoping against hope that the shell of a human before him, unlike the countless others in the past, actually heard him. Understood him. That he would never see this young man again and further hoping that he didn't end up dead because of the agreement.

"Good luck," Schpicer said. The gavel came down.

"Next."

14

HENRY'S ACADEMIC SCHOLARSHIPS DIDN'T ADD UP to much money, despite his performance. He valedictoriously graduated from high school, gave the speech though not wanting to. The Catholic church gave him some money towards college, but not much. He achieved some government money, but that too wasn't enough to cover any meaningful tuition. Several schools offered to give him a partial ride, but it certainly wouldn't cover nearly enough of the high tuition. Henry didn't know what he wanted to study anyway. He had the brains to do anything he wanted to, any career he desired was at his feet. Nothing fancied him, not that he had the money for college anyway. The promised four years of scholarship money didn't add up to one semester at a decent school, let alone the eight semesters for a Bachelor's degree.

The summer of '89 was an eventful one, too busy to focus on school anyway. Margo was still AWOL, a circumstance that was unlikely to change. Jimmy was trying to fight off his own demons. College would have to wait, indefinitely.

The owner of Stewart's would have gladly let him work there for as long as he liked. He didn't believe the rumors, nor could anyone prove to him that a theft had ever existed. The charges were dropped in any event, so the accusations must have been false.

For Henry, the job simply wasn't going to pay any bills. His mother was struggling to keep the Mallor Street house. Struggling and failing. They were forced to move into the rundown cottage on Carver Pond. Tommy didn't put up a fight. He couldn't have cared less about the place since he didn't go there anymore. The cottage was falling down and the senior Devlin had better, more important demands on his time. Henry needed a better job to help fix the place up, make it a proper home for his mother.

He found a job at Ashmont Iron Works in his hometown. AIW was established in 1945, servicing all of New England with steel fabrication of nearly every industrial application. They were the go-to supplier for construction companies in need of fabricating, welding, and erecting steel in the neighboring six states. Henry didn't belong to a union, nor did he care to, so he ran a forklift in the warehouse.

Henry started working at AIW the week following his graduation and continued on through the summer, sucking up all of the overtime as given to him in order to pay the Craver remodeling costs. The place on Carver Pond needed to be fixed, though the necessity became more urgent.

Henry financially supported Faith through her pseudo-foreclosure, the bank taking the Mallor Street house while releasing claim to the cottage on Carver Pond. Fortunately, the Mallor house was resold without the need for the Devlins to make up any difference, thereby alleviating any need for the bank to repossess the collateral, not that the cottage would have yielded any substantial money to pay the debt.

Money was spent by the fistful to bring the small dwelling to a state of livability. He worked and sucked up as much overtime as they would give him. That summer was spent working or sleeping with very little else filling the spaces between.

Until one day in late summer, a visitor came to Ashmont Iron Works.

Henry's supervisor, Bradbury, flagged him down in the warehouse while he was on his forklift, as usual. Bradbury liked Henry because he kept to himself and always worked the extra hours when asked. Henry didn't get visitors and never took a break one-second longer than was required of him by law.

"Devlin! You've got a visitor here. She says it's very important," Bradbury shouted above the noise of the industrial equipment, though he was only a few feet away.

"*She*?"

"I didn't get her name. Wicked pretty. Look, if you need time let me know. You've got some time on the books."

"I need to work," Henry said as he got off his forklift.

"It's paid time. Everybody get's it. No favors. If you need it, you need it."

"Yeah, okay. Thanks. Pretty huh? Where's this visitor?"

"Front offices."

Henry made his way across the multiple football field sized warehouse toward the front offices. When he arrived, he was stunned by who was seated in the reception waiting room.

She sat on one end of a couch in a sundress, legs crossed, leafing through one of the fanned-out, outdated tooling magazine from the reception area coffee table. Her head lifted up when Henry came through the door.

"Kat. Are you okay?" Henry took off his blue hardhat.

She stood, gently tossed the magazine to the top of the pile and straightened her paper-thin dress.

"Yes. Well …. No. Is there someplace we can talk?"

Kat could solve him with a smile, even a fake one as she was putting on just then. Whatever the reason for the visit, which was promising not to be good, Henry was in.

"Sure. There's a picnic table," he said. Henry showed her outside. On the other side of the parking lot was a small grassy area nestled with a few trees. A picnic table was set up there for the employees who dressed up in the offices to take their breaks or to have a smoke. None of the workers in the warehouse used it, though they did procure their daily coffee and snacks from the snack wagon that parked on that end of the parking lot.

As they approached, Henry asked Kat if she wanted a coffee or lemonade or something.

"No thanks. So, I didn't see you at any of the graduations parties. I thought for sure you'd be around. I wanted to tell you that your speech was great. Really great."

"Thanks. I haven't really been around. I don't really fit in with those people. After the big mess on the Cape …. They were all quick to send me down the river. Those same assholes were trying to get beer from me a few days later. I hate this fucking town."

"It's big and it's small," she concurred.

They sat on the picnic table across from each other. They were alone with the exception of the operator of the weenie wagon twenty feet away, who was ogling Kat. The operator was unsuccessful in trying to be discreet.

"Eyes on your own paper, Chief," Henry called to the weenie guy. Once satisfied that the lech had turned attention elsewhere, Henry turned his back to Kat.

"So what's going on? It's not that I don't want to see you, but …. You know," he said. "I've called you probably a thousand times and you're never home or return my calls. It's not like we've really—"

"—I know, I know. But I need your help. You're the only one I can talk to about this. If there was anyone else …."

"Wow, flattery. I want to help. Seriously. Whatever it is, I'm glad you came to me, even if I'm the last person on the list."

"It's your dad."

"Oh." Henry looked at his hands which were folded on top of the table. Tommy was the last thing that he wanted to hear or think about.

"And my mom too. They've been …. Wow, this is so hard to say."

"You don't need to say anything. I know."

"You know? How long have you known?"

"A long time."

"How long? I just found out about it. My dad is losing his mind."

"How long has he known? Did your dad just find out?"

"I think. Why? You didn't answer my question, how long have you known?"

"It's been going on for years, Kat."

"And you've known about it the whole time? And you didn't say anything?"

Henry looked up at her. Even when she was hurt and sad and angry she was radiant.

"And what would I have said? 'Hey, girl that I've been infatuated with for as long as I can remember, I know that we've had more weird moments than good, just thought I would add another one to the weird column.'"

"They need to be stopped, Henry. It's a mess."

"Isn't this really between your parents?"

"And *your* father."

"In terms of biology only. I haven't even seen the man in …. Well, I don't even know how long."

"He was shitty to your family? Sorry for you, but he's being really shitty to mine. How many lives does he have to ruin? My father won't do anything. He is a complete wimp. His take on it is, 'If she doesn't love me anymore, there is nothing I can do about it.' I know he still loves her, but for some reason he isn't fighting for her. He's cracking up with his hands in his pockets, and I can't just sit around and watch."

"Would it help him get off his ass if he knew that your mom isn't the only one?"

"What do you mean? He has other women too?" Her anger was taking over. Her scowl was forming a line between her eyebrows, one that would eventually turn into a wrinkle with age. Henry thought it to be an adorable feature.

"I don't know for sure, but I would bet," Henry said.

"Zebra can't change his stripes kind of thing," she added while shaking her head in disgust.

"He's more like a donkey, but yes."

"So what do we do?"

Henry looked around the mini park and thought for a moment.

"My boss said that I've got some time coming to me. Do you want to go someplace and figure this out?"

"Yeah, sure."

They walked toward the side parking lot where the warehouse workers parked every day. The visitor lot was in the front of the building where the offices were located.

"I'm parked in front, Henry."

"We can take my car. We'll come back for yours later. No sense in taking two cars."

"Where are we going?"

"Wherever we want."

Bradbury had a clipboard in his hand when Henry and the visitor appeared around the corner. He was in the receiving bay when he spotted Henry. He watched the comely visitor get into the passenger seat of the employee's 1977 AMC Gremlin. He continued to watch as Henry closed the door for her. As his employee came around the rear of the car, the two men made eye contact.

Use It Up

Henry received the thumbs up, giving a nod of appreciation to his boss.

He got into his car and drove away.

HENRY NEEDED A SHOWER BEFORE VENTURING anywhere with Kat. He smelled like metal shavings, exhaust, and body odor. He drove Kat to Carver Pond so he could change clothes.

"This is your place? It's beautiful," she said as the pulled into the drive.

"It's old and it's not mine. The bank took the old house, so we don't live on Mallor anymore. Tommy's father built this forever ago. It's falling apart but we had nowhere else to go."

"Your mom's here too?"

"Yes. But not now. She's at one of her jobs." He didn't mention Jimmy since she didn't ask and failing to see the need to disclose more family indiscretion. Keeping appearances was still a Devlin trademark even in the worst of times.

"Losing your house must be terrible," Kat said. "But this is much better, don't you think?"

"No not really. Like I said, it's falling apart."

They left the driveway and went inside the cottage.

"I love it. It's quaint. The pond is gorgeous."

"Glad you like it. I'd give you the penny tour but I wouldn't know how to make change. Everything is where you'd expect it, make yourself at home, I'm gonna hop in the shower real quick."

"No hurry. Is your mom coming home soon? I don't know if I can face her just yet."

"Why? You didn't do anything wrong."

"It's still embarrassing."

"You don't have to worry, she'd be more embarrassed than you could ever be, believe me. Anyway, she won't be home until really late. My mom goes to her night job directly from her day job," Henry said and closed the bathroom door behind him. Again he didn't mention his brother Jimmy, who these days was either trying to find work or at a meeting to uphold his sobriety.

There was only one bathroom in the cottage, though there were three doors to get into it. One door from the living area, and one from each of the two tiny bedrooms. Henry turned on the water to get it hot, which took a while, and got some clothes together.

By the time he disrobed, steam was starting to come from the shower. He got in and went about his business. Henry was in full lather when he received company.

"I forgot to ask if you had to use the bathroom before I jumped in," he called from the shower. "We only have the one bathroom, sorry."

The shower door opened behind him.

"Room for two?"

Kat entered the shower, without garment and unabashedly stood before him. She looked stunning. Sculptures of perfect women had been created with more flaw than Henry could point out on Kat.

He had fantasized about being intimate with Kat so many different times. So many different ways. Scenarios. This was the moment that he had waited for yet had never envisioned this. His mind ran riot while his body took over.

She pressed her slender body against him, her small breasts against his ribs. They embraced while the hot water from the nozzle ran down on them. The suds running down from his body, transferring to hers.

They kissed while she ran her hands all over him. She rubbed and stroked, Henry nearly succumbing.

He turned off the water and the two were still entwined as they left the bathroom for the bed. They hadn't bothered to dry off, the sheets of the bed did the job while their wet bodies writhed and kneaded into one another.

The moment wouldn't wait. Release was followed by euphoria and a desire for more. And so it went, using each other up past the point of spent. They took each other in, rolling and grinding and suckling and draining each other at long last. Over and over and over again.

"I could sit here with you forever," Kat said. They sat on the back porch, looking over the pond as the sun was setting. The warm colors fading further toward darkness. Henry remained quiet.

"A penny for your thoughts," she added before taking a sip of her iced tea.

"Just enjoying the moment. It's the only one I've had here. I used to fish out there with Tommy. Winters on the ice. Summers. But there was no joy in it. I may have felt some happiness at the time, but it wasn't real. No matter what I did, it was always wrong and it ended with a beating."

"Always? That's awful."

"Either me or Jimmy. If it was leaning toward me, Jimmy would egg him on. Save me from a beating if possible. He always got it worse because he just wouldn't shut up and take it. He always had to push it."

Henry paused for a moment before adding under his breath, "No wonder he turned to drugs."

"I'm so sorry." She turned to him, reaching to him in the chair next to her, stroked his hair and neck.

"I don't think he hurts my mom," Kat said. "I hope not."

"No. He wouldn't. Not women. Anything but. He killed my dog out there." Henry pointed out on the pond. He never learned exactly where, only that it happened on the ice.

"Your dog? Why would he kill your dog? Any dog for that matter?"

"Because I loved it." Henry looked down at his lap. A tear formed in the corner of his eye but he refused to let it fall in front of Kat. "He killed everything I ever loved in one way or another," he added as he looked away from her across the pond. "I could get a sunburn talking about all of the horrible shit that he's done, but you don't want to hear it as much as I don't want to think about it."

"Oh honey," she said and left her chair to sit on his lap. She kissed him as gently as she could. On his forehead. His nose. His neck. His lips.

And they made love again.

Henry awoke early the next morning, the other side of his bed was empty save for crumpled sheets.

He rose and searched the small cottage. His mother was home, sleeping in her room. She would be getting up soon, off to work then work again as she did every other day.

No sign of Kat.

He went out onto the back porch, she had seemed taken with the spot and the view. But she wasn't there.

103

No note on the counter, nor one back in his bedroom. She was gone.

Where did she go and how did she get there? I drove her here, he wondered.

Henry got dressed and went to Ashmont Iron Works.

Kat's car was gone.

Henry's supervisor, Bradbury, spotted him in the parking lot.

"Are you working today?"

"No. I just came to see about her car. The girl from yesterday."

"Uh huh. I wasn't sure I was gonna see you today," his boss said.

"Yeah, me neither. I need the day. If that's okay."

"Sure. Like I said, you've got time on the books. I hope you have fun."

Henry shook his head, staring at his shoes.

"Not gonna be any joy today."

16

ANY POST-COITUS AFTERGLOW WAS LONG USED UP BY the time Henry had risen to an empty bed, empty cottage, and empty parking lot. He couldn't help but feel as though that he had lost her again. Kat had vanished without so much as a word or note, kind or otherwise. What had he done this time? What had happened that sent her away?

These thoughts rattled around his brain long enough to remember the initial reason for her visit. Tommy. His supposed father.

Wonder and longing turned to anger. Another casualty of Thomas Devlin. The man had vaporized but was still wreaking havoc from behind the scenes, still destroying lives like some unseen gremlin.

Henry decided there in the parking lot that he was going to make his stand. The final line in the sand had been drawn. Kat was that line. She was everything that he ever wanted and she had been crossed. He got into his AMC and headed to the last garage that had the misfortune of giving Tommy work. The shop was ten miles away, the short trip didn't do much to cool down Henry.

Of course Tommy wasn't there. Long fired regarding the quality of work. Tommy viewed his work as incomparable, others needing to follow his ethic. The reality was that everyone else including the owner concluded that Tommy Devlin's work was slipshod. When the choice came down to "them or me" — there wasn't a choice.

The owner, in an effort to thin his competition, gave Tommy Devlin a glowing recommendation at another garage that had just opened on the other side of town. The owner told Henry that he didn't know if the arrogant sonofabitch remained in the employ of his competitor, but for the sake of his own business, he hoped so.

Henry sped over to Lynch's Auto Body & Repair, then finding the man he sought. The four bay doors were open, each with a car in it—some on a lift and some not—Tommy looking up at the undercarriage of a Saab near its manifold in bay number two. The clangs of metallic hand-tools and the buzzing of air tools could be heard above the shop radio playing classic rock from outside the garage.

Without making announcement or alerting anyone to his presence, Henry walked into the second bay undetected, threw back his right hand, and put every ounce of muscle and weight into his punch. The very definition of a haymaker.

Tommy never saw it coming. A shadow moved, catching his attention, turning to his left just in time to catch the full effect of a sucker-punch that had some serious stank on it. Nearly two decades of torment went into the blow, added to the newly acquired anger he felt for Katherine Bradar's despair.

The compressed air impact wrench Tommy was using and the attached hose fell to the concrete floor. As did Tommy himself. Henry's father recovered quicker than one might expect. Through broken nose and split lip, and while trying to pick himself up off of the greasy floor, he screamed at his son.

"What the fuck! Have you lost your goddamned mind?"

Every mechanic in the bay then dropped what they were doing to watch the show. Not one employee made an attempt to help the senior Devlin. Whatever beating he had just taken, or was about to take, the coworkers were fine with it. Tommy had no friends there. The only movement that was made, other than power tools being shut down, was the mechanic in bay number one closing the blinds of the observation window so the customers waiting for their vehicles inside wouldn't be privy to the show.

Henry picked up the four pound air wrench that Tommy had dropped, which to a layperson would look like a beefy drill.

"Stay away from her. Stay away from all of them," Henry said.

Tommy backed up toward the front of the lifted Saab and an enormous Snap-on tool box. "What are you talking about?"

"Mrs. Bradar. Kat. Mr. Bradar. Stay away from that family. You've fucked up your own, isn't that enough?"

"Oh you're a big man now? You think you can tell me what to do?" Tommy reached and grabbed the first object he could find out of the top of the toolbox. He came up with a socket wrench, which made him sorely outgunned.

"I'm warning you. Don't let me catch you anywhere near them," Henry said.

"Or what?"

"You need me to show you?"

"I've been kicking you ass since the day you fell out of your mom's twat, Kid. Today ain't gonna be any different."

Henry swung the heavy air tool from the attached hose like a medieval ball and chain weapon. The business end came around and hit Tommy from three feet away on his left forearm as Tommy was trying to defend himself. Upon impact, Tommy howled at the immense pain, his radius instantly fractured.

The tool continued around and Henry lifted his right hand above his head, swinging the tool around to strike again. The heavy device came left to right, circling and accelerating for another blow. This time Tommy was hit in the shoulder, doing additional damage to his left side. The blow glanced off his shoulder and struck his cheekbone.

Tommy was in a bad way and fell to the floor at the foot of his large toolbox.

Henry didn't swing the tool around a third time, though the lesson wasn't over. He bridged the space between them, kneeling down on top of Tommy's thigh, he began to wrap the air hose around his father's neck.

"Go to hell," Tommy managed.

"We're already in it. Hell is here and now, right here with me. Believe me, this last bit is only going to seem like an eternity."

Henry drove another punch to his father's face. The blow was unnecessary and adding to the enormous damage already done to the man. And yet another was delivered. And another. Henry would continue to beat him until he heard the words that he finally heard.

"No more," Tommy gurgled through the pain and crimson. Blood, spit, and broken teeth flowed from his mouth along with the garbled words.

"What are you crying? I'll give you something to cry about."

"No. Please. No more."

Henry tightened the hose as much as he could around Tommy's neck, but with amount of compressed air in the hose he wasn't able to wrap the hose as tight as he wanted. Tommy was struggling to breath, but not because of the makeshift noose. He had a broken nose and a mouth full of blood, not enough air was getting to his lungs. Tommy coughed and gurgled and spat crimson in an effort to clear a passageway.

"How does that taste? A little bitter? Like blood?"

Tommy gurgled more. Blood continued to expel from his mouth. His face damaged, swelling, and bleeding as well. He wasn't able to speak any longer, garbled or otherwise.

"I learned from the best, huh? Payback is a bitch."

Henry punched his father one more time in the face with all the gumption he muster. The Kansas song *Carry On Wayward Son* was playing on the shop radio which drowned out the police sirens.

The Bridgewater PD arrived to find a suspect with bloodied knuckles and a victim who was all but unconscious. The ambulance hadn't yet arrived, but the victim would be taken to the hospital once it did, and both the paramedics and the ER would have some work to perform. The person slumped, bloodied and beaten on the floor of the garage was in a bad way.

As Henry was being pulled toward the police cruiser in handcuffs, he yelled to his father.

"Stay away from them. You hear me? Stay away from all of us."

His Miranda rights were read to him, including the right to remain silent, above the music in the background.

"Don't you cry,
Don't you cry no more ...."

HENRY ROSE FROM THE SURFACE WHICH POORLY imitated bedding in his cell when he heard the distinct sound of metal on metal. Doors were opening, meaning that someone was coming, presumably the guard who presided over those that awaited a court hearing.

"Get up, Devlin. You've got a visitor."

Henry knew it wasn't his mother. She had already come and gone. She was thoroughly disgusted with him, with all of her children. So much had happened in recent years. Faith's oldest had run away long ago and hadn't made contact since, which was a constant worry. Jimmy had finished rehab as ordered by the court, now under the watchful eye of a probation officer. Henry had had a minor brush with the law but was thankfully freed from that mess. And now this. She couldn't take any more. She wished Henry luck with the new legal fix he was in and stormed out of the jail's visitation center. She said she would pray for him.

It had been three days since Henry attacked his old man at Lynch's garage. He was in jail awaiting transport to a more long-term facility, the prosecutor taking their time for some reason he hadn't been made aware of.

His arraignment hearing hadn't gone so well. The Plymouth County DA saw the accused's recent record, slipping through the hands of the Falmouth PD and the Barnstable County DA's office. He was not about to let what was becoming a statewide nuisance get bail. The prosecutor fought to get remand, which the presiding judge agreed to. Bail was denied, Henry would wait for his trial behind bars. The charge of attempted murder kind of has a big price-tag.

So Henry cooled his heals in a holding cell. Fortunately it was private, though the guard said that if the facility had a surge of arrests he would have company. He would not have that same luxury when and if he was transferred to another facility while awaiting trial.

And so he wondered who could be calling. His new lawyer? The new one seemed better than the first, though he didn't have any complaints about the result of his previous case on the Cape.

The new public defender was a female who seemed to have a rather large chip on her shoulder. Maybe because she was nearly as wide as she was tall, maybe because she wasn't taken seriously by her colleagues, maybe another reason all together. But she was a feisty one, assuring Henry that she was on the case, her track-record spoke for itself. He appreciated her enthusiasm and her salesmanship, but he didn't really have another option. What was going to happen, was going to happen. He would put his trust in the court-appointed, short-round attorney, hoping for the best but expecting the worst.

If he paid for a lawyer, it would take every nickel he had saved and then some. That money was for the cottage. Or for college, though he now realized his chances of actually going were between slim and none. He felt as though he was stuck with his current attorney, but he also felt he could have done and paid for worse.

Henry stuck his hands through the slot in the door to be handcuffed. Once he was restrained, the door opened and he was escorted to a glassed room where he was seated in a stall.

It was Kat.

She looked good. She always looked good. Her cute worry-wrinkle was back.

Kat picked up her phone, Henry picked up his.

"Hey," she said.

"Hey back."

"I've been trying to figure out if I should even come see you. What I would say if I did."

"You took off. That morning. You left with no word."

"So that's why you did this? Look at you. You look like …. I don't even know what. That jumpsuit."

"Yeah. Red really isn't my color."

"I didn't know you had a sense of humor. This isn't funny, Henry."

"What am I gonna do? Cry?"

"I feel like this is partly my fault." She slumped on her stool, she held her head with the hand without the phone receiver in it. Both elbows were on the small counter in front of her.

"Long history there, Kat. Not your fault. You asked me to take care of it and it got out of hand."

"Out of hand? I wanted you to talk to him, reason with him. Not kill him."

"He's dead?"

"Not yet. But he's not doing very well. My mom's been at the hospital the entire time. The affair isn't a secret anymore and she's not making any apologies about it. I think my dad finally realizes that it's over."

"I'm sorry. I don't know what to say," Henry said. The look of bewilderment not lost on Kat.

"I'm sorry for you. I've been following the papers and news since it happened. They're waiting to see if he dies so they can charge you with murder.   My mom says that he has been in and out of

112

consciousness, but that might be because he is so heavily drugged up. She also didn't want me to come here. She hates you."

"Do you hate me?"

"No. I don't know. I'm confused, Henry. We never should have …. "

"Don't say it. I don't want to hear where that was going. When I get out of here we can—"

"—When you get out of here? Are you kidding, Henry?"

"I lov—"

"—No! No, you don't. You can't say that. It would never workout with us anyway. Your dad. My mom. Us? I'm leaving anyway. I leaving and I'm not looking back. I came to say goodbye. I guess that's why I'm here. To say goodbye."

"Where are you going? When I get out of here, I can come find you."

"You're going to trial for attempted murder at the minimum. Maybe he deserved it, maybe not. Maybe YOU deserve this, maybe not. In any case, you're not going anywhere, not anytime soon. I've got Stanford. I've got a life ahead of me. This? This is too corrosive. There will never be an us. That's what I'm trying to say, there can never be an 'us'. It's not meant to be."

"You don't know that."

"I do, Henry. And I also know that you need to think about you right now. Forget about me, okay?"

"Kat."

"Goodbye Henry." She hung up the phone.

"Kat!"

She put her hand against the glass for less than a second, turned and walked away.

"Kat!"

Henry watched her leave the room on the other side of the glass.

"No, no, no ……. *KAT!*"

But she was gone.

18

THE FIRST SNOWFALL CAME LATE THAT YEAR. Thanksgiving had come and gone, Christmas was less than a week away. It was Jimmy's second holiday season since his stint in rehab, and although he hadn't had a relapse, he was still under Faith's very watchful eye.

The dusting of snow was like dandruff amidst brown hair. In New England, Christmas isn't Christmas unless it's white. It didn't seem like Yuletide in the community until the snow fell, and it was especially true for the Devlin's even when it did. Margo still hadn't been heard from, though after these years it seemed less likely that she ever would. In addition, Henry was due in court for one hearing or another. Two family members being unavailable to come together in the season for gathering, for whatever the reason, rendered the holidays without celebration.

They had no money for exchanging gifts in any case. Faith was still working two jobs just to make ends meet. Jimmy was having a difficult time finding and keeping work even with help from his probation officer, so he was another mouth to feed with little or no income. The cottage on Carver Pond still wasn't keeping out the cold and every extra dollar went to heat them and the outdoors.

The dusting happened overnight. Faith was inside waiting for the winter-fighter in her car to kick in when Jimmy came out of the bedroom in an oxford shirt and dress slacks.

"You have an interview today?"

"No, Ma. Henry. He's in court today. I figured I'd go and see him, show some support."

"Oh. Well, I'm running late. I can't give you a ride."

"I'll figure it out. You're not gonna go?"

"I've got to work. Somebody has to work. This place doesn't heat itself."

"I'm trying, Ma. It's all part-time seasonal help this time of year. The economy is in the shitter and I've got to check the damned felony box on every application. All I get is temp or part-time work. I'm gonna have to go through this all over again next month when the holidays are over."

"You sound like your father."

"Don't you say that! Don't you dare. You stood by and watched it all happen and then you wonder why it turned out the way it did. I'm doing the best I can. Nobody will give me a shot. I've been sober, I go to meetings, and I've stayed out of trouble. What more can I do?"

"So this is all my fault? I was young and I did the best I could and this is the thanks that I get."

"Everything I just said and you gotta start with the whoa-is-me shit?"

"Will you please watch your mouth? I am still your mother and you live under my roof."

"Believe me I wish that were different, Ma. I envy Margo, ya know. She got out and never looked back."

"You think she left because of me?"

"You and I both know she left because of you. Because of what people were making her do. Because of Tommy. The whole thing. I woulda left if I could."

"So Henry's situation is my fault too?"

"Henry did what he did and I don't fault him for it. Maybe if you would have stepped in when we were getting our asses handed to us ....
"

"You were learning discipline. Everybody always said how well-behaved you kids were."

"Yeah, if they only knew right? Tommy deserved what he got, probably worse. I wouldn't have shed a tear for him if he died. For Henry I would have, but not your husband."

Tommy had spent six weeks in the hospital once he regained and held consciousness. His face was reconstructed, nose and cheekbones, and his physical wounds were healing. He hadn't been seen or heard from by either Jimmy or Faith, but then he wasn't expected to be.

Faith's eyes were filling with tears. She looked out the window to see that her car was thawed enough to drive.

"I've got to go to work," she said and closed the front door behind her.

"All rise. The Honorable Judge Greely presiding." The judge walked through his chamber door and up the two steps to sit in his seat on the bench. When he arrived at his perch he told the courtroom that everyone could be seated.

The Plymouth County prosecutor, Brad Tatum, sat on his side of the courtroom closest to a jury if one had been convened. His second chair was as absent as the jury, this hearing wouldn't require either. This appearance for the defendant would be short, as it was a formality in finalizing evidence that was to be submitted at trial, and to set a date for jury selection.

Unlike trials seen on television, courtroom drama in real life is quite different. Meaning non-existent. Court proceedings in real-life are usually quite boring. On TV, the prosecution and the defense always have some big trick up their sleeve. One piece of evidence or a key witness that comes to light from seemingly nowhere. This just doesn't happen. All evidence and witnesses that will be showcased for either side in a trial have to be fought over and decided upon prior to the start of said trial. The two lawyers give legal arguments at an evidentiary hearing before the judge, making motions as to why the other side shouldn't be allowed to use evidence that may be damaging to their side of the case. Then the judge will either allow or disallow said evidence or witness. On a rare occasion, a disallowed piece of evidence or witness may be re-allowed because the other side opened a door previously closed by the judge. This rarely happens and when it does occur, it is because of inept representation.

Henry's hearing was the final formal meeting to solidify all of those pieces and to set a date to select from a pool of people selected for jury duty.

On his side of the courtroom was his court appointed, ad hoc legal representative, Sheila Lang. She was young and eager, what she lacked in aesthetics she made up for in skill. Had she been any shorter, she would have qualified for a special blue hangar for her car and convenient parking wherever she went. Had she been any wider, she wouldn't have been able to sit anywhere without a customized chair.

"I've read all arguments," Judge Greely began, "Both of your briefs were very thorough and I have made my rulings. Those are the following:

- One. The statements gathered at the scene cannot be entered into evidence as they cannot be corroborated since they have not been made available for defense deposition as per the Milenneau Rule."

118

"Your Honor," Tatum interrupted, "The defense either not having the ability or the time to interview the witnesses is not—"

"—It's black letter law, counselor. The statements are out but you can bring the actual witness forward for sworn testimony at trial. Which I was about to say as item number two before I was rudely interrupted.

- Three. The affidavits taken from the hospital staff are not to be presented at trial, pursuant to the Hearsay Rule. They are also inflammatory and outweigh their probative value."

"Your Honor, the statements goes to state of mind," Tatum said.

"The statements can be used in a civil proceeding, but not in a criminal trial, counselor. The alleged victim's state of mind has no probative value in criminal court. One more outburst and I will find you in contempt. Am I clear?"

"Yes, Judge."

"And the last one on my list:

- Four. The blood and fingerprint evidence from the garage is in. Ms. Lang, you are free to bring forth any experts to refute them, but the evidence can and I'm sure will be presented at trial.

"Now is everybody unhappy? Good. That means I'm doing my job."

Henry's attorney knew better than to interrupt the judge while he was making his evidentiary rulings, plus they were going her way, save for number four. But now that he was finished, she spoke up.

"Judge, now that you've made your rulings, I would like to enter a motion to dismiss all charges for lack of evidence."

It is customary to ask for a dismissal in virtually every facet of a trial. And those requests are almost always denied.

"I object your Honor," Tatum said.

"I'm sure you do."

Lang then asked, "May I approach?"

"Yes."

She waddled a few steps forward, handing the clerk a blue form. The clerk gave the form to the judge.

"There are no eye witnesses that will come forward, your Honor," Lang said when she returned behind the defense table. "The statements were ruled inadmissible and those who made those statements to the police have not made themselves available. My client has the right to confront his accusers. Even the alleged victim is refusing to testify."

"*Alleged* victim? Is she kidding, Judge? The man was in the hospital for six weeks and is still rehabilitating. He had to have his cheekbone reconstructed and is now legally blind in his left eye."

"Which could have come from any number of things," your Honor. "He did work in a garage where there were all sorts of tools and dangers. All evidence being produced is circumstantial and doesn't meet the standard for trial. The blood, my client's knuckles, the tool in the garage, the damage to the alleged victim …. Circumstantial, all. Not one piece of actual, admissible evidence ties my client to the cause of the physical damage at the scene."

"So how does the defense explain everything that happened?"

Lang shrugged her meaty shoulders. "We don't have to. And since you don't have anyone who will explain it, having actual first-hand knowledge, any theory about my client's guilt is purely academic."

"The victim was the defendant's father, so naturally he is reluctant to testify against the defendant. If we could have a continuance, Judge."

"Keeping my client in holding without bail while the Mr. Tatum goes on a fishing expedition is unconstitutional. If he cannot make a prima facia case then—"

"—Enough! Both of you," Judge Greely said. The judge didn't want to let the defendant go if truth be told. As a Jurist he was supposed to be impartial, but the evidence that was brought forth by the Commonwealth was ugly. To Greely, it wasn't a question of *if* the son committed the crime, it was a question of if the evidence should legally be allowed to be put in front of a jury. Most of it was not since there was no corroboration.

"As much as it pains me, Mr. Tatum, unless you can bring forth someone who will testify under oath in court that they witnessed the defendant accost the victim, there isn't anything I can do except to let him free."

"Judge, I still have the blood and fingerprint evidence at the scene and the police officers who arrived at the scene," Tatum said without hiding his desperation.

"That blood could have come at any time, as well as the fingerprints. The police can only testify to seeing the alleged victim on the ground and my client in the vicinity, according to the police reports. He could have been trying to help his father, lift him up. He may have been the person who called the police for all the prosecution knows," Lang said.

"Ha! Are you going to say that with a straight face? Your Honor, please."

"At worst it was a mutual fray, but the Commonwealth can't even prove *that* beyond a reasonable doubt," Lang added. "If so, ergo, and therefore, the case should be dismissed immediately."

"She has a point, counselor. You've not indicted with any lesser-included charges. Do you have any direct evidence that the defendant attacked the victim to the level of attempted murder?" Judge Greely already knew the answer but he had to officially ask for the court stenographer to type into record.

"Not at this time, your Honor, but—"

"—Then I have no choice but to dismiss this case with prejudice."

"I would like to declare notice of appeal, your Honor," Tatum said.

"Duly noted. Good luck with that Mr. Tatum. If you can come up with sufficient evidence for the lesser crimes within the statute of limitations, you can refile." Greely turned to the defendant, Henry Devlin, who was in a borrowed suit instead of a jumpsuit thanks to his borrowed attorney. "I would advise that you stay out of trouble, young man. This is the second time that you have been brought to justice in a year. Don't let the fact that you are again being dismissed fool you into thinking that you can continue this behavior. Having said that, you are free to go Mr. Devlin."

The gavel came down.

Henry hugged his short, round lawyer.

"I knew you would do a great job. I couldn't have hoped for a better outcome." It was then that he noticed his brother Jimmy in the back of the courtroom, who was giving Henry a thumbs-up.

"Just remember that it's over but it's not. Tatum doesn't like to lose, and he doesn't give up. He will keep digging. Our hope is that everybody just keeps the party line. And there's not likely to be a civil trial if they can't convict you in a criminal one, so you've kept that at bay as well. For now. The judge was right in telling you to keep your nose clean. You're playing with fire, Henry."

"I will, don't worry."

"Your father refusing to testify was about as big a gift as you can get."

"Well, other than not pulling out before impregnating my mom, that's about the only thing he's ever done for me."

19

TO SAY THAT THE WELCOME HOME CELEBRATION WAS muted would be as understated as the phrasing. Henry had some formalities to take care of prior to leaving the courthouse, but afterwards left a free man with Jimmy. Once putting the courthouse in their rearview, they went straight to the cottage on Carver Pond. It was just as run-down as it was the last time that Henry had been there, the few modifications Henry had made prior to being incarcerated not withstanding. The last time he'd seen the place was the night that he had spend with Kat.

Faith wasn't a drinker, never had been for all the children knew. On the irregular summer vacations when they all pretended to be having a good time, they hadn't seen her take a drink. If hard pressed, Henry would state on his life that the only alcohol his mother had ever put to her lips was the consecrated wine for communion. Faith partook of holy wine only on the high holidays of Easter and Christmas, which was a mixture of red and white Reunite diluted with a healthy amount of water. She would let the liquid touch her lips after taking the Eucharist, bless herself while making her way back to her pew, and get down on her knees and pray until the end of the mass. She could have taken a good, hearty guzzle of it and she still wouldn't have gotten a buzz from it, as skinny as she was. Jimmy had taken a good long pull from it one Sunday at mass and felt nothing because it was so watered-down. He felt more from the subsequent ass-whooping for having had the audacity to pull such a stunt.

Because she didn't drink, there wasn't any alcohol in the house. Additionally, Jimmy's probation officer had inspected the house from top to bottom after he was released from rehab to ensure there weren't any substances in the house as mandated by the court. His PO warned him that henceforth surprise inspections could come at any time, as well as his random piss tests.

Jimmy offered to stop by the packie on the way back to Carver Pond if Henry wanted to unwind, but Henry said that he didn't. He liked the occasional bottle of suds or a shot of something stronger, but not enough to drink alone. Not enough to test the limits of Jimmy's willpower.

"I'll stick with my usual glass of rain, but I'll be okay," Jimmy said. "Really. I'm cool with it if you want to get a buzz on."

But Henry really didn't.

There was nothing to celebrate as far as he was concerned. He was out of jail, which was good, but he had nothing on the outside. He and his brother were starting to get on, but there was a past no matter how much they tried to chalk it up to water under a bridge. Any time they had attempted to bond, there were always substances involved and a tragedy of one sort or another.

Henry and his mother weren't as close as they once were. He had been her favorite, he thought, probably because he was the youngest. They shared music but not often in days and weeks before his incarceration. He was the only one left after Margo ran away and Jimmy was in rehab. Her eldest children had disappointed her too deeply for Faith to simply turn another cheek, though she pretended. And now Henry. He had disappointed her the most. She hadn't gone to any of his hearings. Hadn't visited—other than his initial arrest—while he was locked up.

College, for Henry, was put on hold before he was arrested for the assault on Tommy. He had been saving with the hope of starting the following fall, once the cottage was made livable. But he couldn't save while he was locked up. He didn't even know what he wanted to study if he went to college. It was more of what he was supposed to do rather than what he wanted to do. Henry was always told how bright he was and how he could do anything he wanted if he got an eduction. Henry always felt that was a fine plan if there was some sort of direction he felt drawn toward.

But he didn't.

Lack of money to fix the mess around them and to go to school were more reasons for his disinterest in celebrating. Unsure of his status at AIW, his ability to earn a paycheck was in question. His supervisor liked him, but would he take him back? His rudderless future was the cause for his melancholy. His funk. Though not the real cause.

The actual impetus for depression was Kat. She was all he ever wanted, the girl of his dreams. The partner with whom he was supposed to grow old with. He would have gone to college and done all of the stuff he was supposed to do just to have a life with her. He'd shovel shit for a living if that meant that he could be with her. But that was now impossible. She had told him so. She was a bright star on the rise and Henry was an unwanted heavy anchor that would hold her down. Every feeling he had for her, every sentiment, was unrequited. That is what hurt the most.

Henry was lost in both direction and purpose. He felt like he was in the middle of a vast desert; nothing around him in any direction; no way out; alone; devoid of sound; bereft of any feeling.

The only bright light, far off in the distance, was his freedom. He was no longer in a four by ten cell. No longer under the strict regimen of the Plymouth County Sheriff's Department. He was free to do nothing with his life, free to use up whatever time he had left in this existence.

Jimmy knew how his brother was feeling even if he hadn't said it yet. He knew an emptiness that couldn't be filled like only an addict can. Jimmy spent every minute of every day yearning to feel. Drugs did that. The hole that was inside him pined for occupancy, a void that he feared may never be resolved. He saw that in Henry. Only his brother's drug was a woman. Not just any woman, *THE* woman.

Though Jimmy hadn't felt the same way about another person, he understood what it was like to want from the base of his being. To need. Jimmy needed drugs and alcohol like he needed air. It was silly, of course, though his body craved the substances just the same. That is how he imagined his brother was feeling. His body craved Katherine Bradar like his lungs craved air. He hoped that Henry's suffrage would not be as prolonged and as painful as his.

Jimmy wouldn't let them both wallow. It was time to set a course, time to make new plans. Henry was free, and Jimmy was bound and determined to make sure that his brother appreciated it. He was bent to raise Henry out of the dumps. If Henry wouldn't do it for himself, he was damn sure going to do it for his younger brother.

The two made dinner together. Faith wasn't home, she was working her second job at that hour. She would eat the leftovers when she came home much later in the evening. Or maybe she wouldn't, it came out awful. The two brothers laughed and pretended to eat it by moving it around their respective plates, neither being shy about joking that a starving person would likely reject it.

They listened to music while they stared out at the nearly frozen pond. Some of the albums were from Faith's large collection of vinyl records—her only possession of value—some records were Jimmy's, but most were Henry's. He had a keen ear and an encyclopedic knowledge of every band, album, and those who had collaborated to produce them.

Most importantly they talked. They spoke to one another like they had never spoken with each other before. The two conversed like two people without a past who had instantly bonded. Like they hadn't shared any past. There was no blame language, no bitterness, no rivalry, no condescension, no baggage. Every word was listened to without prejudice or pre-conceived weight.

They spoke of times past as if the events were being heard for the first time. Like they hadn't already lived them and the occurrences had happened to other people. They spoke about their respective sadness and how they hoped their futures would not imitate the past.

The two spoke and listened and reflected and advised.

And for the first time in their lives, they became friends.

20

HENRY'S RETURN TO FREEDOM BECAME A VERY BUSY time for the Devlin boys. There was a new vigor, a new sense of purpose and an urgency therein. The new friendship between them brought about a new resolve to live life, to appreciate one another and to do something worthwhile.

Henry got his old job back at AIW. He sat on the same forklift, moved the same inventory from truck to shelf to another truck destined for a final destination. Bradbury, his former supervisor, was promoted to warehouse manager, he made the decision to bring Henry back in less than ten-seconds.

It took a bit more convincing in getting Jimmy a job there. Jimmy had a record and a recent habit, where Henry had been released with a relatively clean record. Accused and released without conviction, let alone a trial, was much different from pleading guilty to charges and current probation. Henry vouched and promised and begged. The decision to hire Jimmy Devlin took less than ten minutes.

The job made Jimmy's PO happy. It made Faith happy, though she was never around to say just how much so. She continued to work her two jobs, six days a week, spending Sunday in a state of prayer.

Henry started taking core classes at the community college in January. He went three nights a week after getting off of his forklift. Henry still didn't know what he wanted to do with his life in terms of career, he just knew he didn't want it to be at Ashmont Iron Works. The career counselor at the college told him to start with the required coursework for a general studies, liberal arts degree—maybe a couple of electives—then see where his interests leaned. He found the classes easy and again found himself in the similar situation of being the smartest student in each of the classes.

Jimmy became quite good at reading the drawings and fabricating the steel structures that needed welding. He rose quickly in production, joined the union, and loved the work. He was also falling for one of the girls in the front office. He had been out on several dates with her and they were getting on nicely. She loved to ride on the back of his new-to-him Harley Davidson Fatboy. Jimmy said that she loved the vibration.

When Jimmy wasn't at work or out with this girl, Samantha—who he called Sam—he was sharing a room with Henry again, though he'd been sleeping elsewhere as of late. They continued to live with Faith on Carver Pond though they never saw her.

Money was saved and money was spent to make the cottage a home.

The structure was made more sound. New windows were installed and the walls re-insulated. The roof was re-shingled, the deck on the back which faced the pond was torn down and built again. The kitchen was updated, as was the plumbing and electrical. What the boys could do, they did themselves. The rest came from help from the men that they worked with who donated their time and skill.

By October, the cottage had been remodeled into a reasonably nice place to live. It was small and cozy and virtually unrecognizable from what they had started with.

Henry was amidst his third semester of college, having taken night classes all summer and nearly a full course-load in the fall, while keeping his full-time job at AIW.

Faith was still felt but rarely seen. With everyone's busy schedules, they often slept under the same roof without confirmation. Notes would pop up now and again suggesting that she liked the renovations or asking how a new appliance worked, another note would replace it to give her instruction.

The weather was unseasonably warm. 'Indian Summer' had lasted months rather than weeks. All of New England shared mixed emotions about the mild autumn temperature. While sweaters and cold-weather clothing remained in closets, the leaves weren't changing colors which kept the out-of-towners away. The economy was suffering and the ski resorts were worried about how they'd fare the upcoming season.

Halloween fell on a Wednesday that year. Henry would never forget the day for as long as he lived. He went to work as usual. He sat on his forklift, moved shit around the warehouse as usual. He completed tasks that required less than ten percent of his brain function, as per the norm. The police officers that were following his new boss—a guy everyone called Pinky for some reason—through the warehouse was not the norm.

They were a distance away yet coming directly toward Henry. He noticed them in his periphery and parked the conveyance while he assessed the situation.

"What is this now? I haven't done anything wrong," Henry said to everyone yet nobody in particular. And nobody in the group responded. Not until they bridged the interval between them.

"Henry Devlin?" The older of the three policemen took charge. "Can you come down off the lift and come with us please?"

"No. Not until you tell me what this is all about."

"Henry you might just want to go with them," his new supervisor said.

"I didn't do anything."

"Nobody is saying that you did. We just want to speak to you privately. Can we do that?"

"No handcuffs?"

"No. Handcuffs won't be necessary. You aren't under arrest now nor do we intend to place you under arrest after we speak."

That seemed to mollify him for the moment, though suspicion had reached a pinnacle. He followed them into the front offices, an empty conference room their destination.

They walked past Sam, the girl Jimmy had been seeing. She gave Henry an inquisitive look, Henry shrugged to communicate to her that her guess was as good as his. He hadn't the first clue as to the purpose of the gathering.

"Please have a seat Mr. Devlin. Can we get you anything? Water?" The lead policeman not only took charge of the other officers, he was taking charge of a conference room that wasn't his to commandeer.

"No .... Thanks anyway. Okay, I'm officially freaking out. What the fuck is going on?"

"Your brother, James Thomas Devlin, works here. Correct?"

Henry looked at his boss. Then back at the cop.

"You know he does. What did he do now?"

"Is he here at work today?"

"How should I know? I'm not my brother's keeper." He looked back at his boss who was staring at his steel-toed boots.

"Pinky, you don't know?"

Henry then turned back to the cop in charge. Somebody needed to give him answers and the uniformed flunkies weren't saying anything. "He would know. He's the Super."

"Yeah, we know he's not here," Pinky said.

"Then why are you asking me? Is somebody going to tell me what in the hell this is all about? Ten more seconds and I'm walking out of here."

"According to his PO and the records here, he has the same address as you. You both live together, correct?"

"Is that a crime?"

"No, not at all. Did he come home last night?"

"He may have had a date, the girl is right out there. Go ask her. Is that what this is about? He's dating someone in the office? Is that a no-no? Does that violate some law and so you're fucking with his probation? Last I knew it's not against company policy. You can't fire him for that."

"We don't care who he's dating, Mr. Devlin," the cop said.

"Neither does the company," Pinky said still examining his boots.

"Just call me Henry. Did he have a drink? Dirty piss? WHAT?"

"Last night was cabbage night," the cop said.

Henry's mind raced. Cabbage night is a ritual for young punks. The would-be holiday is a staple in New England. Teenage boys who like trouble, and those that want to be boys who like trouble, go out after dusk the night before halloween and toilet paper neighborhood trees. Egg some cars. Smash the artistic fruits of labor spent on pumpkin carving. People used to joke about making sure to give out good candy on halloween so that the kids wouldn't make a mess of your property the following year. The ultimate pay-it-forward.

Henry had seen the detritus from the previous night's festivities on his way to work that morning. He remembered when he used to pull the same shenanigans. He also remembered the beatings he suffered after his father found out about it.

Only he and Jimmy hadn't TP'd anybody's house in years. They were trying to get past the more serious trouble they had gotten themselves into more recently.

"And…. Am I supposed to keep guessing? Did he egg a cop car?"

"No."

Henry stood up violently. His chair rolling a few feet away from him. He was on the precipice of a melt-down.

"Then I give up. Either say something or let me get back to work."

"There's been an accident, Henry."

He went to sit back down but there was no longer a chair near his posterior. One of the underlings brought it under him in the nick of time.

"Some knuckleheads took smashing pumpkins to a new level last night. They decided to drop them down onto oncoming traffic on the 24 from the overpass. Cars doing sixty-plus getting pumpkins dropped on them from the bridge above. There was damage. And panic, which created more damage. It was warm. Your brother was on his motorcycle. And it's a God-forsaken mess, Henry. I'm so sorry."

"My brother?" Henry was about to be sick. Jimmy liked to ride motorcycles as much as possible, until snow flew if he could get away with it. The unseasonable weather allowed him added time on two wheels. The girl he was seeing liked the Harley also, an added bonus for continuing its use beyond the usual riding season.

"Direct hit to the concrete barrier. There were no tire-marks on the highway, so it looks like he didn't even have time to brake. It happened in all of an instant. He had passed before any emergency personnel arrived on the scene, before the ambulance arrived. By all accounts he didn't suffer."

"Oh fuck no. No. No way. He was clean. He was getting his life together. This can't …. I mean …. We …. He …."

Henry couldn't say anything else. What was there to say? How does one process that kind information? His brother. His brother who was only ten months older. The man he had gotten to know so well in his sobriety. His new best friend. Jimmy was dead.

Use It Up

Real men don't show emotion. Real men don't cry. Not in front of other men. Not in public. Not ever. That is how he was raised.

Henry Devlin wept.

21

CATHOLICS HAVE A MORBID FIXATION WITH VIEWING their dead. There simply was no communicating to Faith Devlin, a devout Catholic, that a closed casket was not an option. No way to get through to her that what was left of her son was not, nor could not be fit for viewing. She wouldn't hear it. If she had heard it, the information wasn't registering in her brain. So she continued to seek out somebody who would tell her what she wanted to hear. It took five funeral homes, seven morticians, before someone said that they could accomplish an open coffin as per the custom.

Father Donovan had given spiritual guidance to all of the Devlins over the years. He had advised on Faith's marriage and the church's take on divorce; the schooling of the three children as well as their sacraments of baptism, first communion, and confirmation; seen her sit front and center every Sunday; taken every confession no matter the severity of sin; and he would ensure a majestic send-off for her son James with the help of Bishop McCaffrey, who also knew the Devlin family quite well.

There was a public viewing, though the people looking for closure would have to use their imagination. The person in the casket did not look like Jimmy Devlin. The mortician had done what they could, but it simply wasn't enough to make what was left over from the accident look like the departed.

After the viewing, Saint Ann's would host a vigil the night before the big mass. The funeral would have all of the bells and whistles. Robes and incense and holy water and choir with a pipe organ.

For someone who had always been uber-concerned with appearances and what the neighbors would think, Faith couldn't reconcile that ethos with her inability to hold herself together. The crying jags were as ferocious as they were frequent. Each tantrum bookended with fervent prayer. It worked in her favor. The faithful swarmed around her to give comfort. Solace in that her son was in a better place. Jimmy was nestled in the bosom of God.

None of it gave comfort to Henry. Nor did any eulogy. Nor any of the readings from Job or Psalms or Romans or Corinthians or Luke or Matthew. He thought it all bullshit. For what sick and twisted purpose would this God allow someone in the midst of redemption to be struck down in such a way? This was the work of the most kind and benevolent on high? More like a grimalkin puppet master batting around his mousy subjects before he kills them. His mother could prostrate herself on bended knee before her omnipotent maker, but he would not. Never again.

The current in the river of Henry's despair was nearing the metaphorical waterfall when he saw her.

It was during the mass. The funeral. Jimmy lay in his casket below the altar while various people read and eulogized. Henry's thoughts took him away, to another time and place. He shifted to his left. Tucked in the rear corner of the cathedral, behind a large pillar, under a painting of the fifth station of the cross—where Simon of Cyrene helps Jesus carry his cross to his own crucifixion—was his sister.

Margo had come home. Wherever she had gone, whomever with, she had obviously been informed of Jimmy's death. She had returned from hiding to say goodbye. Henry couldn't believe his eyes. Was she real? Was the incense playing with his eyes? He wanted to go

136

to her in the middle of the mass.   He wanted to ask her a million questions. He wanted to feel the warmth of her embrace.

He needed his big sister.

Henry went to her.   She was crying but smiled as he walked down the aisle toward her. If people were looking at him he didn't know it or care. If his mother was aware that her daughter was present, she didn't show it. He wondered if that was proof that he was hallucinating.

But he wasn't. They didn't say a word to one another. They held each other while the mass continued.   Henry was much taller, he held her cheek into his chest. His chin rested on the top of her head. She smelled like Margo. She smelled like she had never left. There was no scent of new lands or adventures. Just Margo. He hissed the top of her head. Her shampoo an elixir of life.

Of hope.

With the exception of Tommy, people came out of the woodwork to pay respects and show support in various ways. There were cakes and casseroles and pies and greeting cards from every manufacturer. People were in and out of the small house on Carver Pond.

It may have been a coping mechanism, but Faith continually thanked her God that she had a decent house for people to visit in her time of need. Imagine her embarrassment if while she was an emotional mess, her place of residence was as well? That was the gist of it, if not her exact words. Henry found it maddening.

To her credit, Faith didn't press too hard on where her daughter had been all this time. And to Margo's credit, she didn't relive the events leading to her departure, nor did she sling any blame for it.

They got on cooly yet civilly. The house was too small to avoid one another completely, but the two women afforded the other a wide berth.

Henry was attached to Margo's hip. He learned about her drive cross-country. About her settling in a place called Sausalito on the other side of the country, on the other side of the Golden Gate Bridge from San Francisco. How she had found the place that she now loved and the new person. Her life was full and rich and genuine. In other words, the opposite of Bridgewater. And she would be returning in a few days.

Henry was fascinated. He wanted to experience something other than Massachusetts. Something other than the facade of what he was building, or not building as was the case. He wanted to go with his sister. He wanted to go to California.

Margo told him that he was more than welcome, he could stay with her and her boyfriend for as long as he wanted. They needed to make up for lost time and Northern California was filled with good schools. He could transfer his credits there and finish what he had started at the community college. There was just one problem with this plan.

He had to break the news to Faith.

The reaction was worse than even Henry had expected. Faith took the news as though she was losing all three of her children at once. Jimmy was dead, and as far as Faith was concerned, California was the same thing. Margo had been gone for years and feared to be dead. And now Henry was going to leave.

"You're killing me. You know that right? I hope that you both are happy with yourselves. Is that what you want? You want me dead?"

She went on and on like that for two days. When guilt didn't work, she prattled on a slew of logistical reasons why a 3000 mile move was the height of stupidity.

"What about school, Henry?"

The solution was presented. He would transfer. She made like she didn't believe him and that he would drop out of school for good.

"How will you two live?"

Margo has done fine and Henry will live with her, they explained over and again.

"What about money?"

Henry had money saved and living with Margo wouldn't cost much.

"What about me? What about this house?"

They were getting close to the real reason she didn't want them to go, Henry thought. As much as his mother loved him, she was worried about herself both personally and financially. Worried about being alone, Henry saw it in her eyes. She was worried about survival.

Faith wouldn't divorce Thomas Devlin. She was listening to the church instead of taking care of herself. She couldn't find someone to share her life with, not while she was married. Taking up with another man while still married to a man she never saw was still a sin. Faith prayed to her God that he would take care of her. That he would provide for her through Henry. And her youngest son was abandoning her.

Henry explained that the renovations would make it much less expensive to heat. Utilities would be cheaper. Finally, the house was paid for. She worked two jobs and had for some time. She would be fine. Financially, she was taken care of. Henry couldn't do anything to solve her loneliness. He hadn't been able to solve that while they lived under the same roof.

"You'll never come back to visit." Her final justification. She may have had a point. Henry didn't plan on returning. Ever.

Her Lord knew that she would never set foot in California.

22

HENRY HADN'T FORGOTTEN THAT HIS BROTHER had just died. He would carry that with him in his heart every day, and would for the foreseeable future. The saying, 'Time heals all wounds' may be true. Thus far in Henry's life, however, that sentiment hadn't panned out. He felt more like 'Time will tell'.

He was enjoying Sausalito and the greater San Francisco area despite his melancholy.

He spent his days on the beaches and hiking paths. He loved the Pacific Ocean. It was nothing like the Atlantic. Nothing like Cape Cod back east. The sand was softer, the air less humid and damp—the smog burned off by eleven in the morning every day—the surf taller and more cleansing as it crashed against the beach. It was a new beach with every wave. It was metaphorical. A new beach meant a new start.

He got a job doing minor landscaping and maintenance at the National Park Arts Center. It didn't pay much and it was only part time, but it was more than what he needed. The job was not a career and certainly didn't require much in the way of thought or brainpower, though it did allow him to save a little money and to send some to his mother in an effort to assuage his guilt.

The first paycheck went toward a beat-up Toyota Corolla. The tan two-door had almost a hundred fifty-thousand miles on it and the manual stick stuck from time to time, but it ran well enough for Henry. It didn't take him long to sort out how to get around, everything was off of one freeway or another. He would intentionally get lost and try to find his way back to Margo's place, then head back out to do it all over again. He wasn't spending as much time with his sister as he had originally thought or wanted, unfortunately. She had other demands on her time.

Once such claim on her time was her boyfriend. Her live-in boyfriend to be exact, the one with which she'd lived for some time. The one that Henry hadn't decided if he liked in the early stages. The two of them hadn't hit it off directly out of the gate because Margo had omitted the fact that her brother would be moving in. The omission had caused a rift, which became a chasm over time.

Paul was Margo's new love, but he might as well have been the old love. Old because he was older than her to be sure, and also because he was the replacement for the original one that was forbade. Andrew Benning was currently housed by the Department of Corrections in the Commonwealth of Massachusetts for statutory rape, but he was incarnate in Paul Bowers. Though the two men were three thousand miles apart, they looked very similar and had similar occupations. Henry wondered what he and his sister could possibly have in common as Paul was 46, Margo was about to turn 22.

They were nearly a quarter century apart, but never far from the other's side. They touched each other and held each other and pet each other publicly like nothing Henry had ever seen before. The public displays were the exact opposite of everything that he had seen growing up. He wondered if this was the way that normal couples were supposed to interact, or was the touching more a point in negating the possibility of others misjudging them for father and daughter? Were the displays designed to proactively communicate the nature of their relationship and avoid any awkward assumptions? Is this how hippies live?

In any event, the relationship had been happening long before Henry ventured west and was likely to continue with or without his tacit approval. He was a guest and he needed to keep his feelings to himself, even if Paul had made his crystalline.

It was plain that Henry was an intruder and the sooner the uninvited guest moved out the better. Paul had said so without as many words—yet still in plain language—and not in the presence of Margo.

The holidays came and went though they didn't feel the same. It didn't feel like Thanksgiving. Nor Christmas. Canary Island Date Palm trees and a lock of snow weren't the only reasons. Tensions were palpable, the household lacked merriment, and rendered the season anything but festive for Henry.

The ball dropped in Times Square three hours before they sang Auld Land Syne in Cali. Dick Clark wasn't *rockin'* anything by the time midnight rolled around on the West Coast. Henry was thankful for a new year, but he still didn't feel like celebrating.

While Henry found each new day a new beginning, California still lacked something. What that thing was, he couldn't quite place. There was a hole in him, a hole that needed to be filled but with what he didn't know. He loved Sausalito and the Bay area, but he was still searching for something. He resolved to figure out what that was in the new year.

Faith had been right to worry about Henry leaving for California. She feared that he wouldn't be back. That once he tasted life outside of Bridgewater, outside of Massachusetts, that he wouldn't want to return. She was further troubled by the thoughts that California would change her son and not for the better. She watched the news. She never read tabloids but would always see the gossip on the front pages while waiting in the checkout line at the grocery store. California was a sinful place with half-naked women and drugs and Hollywood and surfers and hedonism.

And her son wasn't returning. He didn't return either in person or her phone calls. Whenever she would call, her son was never in Margo's apartment. He either wasn't getting the messages, Faith thought, or he had gotten them and didn't want to speak to his mother. She received checks in the mail now and then, which she found helpful, though she wanted to speak to her son. She hadn't had many heart-to-heart conversations with him. Ever. Certainly not after his legal troubles. Not while they lived together on Carver Pond. They hadn't listened to records like the once had. But she could have. He was in the next room back then, not 3,000 miles away. Faith wanted to tell Henry that she missed him. That she loved him. That she wanted him to come home. Faith promised herself that she would work up the courage to say those things if and when they spoke. Yet they didn't.

California was already changing her youngest child, and not for the better.

On the other side of the country, Henry did get the messages and the verbal chiding from his sister that he should call his mother back. He told his sister that she hadn't wanted to talk to him this much when they lived under the same roof. Margo's response was that she and her mother's relationship would never be repaired, but that Henry still had an opportunity to have one with her. He would nod and placate his sister, but Faith's phone calls remained unanswered.

Henry wasn't anywhere near Hollywood or Drugs, though San Francisco was changing him. He grew out his hair which became a lighter shade of blonde as he worked and played outside every day. He looked Californian. He felt Californian. What he wasn't looking was backwards. He certainly didn't want to call back or think back to days on the East Coast.

Those thoughts were painful. He was tired of pain.

Use It Up

Henry decided that he wasn't going back, not that there had ever been a plan to.

23

COLLEGES AND UNIVERSITIES ALL OVER THE COUNTRY like to assemble tours in the spring. The flowers are blooming, the campus greens are well manicured, the students are wearing less clothing after the winter weather has subsided. California schools are no different either in the north or the south.

Henry decided to take in some tours in the early spring of 1990. He hadn't lived in California long enough to qualify for in-state tuition, but he wanted to get the ball rolling. He had savings and he still had a bit of scholarship money left to help him. He could always apply for more, or for financial aid. It was just a matter of which school fit him best and what he wanted to do with his life. He still hadn't found himself or filled that missing piece, he hoped that a new school would provide the answer. But an answer hadn't presented itself when he toured any of the schools in San Fran, or Daly City, or San Bruno.

He continued south in his decrepit Corolla on the 280, grinding his transmission in the freeway traffic. He was headed to Redwood City where a lesser known school offered a wide variety of disciplines and was inexpensive compared to others in the area. The bumper to bumper traffic was heating up more than just his transmission—Henry was nervous about what his temperature gauge was reading—when he saw the sign for his exit five miles ahead. Was the car going to make it without a break? He needed to take the 84 but he needed a rest stop sooner. California had fewer of those than New England. His eyes remained keen on every sign, hoping to find an easy place to pull off, but he found one that shocked him instead.

Five miles ahead was the 84, ten miles ahead was Stanford University.

He couldn't believe his eyes. All of this time he was living only an hour away from the woman of his dreams. The one that had gotten away. Kat had been here the entire time, he presumed. Isn't that where she said she was going? And was it the same Stanford? Of course it was. How had he not known that it was right there this entire time?

He thought about her often, those thoughts subsiding into despair at what could have been. It was the only thing he wanted to think about in terms of his past. Or when contemplating his future. In another time, another world, who knows? She was gone and so far away. But she wasn't. She was there, ten miles away.

It was a sign. Literally. But there are signs and then there are signs. This one was both.

He limped his melting car onto Sand Hill Road off the freeway and headed toward *THE* Stanford University. The campus was massive. And Beautiful. And the people were friendly, all-too eager to give him directions to where the undergraduate admissions office was located.

The admissions office was willing to help him—up to a point. No, the girl in admissions didn't know Katherine Bradar. No, she couldn't tell Henry where she lived, she further explained. What she could tell him was that *if* she adhered to her class schedule, and *if* that schedule hadn't changed for some reason, then she was at the address she was willing to provide since it was a public building.

The admissions woman passed Henry a piece of paper with a handwritten address in big, feminine letters under the heading **Tort Law 210.** The class would start in just under an hour, she said. Henry must have looked a bit puzzled, the young lady behind the counter further explained that the Katherine Bradar he was seeking was a prelaw student. Tort Law 210 was requisite for graduating in that course of study.

It took him longer than the forty-five minutes he was afforded to find the address. He had to stop three times to acquire help and direction, all on foot. He crossed four quads of various sizes and shapes before he arrived on Galvez Street where the class had already begun. The bookstore was basically next door, so Henry decided to kill some time inside. Plan B would be to catch her on the way out of class.

He spent another fifty minutes inside the bookstore going over textbooks for sale, fantasizing about which books would be required of him when he attended Stanford the following semester. Allowing for a ten-minute leeway in case Tort Law 210 let out early, he crossed Canfield Court and waited on a bench for Kat to exit the building. Henry strategically placed himself at a remove where he could reconnoiter the several doors of possible egress. He became nervous as time passed without seeing her. A door would open and a person or a small group of students would exit the building, but not Kat. He speculated that she could leave the building from a different side, was planning to relocate after an interval, in fact, when a small group of people spilled out from said building thirty yards away.

The group walked along the path toward Canfield Court as one, yet carried on in fragmented conversations. Kat was speaking with a tall, lanky man on the left side of the cluster.

Henry rose from his bench and approached her and therefore the flock of prelaw students. She hadn't noticed him when he did so, hadn't noticed him as he walked toward her on the path closing in. Kat was still turned toward the lanky male student in conversation when Henry stopped in front of them, blocking her and her colleague from passing without melding into the main body of pedestrians.

Kat stopped, both physically and in mid-sentence, interrupted by an unnamed person who was blocking their progress along the path.

She froze. It took her more than a few seconds to believe her eyes, more than a few seconds to regain the ability for speech.

"Hey Kat."

She and her companion remained reticent.

"Surprise," Henry continued after the awkward pause.

"Henry. Wow. How? I hardly recognize you. What are you doing here?"

The rest of the small group had moved around Kat, her companion, and the person obstructing their progress. Her look of confusion not lost on either of the men.

"I'm thinking of going to school here," Henry said. "I thought I'd look you up."

He looked to Kat's friend and introduced himself. "I'm Henry. We grew up together. We were a couple before she moved out to California."

The stranger stuck his hand out to shake hands and was about to make introduction when Kat stopped him.

"No. NO. This is not happening. Henry, you can't just travel three thousand miles and pop in on somebody. I have a new life—"

"—I just want to talk to you."

"About what, Henry? What is there to say? I thought things were pretty clear when I left you. In Jail. I can't get mixed up .... " Kat shook her head and trailed off, whatever thought she was trying to convey was being shuffled in her brain and remained there.

Her friend came to aid. "Look, Henry is it? Maybe it was a bad idea to—"

"—And this has nothing to do with you. So whatever you were going to say, don't say it. I just want to talk to Kat for a few minutes. Can you give us a minute there, GUY?"

The stranger looked at Kat, who was visibly shaken, knowing her male friend's only two options were to either stand down or risk the possibility of a physical confrontation. He was not a fighter and his skepticism was very apparent to Katherine.

She knew Henry was capable of violence, she had seen his handiwork on his own father. The pictures were all over the news after it had happened, even the black and white photos in the newspapers were gruesome.

She pumped her hand toward Henry like a traffic cop attempting to bring oncoming vehicles to a halt. Henry took a few steps backward while Kat turned her back to him in order to confer with her male friend.

She whispered to the lanky stranger, asked him for space and handed him her bag. She called him Chad or Thad or some name that was more blue blood and than blue collar. She then thanked him, kissed him on the mouth and left him standing on the path while she walked toward Henry.

"Come with me, you." She led him on the path crossing the quad.

"Is that your new boyfriend?"

"He's a friend, Henry. You don't get to interrogate me, okay?"

"It was just a question."

"I know what it was. What I don't know is what you're doing here. You can't just show up out of the blue."

"But you get to?"

"What are you talking about?"

"You show up at my job, tell me that you need help, no notice …. I drop what I'm doing and help."

"I hardly call getting arrested a big help, Henry."

"I got carried away.   But that's all in the past.   That's three thousand miles in the rearview. I'm here now, so we can pick up where we left off."

"No, Henry, we can't. That was a mistake. We never should have done …. We never should have gotten involved.   We definitely can't now."

"Why not?"

"Because our past is too corrosive for any meaningful relationship. I'm not even sure if we can be friends, Henry."

"I don't want to only be your friend anyway. Are you trying to tell me that what we did meant nothing? That the pond was nothing?"

"Don't be so immature.   It was nice, yes.   Of course I felt something. But that was then. That's over with, Henry. That was another life, a life that is gone and not to be relived."

"You're talking like it happened a decade ago. What's changed?"

"I've changed."   They stopped walking across the quad, she turned to face Henry. "Everything has changed. I've moved on and I don't want to look back, okay? I'm happy that things worked out and you're not going to spend the rest of your life in prison. Really, I am. But you should make something of yourself, Henry.   Do something worthwhile. Move forward, don't live in the past. I told you when we were talking with glass between us that you should forget about me. I meant it then, I mean it now."

"Would that I could.   There is no way I can move on without you."

"Of course you can. You are the smartest person I've ever known, Henry. And look around you, there are a ton of smart people here. You can do whatever you want."

"I want you, Kat. That's what I want."

"You can *DO* whatever you want, you can't *HAVE* whatever you want. That's not how life works."

151

"Then what's the point? What kind of universe allows you the freedom to do what you want but not be able to share it with whom you want?"

Kat sighed with both exasperation and for effect.

"I don't know, Henry. I guess a cruel one."

24

HENRY SPENT THE FOLLOWING FEW HOURS meandering about the Stanford University campus, rudderless and numb to his surroundings. The sun began to fall from the sky, the ensuing darkness a metaphor for the black and bleak future he envisioned for himself.

He had always wanted Kat. For as long as he could remember, since the moment he first noticed her in class at Saint Ann's. From the first time that he understood that he appreciated females, that he was attracted to them, he had measured Katherine Bradar against all others. None came close. Kat was the woman by which the sex was judged. She was why songs were written, why love had a name.

And she was gone. Again.

She had rejected him, rejected what made sense. Rejected a life where Henry would devote every day to the pursuit of making her happy.

He could never have her, never make her happy. She was happiest without him, she had said, which made it that much more heart-wrenching.

He couldn't talk to her, hold her, know her or admire her. Her beauty would forever be treasured by another. Someone else would share her body and soul. Not because she was a world away, not because she was beyond his reach. She was right there, just beyond his grasp.

And that was the damnable misery of it.

He had moved out to California to start over, only subconsciously did he know why. He'd been searching for answers since his brother died in October, trying to find his place, trying to find what he'd been lacking. The answer to the hole in his heart, the one that desperately needed to be filled, was only an hour south of him the entire time he had lived in Sausalito. Was it fate that led him west in search of a new start? South? Was it fate that made his car want for a rest at the point where Kat was studying? And was it that same fate that made her so unattainable?

These thoughts consumed him as he walked around campus, anesthetized to anything other than Kat's face. Her beauty. Her memory.

Henry found a payphone near the parking lot where his car was parked at Stanford and pumped a few quarters into it. Margo answered on the third ring.

"Hello?"

"Margo, it's me."

"Henry?"

"Yeah."

"What's happening? I was just talking about you with Paul. I haven't seen you in a while. Is everything okay?"

"No. Nothing is okay."

"Where are you? Are you in trouble?"

"I'm not in trouble. Not like that. Where are you?"

"You called me at home, Henry, you know where I am. You're scaring me. What's going on?"

"It's all over Margo. She doesn't want anything to do with me."

"What are you talking about? Who is she?"

"Kat. She's changed. She said that she changed, but I don't see it. I don't understand any of it."

"Kat …. Like down the street, Kat? Katherine Bradar? *The* Kat? Where are you?"

"Stanford."

"Jesus, Henry. You drove down to Stanford? What did you think was going to happen? There are plenty of other girls out there. I can fix you up if you want. You're a good looking guy, and smart. At times you can be funny …. What is so special about Kat?"

"She's the one that I want, Margo. Simple as that. We have chemistry. We belong together. She can deny it all she wants, but deep down she knows it's true."

"Well, you keep going back to her, and she keeps running, so you're gonna have to move on. Whatever her motivation for 'denying it'—as you say—she's obviously made it clear that she doesn't want to be with you. I'm sorry. Just come home."

The operator told Henry that his time for the long distance phone conversation was almost up. He needed to either hang up or feed more money into the payphone. He chose to feed the slot but he wasn't sure why. There wasn't much else to say.

After the coins were deposited, after a pause to collect thoughts that weren't aligning, he continued.

"You're gonna tell me not to chase the same girl, Margo? You keep going back to the same guy. Paul is Andrew Benning all over again. Only Paul isn't a convicted child molester. At least not that we know of."

"Fuck you, Henry. You've had a shitty day, so now you want to take it out on me? Andy didn't do anything wrong and you know it. Mom had to feel like she was protecting me, so the poor guy had to pay."

"The Commonwealth of Massachusetts seems to think that he did do something wrong, and he's paying a hell of a price for it," he said.

Margo didn't say anything for a few moments. Henry could hear her beginning to cry and Paul asking why in the background. She appeased him somehow and then continued with her phone conversation.

"You wanna keep stalking Kat, be my guest. I don't know what you expected. She moved three thousand miles away from you, away from Bridgewater, she doesn't want relive the same life."

"Like you? Is that why you moved out here, Margo?"

"Whatever. I'm not gonna let you piss on my life. You're hurt and I can tell that and I'm truly sorry. For what it's worth, I'm sorry Henry. It's been a tough road, especially lately, but you've got to get over it. It's hard but I know what I'm talking about. Just come home and we can talk about it if you want."

"I'm not coming home, Margo. It's no home anyway. Paul doesn't want me there, I don't belong. I don't know where I belong anymore."

"What are you saying? Where are you gonna go?"

"I'll let you know when I get there."

"You're scaring me, Henry. What about your stuff?"

"Take care of yourself, Margo."

"Henry? Henry? *HENRY?*"

She was yelling into her phone, but nobody was on the other end.

It started to rain on Henry's walk back to his car from the payphone. If he had thought about it, he might have found it appropriate for how his day had gone. But he didn't think about it. He wasn't thinking about much of anything. His brain was handling the basics and not much else. His heart pumped. His lungs took in oxygen. Blood moved through his arteries, veins, and capillaries. Other basic systems chugged along as well with the exception of digestion, he hadn't taken in anything to digest. Nor did he have any interest to.

He got into his beater Corolla and started it.   There was a hodgepodge of crumpled clothing on the seats in the back, on top of his records in the far back, and on the floorboards. Virtually all were in need of the laundry but had the advantage of being dry.   He changed into clothes that were immediately within reach while the car ran.

The wet clothes were draped over the passenger seat to dry. Henry put the car into reverse, backed out of his parking spot and then moved the Toyota forward onto Sandhill Road.   He stopped just long enough to fill up the thirsty vehicle, then headed north on the 280.

An hour later, when he should have stayed on 280, crossed the Golden Gate Bridge and continued into Sausalito, he veered off onto 80 east. He didn't know why other than the direction of west would put him into the Pacific Ocean, the only immediate destination off-limits by car. Some unknown force was guiding him, which took control as he drove. Henry wasn't intoxicated, but he wasn't in full function either.   The car seemed to steer itself onto the 505 and then onto 5 north some interval later.

He stopped when he needed to fill up his tank or to eliminate his bladder. He drank very little and ate nothing. He had no appetite. No aim. No plan. No pleasure in the music that played on the FM radio, he hardly heard it.

Chris Robinson, lead singer of The Black Crowes, belted out *Twice As Hard* through the static and the small speakers at low volume to deaf in ears. Henry wasn't paying attention.

The road would lead him somewhere, he didn't care where.

Part Three

The grunge of Emerald City

25

THE RAIN FELL FROM THE SKY IN DROPS THE SIZE OF balloons. Rivulets of big, lazy, wet rain fell onto all below as it did every day. There were various types of rain, the sole job of the local meteorologist was to inform as to what kind would fall on any particular day. It came down in sheets, or from the side, or so hard that it would ricochet from every direction. It was never dry. Everything existed in a state of wetness. Damp weather begat damp spirits. If it wasn't raining it was threatening to. More than half of one million people lived in Seattle, Washington, six hundred thousand waterlogged souls in search of arid refuge.

Ants marched about the city, moving unfazed by yet another damp and dreary day. All had places to go, things to do, work to be performed regardless of climate. No matter the purpose of scurry, all moved in and out of coffee shops amidst their errands.

Coffee shops were immensely popular. When a person is wet, they want to be warm and dry. Coffee shops provided a place to get out of the weather, drink coffee or tea, and socialize. The hot liquid warms from the inside out, the caffeine lifts energy as well as it raises the spirit. One could throw something over their shoulder in Seattle and the object would land in front of a coffee shop. Music played, usually live. Some played jazz. Some blues. But the real scenes played Grunge.

Grunge was rock music that represented everything that was Seattle. The guitars sounded heavy and wet. The vocals were inarticulate and distorted. The drums hammered down like hard and fast storms.

Use It Up

While the rest of the world was focused on Alternative Rock, Seattle was perfecting it and renaming it.

The show *Friends* didn't exist yet. The coffee shop trend with couches and oversized mugs and live, non-mainstream music didn't come until a few years later, spreading to every city small and large. They all emulated the model Seattle had built on every corner. It was 1991. There was no Chandler Bing, Monica or Ross Geller. No Joey or Pheobe. Long before the world tuned in to see Rachel's new hair style or listen to the latest incarnation of *Smelly Cat,* Gen Xers in Seattle were amped up on Coffee and Grunge.

Henry found one such coffee shop on his adventure north and didn't leave the city. He had found what he was looking for. The Emerald City awaited.

The music was intoxicating. It was part heavy metal, part punk, and Henry loved every distorted chord of it. He listened to bands play small clubs and after-hour coffee shops daily, costing very little money to attend, the bands garnering very little money to perform. Bands like The U-men, The Melvins, and 10 Minute Warning. He could hear the influences of his favorite bands throughout the new records he was buying. Led Zeppelin, Black Sabbath, and The Doors lived on.

He went to show after show. Met people of like mind and interest who all noted Henry's ear and interest. He wanted to know how to create those sounds, how to improve them. He wanted to know he people developing the records that had up to then remained so localized.

At the suggestion of several people he had come to know from going to various shows, he took sound engineering courses at the University of Washington School of Music. He worked at the very first coffee shop he'd visited when hobbling his car into the city. The same coffee shop promoted music and Henry became acquainted with several of the players in the subculture that was finally gaining traction. Grunge had been around since the late 70's and early 80's, only now it was a salable sound. A desired commodity.

Henry met an innovator at school. A man named Geoff Turner, an acoustician at London Bridge Studios, which was located just north of the city in an area called Shoreline. Geoff had spoken at UW and with Henry after the seminar for no more than thirty minutes when he offered the young talent a job, of sorts. More like a meagerly paid internship. Henry was all-too eager to start as a fledgling engineer, the studio had already produced Soundgarden's *Louder Than Love* and Mother Love Bone's *Apple,* both albums were among those that he listened to almost daily. Henry would be working for very little money, and he would be working under other engineers, but he would gain an education that he couldn't replicate at school.

So he left UW.

Instead of classes at the University of Washington, he learned as he helped produce Alice in Chain's *Facelift.* The band had been together for three years and produced an album called *The Treehouse Tapes,* but since they were now under the same management which represented Sound Garden, all concerned were looking for a more professionally produced album. Henry listened and learned. He worked with Jerry Cantrell, Layne Staley, Sean Kinney and Mike Starr under engineer Dave Jerden. It was magical. It was an education. And yet again he was a lethally quick study.

Henry became as isolated personally as he was geographically. He lived and breathed music. He practically lived at coffee shops, clubs and the studio. Henry's work was getting noticed, working with many bands that year. Every one of the people he surrounded himself with were musicians or those that produced them. They became his family.

While everyone was taking time off during the holidays, Henry was busy in the studio putting final touches on the recording, *I Can't Remember.* Layne Staley's voice was unlike any he had ever heard and wanted the heavy music to enhance the lyric, not drown out the vocal. He was alone in the studio, listening and perfecting the various tracks, setting and resetting levels. He took a break only to make a phone call.

He hadn't spoken to any of his real family. He called Margo for the first time since Stanford on Christmas Day of 1991. She was relieved to hear from him, she was more than a little concerned that he was no longer among the living after so many months of not hearing from him. It was a brief conversation, made so because she prattled on about the purported drug problems in Seattle. Henry insisted that she was jealous about his burgeoning success, that he was doing well and happy, and had to rain on his parade. She laughed because she thought he was making a Seattle rain joke. He didn't call again.

He immediately went back to the recording, playing it for the millionth time, yet each time hearing it like it was the first.

"....Bring me down, you try
Feel the pain and keep it all in 'till you die
Without eyes you cannot cry
Who's to blame?

I can't remember, I, I can't

Remember identity
The visions in my mind from screamin' at me
And mama, mama, ooh, my angry brain of
Infancy...."

Margo called the only other person that she thought would care about Henry. Faith insisted that he was living a life of sin though in reality she couldn't possibly know one way or the other. Faith was convinced that her son was doing drugs and engaging in sex outside of marriage. She told margo that she prayed for both of them, as her daughter was living in sin as well.

"Merry Christmas to you too, Mom."

That conversation lasted less time than the chat with her brother Henry.

26

BY MID 1991 HENRY HAD BEGUN TO MAKE A name for himself within the Grunge community. He had blossomed quite fast and was making a little bit of money. With less than a year of working under more well-known engineers at London Bridge, he was taking on projects of his own. By the end of that year he would be working with Alice in Chains, no small feat for someone who had entered the city and the business in early summer the year before.

Henry had an apartment in Seattle proper, complete with a live-in girlfriend. Henry liked her well-enough but liked his work more. He travelled with Geoff to hear bands and to drum up business to pay for the relatively new studio. They would sometimes travel as far south as San Diego, California. One such trip was to listen to two bands, Bad Radio and Mighty Joe Young who were packing small venues like SOMA. The first show was a band called Mighty Joe Young, the frontman was Scott Weiland.

The lead singer was a drug and alcohol addled mess. Henry thought the performance was amazing, a combination of verbose and confusing poetry with heavy guitar licks and sonorous drumming. After the show, when he met Scott, Henry realized that the lyric wasn't poetic license but aimless soliloquy. Weiland was not able to focus on the conversation and seemed more interested in seeking out more fuel for the rock and roll lifestyle. Weiland cut thumb-holes in his long sleeve shirt in order to cover track marks in his hands, a trick Henry had noticed on Layne Staley.

Henry was without sex or drugs and was therefore useless to Weiland. The lead singer reminded Henry of his deceased brother in his days of daze and confusion.

Geoff and Henry spent the remainder of the evening with the remainder of the band, going over materials and plans for the future. The band had yet to achieve proper management and couldn't afford the studio. Later, on the trip home, they would talk about Mighty Joe Young's lead singer.

Henry had said that working with the band would be a chore, while they were musically brilliant, the vocals and vocalist were toxic. Weiland seemed to be more about the lifestyle than the craft, in Henry's estimation.

Geoff pointed out that Weiland wasn't the only artist who had difficulty separating art and the reality of life as a professional musician. That if drugs and overindulgence were distasteful to him, that this was most definitely not the career path for him.

He understood and related. Henry knew what drugs and alcohol had done to his personal music collection, the inspiration that fueled art. With bands like Zeppelin and Sabbath it was obvious. With others, it was logical if not known. The Beatles went from *I Saw Her Standing There* to *A Day In The Life*. The two albums from whence those tracks came were as dissimilar as the songs themselves. Drugs were likely a factor. Experimentation comes in many forms.

Henry appreciated substances as muse, but he had seen first-hand what substances can do as a lifestyle over the course of time.

The trip wasn't a waste, however. In fact, it was just the opposite.

The second band, Bad Radio produced a San Diegan vocalist named Eddie Vedder. He had been working with Bad Radio for some time and was looking to leave. Vedder had been given a demo tape by his friend and drummer Jack Irons. Jack told Vedder that a fledgling band was looking for a drummer and a vocalist. Irons passed as a potential drummer but thought it an opportunity for Vedder to leave Bad Radio and land on his feet for the vocal role.

Which he did.

The new band, with Vedder at the helm, was named Mookie Blaylock after the NBA basketball player. They produced a demo and were signed by a major label, performing shows primarily in Seattle clubs like the Off Ramp Café, where Vedder was forced to relocate.

Mookie Blaylock's incubation to success transformation was instantaneous.

The new label, Epic, required that they yet again change their name, which they did. A studio was booked to record their debut album, and low and behold, Vedder found a familiar face.

Henry.

It had only been a few weeks since Vedder had met Henry, but they had made a fraternal connection, spending time together frequently both personally and professionally.

Henry recorded Vedder for backing vocals in the band, Temple of the Dog, prior to recording Vedder's new band. The TOD album comprised of makeshift musicians from various bands. It was a small project that would attract a cult following.

Eddie enjoyed working with Henry not only because of his skill as an engineer, but their personal alignment as well. Eddie was a surfer, and Henry looked like one. They had a newly acquired mutual friend in Lane Staley. Both Henry and Eddie were relatively new to the professional music business. Both wanted to make their stamp on it. Working together would be fun and it would change everything.

The new band, with Vedder as frontman, was Pearl Jam.

Eddie Vedder, Stone Gossard, Jeff Ament, Mike McCreedy, and the new drummer Dave Krusen made inarguably one of the most important albums ever recorded.   Rolling Stone Magazine in subsequent years hailed the album, *Ten*, as one of the best complete albums ever recorded.

And Henry was there to engineer it.

It was the same argument all over again.

Henry's live-in girlfriend felt used-up and unappreciated, reminding him of how those feelings hadn't changed since their previous discussion.

Henry was never around.   He cared more about his music projects than he did about his girlfriend.   Did he care about her at all? He was rarely home, preferring to spend all of his time at the studio recording music, or going to clubs to listen to new music. Why couldn't they go together like they had when they first met? Was it another girl? She would be okay with a three-way.

Technically they lived together.   The apartment was in Henry's name but he chose not to go home. Henry's take was that she had a free place to live, what was she complaining about?   She didn't need to account for any of her free time. She could come and go as she pleased. Freedom was something to be cherished, right? I'm not the jealous kind, Henry said, spend time with whom you please.

She wanted to spend time with him. She loved him and said that she would do anything to keep him.

He loved his work.

"Don't you love me?"

"No."

It was always another project that kept him from coming home. First it was the Facelift project. Then *Temple of the Dog*. Next was the *Ten* album, followed by Alice in Chains *SAP*. Henry was always working, using the work as an excuse for keeping at bay. In truth, he loved the music so deeply that he didn't consider it work. He had found a passion, none of it transferred to his girlfriend. It was the first time that he had said that he didn't love her, the first time she had heard the words that actions displayed. Yet she didn't leave. She was determined to change him.

By the time *SAP* had wrapped, *Ten* was released and blowing up. The album gained attention not only because it was good, but because there was controversy surrounding it. Nirvana's Kurt Cobain called Pearl Jam a sellout and stated that they were more popular rock than grunge. Vedder wasn't even from Seattle. Vedder and Cobain went at each other's throats publicly, meaning on MTV, which made teenagers eager to see what the fuss was about.

While on their tour for the album, Pearl Jam refused to play any cover songs, other than Neil Young songs—which didn't sit well with teenagers at the time—meaning their fifty-three minute long debut album wasn't enough to fill a complete show. They were forced to either play the entire album; or the hits with copious Neil Young, which fans deplored; or live up to their true name and jam. They extended their three-to-five minute songs into fifteen or twenty, never playing them exactly the same twice.

The young fans who attended the shows recorded them onto cassettes, exchanging the bootlegs like currency. This created more buzz, more official album sales, as well as the sales for concert tickets. While the label loathed the bootleg recordings as they couldn't capitalize on them, they did enjoy the sell-out arenas and potential for more albums.

Pearl Jam, specifically Eddie, loved the bootlegs.

So much so, that the band decided to take steps to ensure the quality of the tapes being produced. Vedder decided the only way to do that was to ensure that the sound at each concert was the very best possible. He knew just the person he wanted to hire for the task.

Henry couldn't say yes fast enough. He needed to get away from Seattle, away from his apartment and the girl therein. His rent had been paid through the end of the year, telling his landlord that the girl could stay until the end of the lease. After that she was on her own.

He took a hiatus from London Bridge Studios.

Geoff was sad to see him go, but recognized the opportunity. He knew he couldn't keep Henry tied down long. Geoff said as much to Henry in their last conversation and further explained that the door was always open. Henry would be welcomed back at any time.

The *Ten* tour crossed the globe several times over and didn't end until the Lollapalooza music festival in September of 1992, where the band was moved up to co-headlining because of their immense popularity.

Henry saw the world and soaked up every minute of it like a sponge.

THE FOLLOWING THREE YEARS WERE A BLUR FOR Henry. He toured and helped record the second album with Pearl Jam, *Vs*. The band seemed to recoil at fame yet always did things and pulled stunts to bring them further into focus, yet not in a good way.

It seemed that Eddie always had a cause and the band as a whole would ultimately suffer for it. Henry admired Vedder for his beliefs and his willingness to use his notoriety to shed light on issues, but the music was beginning to suffer.

What began as foolhardy positioning, became a visceral agenda for the band as they received more blowback. And it was coming at them in swarms.

The band refused to make music videos. After the huge success of the MTV video for *Jeremy*, they refused to make another. The label was seething, as was the cable network.

MTV was *the* platform in those days for promoting music, providing visuals as another means of sensing the essence of what the artist was trying to convey. Because of the popularity of the station, everyone who was recording music to be sold on the market was also shooting music videos. It was big business, high-end directors were in demand to shoot these videos.

Pearl Jam argued that music is to be appreciated and interpreted by the listener, not forced into visuals that are interpreted by whomever directed the video. They wanted to be remembered for their music, not the music video. They preferred instead to play their music live and let the performances speak for themselves. They believed their music and their stance to maintain its purity to be a requiem.

The stance on integrity reminded Henry of one of his favorite bands, Led Zeppelin.

Only the performances didn't speak for themselves. Eddie would conduct a monologue in the middle of every live show. The band would take a break while he got on his soapbox. It was always political, always with whatever salient point was on his mind. These diatribes created yet more controversy.

Pro choice in 1992 was one such cause.

The environment. Who was campaigning for this political office or that. Rock the Vote. Vote for Change. The freeing of various demonstrators. South Africa. If it had a name, Vedder had an opinion on it.

But the one that killed the proverbial camel was taking on the corporation that fed them. They looked that gift camel in the mouth. They took on Ticketmaster, the one and only major concert promoter. The band argued that their prices were cost prohibitive for most people who wanted to see a Pearl Jam show, let alone follow them on tour a-la-Grateful Dead. They further argued that fans were forced to pay an inflated price set by Ticketmaster because they had a monopoly on ticket sales at virtually every venue. You paid their price or you didn't see a show. They argued that their avarice violated anti-trust laws.

When Pearl Jam filed the lawsuit in May of 1994, Ticketmaster obviously dropped all of the band's shows in retribution. Large arenas were off the table. Large clubs and theaters were off the table. Even small clubs in major cities. The band could continue to make albums, but they could no longer promote them by playing live. Jamming live was their bread and butter.

And the albums stopped doing as well. When *Vs.* was originally released, it held the record for the most copies sold in the first week, but sales waned. With all of the controversy and causes, the music was hidden behind all of it. And with the inability to promote new albums, sales suffered further because they couldn't play the music that the fans were yearning to hear live.

The atmosphere among the band-members was miasmic at best. The support team, like Henry, would soon be out of a job.

Some of the band members were taking on side projects, forming new bands. Mad Season was one such project with Layne Staley. Henry wanted to work on the record, *Above,* with all of his being, but was told that he was needed on the non-tour.

If that wasn't bad enough, the other shoe was about to drop. Eddie approached Henry in July 1994 in their hotel suite in Toronto. Geoff was on the phone for him.

"Geoff? It's been a while," Henry said into the phone.

"Yeah, for sure. How have things been?"

"It's been crazy? You must have heard."

"I have. Who hasn't? Sorry about *Above,* everybody wanted you on that record."

"Including me."

"If things get too crazy you can always come back here to the studio. Business is good. Since Cobain's death, bands are popping out of the woodwork trying to fill the void. Nobody will, of course, but we can record as many as we can to prove it."

"Yeah that whole thing was sad. Good thing Eddie patched things up with Kurt. The guy is going to go down a murdered saint, who wants to have to live with the God of Grunge calling your music shit?"

"It sounds like they have bigger image issues than what Kurt said, Henry."

172

"Isn't that a mouthful. With no work, the guys that aren't doing side projects are going to rehab. We're going to lose more to the junk, Geoff, mark my words. Heroine is a problem."

"I hear ya. Anyway, that's why I'm calling."

"Somebody died?" Henry sat down in the chair next to the phone in the hotel suite the band had booked. He was bracing himself for an industry death. Layne? Scott? Chris? And those were just the frontmen that came immediately to mind. After a second or two, Henry asked, "Oh no. Who?"

"Your sister Margo—"

"—MARGO DIED?"

"No. NO. If you would let me finish …. Your sister, Margo, called trying to find you. I didn't know exactly where you were either, or if you were still following PJ around. Anyway, you need to call her. I have her number here. She gave it to me in case you lost it, she said you haven't called her in a while. She said she hasn't seen or heard from you in like three years. She also said that her number hasn't changed."

"She misses me, so she calls you to track me down? That doesn't make sense. Is she in some kind of trouble?"

"No. Well, not that I know of. Look, she called about three weeks ago. I've had a hell of a time tracking you down. I had to call Epic, who didn't get back to me right away. The label finally gave my Kelly Curtis's number, who for a band manager, takes his sweet time returning people's phone calls—"

"—I get it, Geoff, you've had a tough time tracking me down. We're always in a different city, and they're all starting to look the same. The point?"

Geoff sighed. "I can imagine. Anyway, call your sister. She has some bad news."

"Did she tell you what it was?" Henry was loosing patience. "What is it? Tell me."

"I'd rather it not come from me, Henry."

"Spill it."

"She said your mother died. Sorry to be the one to tell you, but you pretty much forced my hand. Just call your sister, okay?"

Henry didn't speak for more than a beat. Geoff let the time and dead air over the phone pass without interjection until it seemed that something needed to be said.

"I'm sorry for your loss, Henry. If you need anything …."

"Jesus …. Three weeks?"

Henry hadn't let his anger subside before making the call to his sister. He had learned that his mother had died three weeks prior, and he found out about it from his former boss. The fact that he hadn't exactly kept in touch with his sister, allowing her the opportunity for a timely notification was completely lost on him. Shock and anger were the emotions ruling the roost at present.

"Hello?"

"Margo?"

"Henry, is that you?" The voice coming over the phone into Margo's living room sounded like her brother, but she couldn't be certain. Too much time had passed.

"What the fuck? I find out about mom dying three weeks after the fact?" Henry was practically spitting into the phone on his end.

"It took you that long to call me back," Margo yelled back. "I had to deal with it all by myself. I didn't know what you would want, or how you wanted to see her looked after. It was a mess, Henry. And you weren't around."

"I wasn't around because you didn't tell me. I had to find out from my former boss."

"That was the only way I could reach you, Henry. You never found an occasion to call, let alone tell me where you are. How was I supposed to find you? Mr. Rock and Roll could have been anywhere on the planet while us little people who live in the real world have to deal with real world problems."

"So when did you call Geoff?" Henry was starting to calm down. Logic and command of the facts were beginning to reclaim their hold on him.

Margo's voice lowered a considerable number of decibels with him. "A few days. I'm sorry. It took a few days for me to deal with it. I had to get myself prepared before I could fly home. I called from the pond."

"How did it happen?"

"She just died, Henry. Loneliness? Heartbreak? Who knows? Forty-three is way too young to go."

"Are you kidding me? Faith Devlin didn't die at the age of forty-three from natural causes. Did they do an autopsy? Were you waiting for me to have it done?" Henry's voice was starting to raise again.

"Officially it was cancer, Henry. Untreated."

"Martyr until the bitter end?"

"Are you that shocked?"

"Yes. No. I don't know, Margo. I just found out that my mother is dead ten minutes ago and that she died three weeks ago."

"Well, now you know where I was. I couldn't get ahold of you, so I had to make all the decisions and hope that you approved. Our father wasn't even there. He was just like you, Henry, I couldn't find him either."

"Don't you fucking compare me to him. Do you hear me? Ever!"

"I'm not. I'm just saying that he never showed. His own wife dies and he is off doing …. Whatever or whoever he pleases" She paused out of exasperation before continuing.

"It was all left to me to deal with in any event. It's not like she left a last will and testament. That would have been too easy. She left a letter on her dresser but not addressed to anyone in particular."

"What did it say?"

"Random musings," Margo said. "More advice than anything else. Like whoever read it was scoring the meaning of life. How 'Life is short, use it up to the best of your ability'. And 'God has a plan for us all, a vision. Pray that you find out what it is early, and spend your time on this earth fulfilling it'. I might not have the exact phrasing right, but stuff like that."

"That sounds like Mom," Henry said. "Too bad she didn't take her own advice."

"I know, right? So she didn't have anything of value, other than her sage advice, except her record collection and the house on the pond —not that the house is worth anything anymore. She let it go to shit. All that work that you and Jimmy put into it's all falling down. All used up with nothing put back in. Tommy's father built it, so I don't know if we can even sell it legally."

"What do you mean? He abandoned it. He abandoned our family. He let Mom move in and he forgot about her."

"And he stayed scarce ever since you beat him down flatter than hammered shit, Henry. He is a bastard, but do you blame him? He didn't stick around for a round two."

"So now what?"

"What now what, what, Henry? It's over. Done. The church did a nice mass, the least they could do for her after forty years of wishes on bended knee. She was put into the ground at the cemetery next to

176

Jimmy. I haven't done a damned thing with the pond because a lawyer said the house would have to go to probate. It's still Tommy's as far as the law is concerned, if we want to take it or anything inside of it we have to clear it with him. Probate lawyers cost money and I wasn't even sure if you wanted anything to do with it. We'd have to find our beloved father and take him to court."

"Let me think about it. I want those records. No matter what, I want her record collection, Margo."

"And they are worth a lot of money, and they legally belong to one Thomas Devlin."

"And I don't give dusty fuck! I used to listen to those records with her. That was the only thing that gave her any kind of joy."

"That and church," Margo added.

Henry gave her a loud chuckle over the hotel-room phone thousands of miles away. "You think she went to church for the joy of it? She went because of the guilt. She went out of obligation. When she wasn't praying over her sins, she was asking for the big guy to forgive all of ours. Me. You. Jimmy. Probably Tommy more than the rest of us, but if anyone deserves hell it's him."

"So how do you propose to get them?"

"I'll go there as soon as I can and take them. If he didn't show up to her funeral, he might not even know."

"I put her notice in the paper, Henry. Bridgewater ain't that big."

"I'll deal with him if I see him. But just so you know, I'm not going to sell them. They are worth more to me than money. And she kept them in mint condition, so they're worth a lot. Are you going to want me to get them appraised so I can buy you out?"

"No. That was your thing with her. There was a little money left in her bank account after I paid all of her expenses. She put money away. She lived like a pauper and didn't spend a dime that wasn't absolutely necessary. Anyway, I just went to the bank and withdrew it because I didn't know what else to do. She didn't have a backup plan for retiring, but she worked those two jobs and saved. She certainly didn't put any of it into the house. I still have what's left over, which isn't a landfall by any stretch. I don't know if we are even or not, but who cares? When and if we can sell the place on Carver Pond, we can sort it out then."

"Fair enough."

"I'm sorry you had to hear about it like this, Henry. You didn't get to say goodbye."

"I said goodbye to her a long time ago. I guess I just realized that now while we're talking. I'm sorry you got stuck with everything, Margo. That wasn't very fair."

"What's done is done. It's just good to hear your voice. I hope the next time we see each other isn't at another funeral. Can we make that deal?"

"There isn't anybody left, Margo. Just you and me. But it's a deal."

28

THE INITIAL PLAN TO LEAVE PEARL JAM AND THE hotel in Toronto for Massachusetts, specifically Carver Pond, would have to wait. Henry found the band members milling about in the common part of the hotel suite. They were mulling as well as milling.

They had received the legal documents with regard to their lawsuit against Ticketmaster. The documents contained the corporation's legal rebuttals that their numerous attorneys would be presenting in the event that the action went as far as a trial. Each band member held a copy that they had received via courier and were arguing over point by point. One of the bandmates would point out one Ticketmaster argument as bullshit, then somebody else would highlight another.

When Henry entered the room, Eddie told him that he wouldn't believe what was said in the drafts they were all reading and tossed him one of the thick, binder-clipped copies. There was nothing that any of them could do, the lawyers would fight it out, but they all seemed invested so Henry played along to get along.

He had gone into the room to tell his employer about his mother's passing and the need for him to go to Carver Pond, but he determined that it would have to wait until a little later. He would need to find a very early occasion, but later.

Henry flipped through the lengthy pages, reading all of the legalese. He chimed in where necessary or when somebody asked him what he thought about this or that, but he wasn't really absorbing much of it.

His thoughts kept returning to Faith and the fact that she was no longer here. He hadn't spent any time with her over the past few years, nor had he made any phone calls. But in the back of his mind he always knew that he could if he wanted to. He could pick up the phone. He could take a few days between shows to fly into Logan Airport, see his mom, then continue on with the tour. But he didn't do any of those things. There were all sorts of reasons why, but the facts remain. When push came to shove, no amount of justification was good.

His mother was dead and in the ground and had been for three weeks. He hadn't said goodbye. Henry thought maybe that was why Catholics had a morbid fascination with viewing their dead before putting them into the ground. It was a chance to look at your loved one and say goodbye in the slim hope that they were watching. What would his mother say to him now if she could? What if she was watching?

None of it good, he reckoned.

All of these thoughts were ever-present amidst the commotion and bickering. His eyes moved from page to page without focus until the last page. There, at the end of the document, he saw her name.

Katherine Bradar.

There were other names as well, all lawyers working for Ticketmaster racking up hundreds if not thousands of billable hours.

How many Katherine Bradars are there? It couldn't possibly be the same one. How long has it been?

Henry looked further down the page and underneath all of the lawyer names was the name of the law firm who represented Ticketmaster. They were from Los Angeles.

"I think I know one of these lawyers," Henry said to the room. It was out of his mouth before he could censor it, before he could mete out his thoughts on whether the attorney could be Kat. His Kat.

The band's manager, Kelly Curtis, looked up from his copy, pointing at it.

"What? You know somebody on here?"

"Oh. Yeah. I think so. It's the same name. If it's who I think it is," Henry stuttered.

"Which one?"

"Katherine Bradar. Kat."

"How do you know her?"

"We grew up on the same street. We went out a couple of times. We ....," Henry trailed off. The entire band had stopped reading to listen to him, only he didn't finish his relaying of the nature of their relationship. The room hung on his lack of explanation.

"So you can talk to her, get their side of things? Maybe you can steer this thing in the right direction," one of them said. Henry didn't know who, he was completely out of focus at the moment.

"Huh?"

Curtis left the sofa where he was sitting and went to Henry.

"Listen we're in purgatory here. The tour is on hiatus until we can get this sorted. If you know this lawyer lady, you need to go see her."

"I'm not sure. I don't know what good it would do. The last time we spoke .... My mother ...." He was stuttering again.

He was halfway to LA with one of the PJ lawyers before he fully realized what was ahead of him.

"I'm here to see Katherine Bradar," He told the receptionist. Henry stood in the lobby with Miles, one of the legal representatives for Pearl Jam.

The receptionist nodded and told them they could have a seat and she would see if Ms. Bradar was ready to see them. They had an appointment scheduled and were ten minutes early.

"I don't even know why we're here," Henry said to Miles as they were taking a seat in the waiting area.

"You're here to see what we can do to blindside the opposition. It would seem inappropriate for you to be here without an attorney, so here I am. Just see if there is some sort of bottom-line for them. Our side wants to go on tour with lower prices and a fair market where other promoters can apply some price competition. Ticketmaster wants to be the only game in town. If they are willing to settle somewhere in the middle, at least get a moratorium, then everyone can go back to work."

"I'm not even sure if this is …. Her," Henry said, trailing off as he saw the slim, well-dressed attorney approaching them.

It was Kat. Of course it was her. The attorney looked as radiant as ever as she walked into the lobby through some glass doors, nearly tripping when she saw Henry.

"Hey Kat."

"What are you—"

"—I'm here with him," Henry said nodding his head toward Miles.

"But this is just absurd. This can't be happening …."

"Kat—"

"It's Katherine," she said regaining her composure, straightening the non-existent wrinkles on her form-fitting business suit.

"Okay. Katherine it is," Henry said.

"I'm very busy and have no time for you. You just show up here unannounced?"

Miles interjected. "In fairness we did have an appointment. He's here with me to have a preliminary discussion over the documents your team crafted and sent to us. We were hoping to speak less formally, without all of the billable hours present."

"And you brought along someone who you thought would facilitate that meeting. Very shrewd, Miles."

"Will you take this meeting?"

"No. I think that would be inappropriate, I am junior counsel in these proceedings. I'm merely one of many who are defending our client. But I would like a word with Henry in private."

"Of course," Miles said.

"I'm glad I have your permission," Henry said to Miles without disguising his irritation.

Kat led him out of the lobby, down a hall, and into a small, windowless office. She let him enter first, and closed the door behind them both.

"What in the hell do you think you're doing, Henry?"

"It's not what it looks like."

"Oh no? It *looks* like you are trying to ambush me. *AGAIN.*"

"And I just said that it's not what it looks like. Of all the law firms in the world, you had to be the one to defend Ticketmaster."

"I'm just a lowly worker-bee. I'm not *the* attorney, I'm *an* attorney. Why are you here? How did they find you?"

"It's just a coincidence. I'm a sound guy for the band. I engineer their albums and make sure that their live stuff is on point. I was in the room when they got a draft of your firm's arguments. I saw your name on it and before I knew it I was on a plane to LA."

"Of all the bands in the world, you had to work for the one that's suing Ticketmaster."

"Funny huh?"

"Oh yeah, Henry. It's a real hoot."

"Congratulations, by the way."

"What?"

"You're a lawyer.   School.   The Bar.   Big law firm in LA. Congrats."

"Oh. Yeah. Thanks. You too. You work for the biggest band on the planet right now and the biggest activists this side of U2. Congrats yourself."

"Mine wasn't sarcastic, Kat."

"You're nicer than I am.   Sorry …. Thank you," she said as she took a seat behind her desk. Henry sat down as well. "Your mom must be proud," she added.

"I doubt that. Somewhere in heaven she's probably going to bat for her sinner son."

Kat changed faces and attitude but didn't respond verbally.

"She died three weeks ago. I was traveling. I just found out two days ago."

"I'm so sorry, Henry. Really. I had no idea."

"How could you?"

"She was so young."

"Yeah. I guess it was cancer. Listen, she never really lived in the first place. We were all terrible burdens and abandoned her. I can still hear her making her speeches. I loved her but …. You know."

"I do actually. I don't really speak to my mother anymore either," she admitted.

"Obvious reasons."

"Not as obvious as you'd think. She broke it off with your dad, I guess. Tried to ameliorate the entire situation, but too much damage had been done."

"Sorry to hear that. She was wrong to hitch her wagon to Tommy Devlin, that I can say."

"You won't hear an argument from me."

"And you're a lawyer," Henry joked.

184

Kat smiled, staring at him.

"Lets go to dinner," Henry said after an interval of silence.

"No. Bad idea."

"We'll go as friends. Bring your boyfriend if you want."

"Subtle."

"What?"

"You were fishing to see if I had one, so you invited him to a dinner that we are never going to have."

"You caught me. We can still eat together. People have to eat, Kat. You pick the spot since your on home turf. The only people I eat with are the band and their groupies. I don't want to have to eat with Miles tonight. Please? C'mon …. What do you say?"

Kat thought about it for a time. The silence and tension was palpable.

"How does eight sound?"

29

DINNER AT THE WATER GRILL WAS EXCEPTIONAL. The superlative food had been a mainstay for fine-diners in Los Angeles for a half-dozen years or so, since the late eighties. The atmosphere, service, and offerings were beyond any expectation.　All of the elegance notwithstanding, Henry found his dining companion to be far superior.

Kat and Henry carried on with ease over the meal.　They spoke of their adventures over the past four years.　Henry had seen the world, Kat was taking the world by storm as an up-and-coming hot-shot attorney. The conversation had no prolonged lulls or points of strain.　The pauses weren't awkward, the exchanges witty yet innocuous.　It was as if the two hadn't shared a past, no peccadilloes or gross misdeeds to weight down the night.

The sexual tension was palpable.

Sly looks at one another from across the tucked-away table begat innuendo.　Innuendo begat prurient curiosity.　It was unescapable despite the cognition of logistics.

Kat looked amazing as usual.　She hadn't changed a bit, it was as if no time had passed since Henry had last seen her on the campus of Stanford.　Her fawn-colored hair had been highlighted; her pouty lips had a more expensive shade painted on them; nails manicured with precision; her petite frame held a designer dress made to accentuate her slight curves; but underneath all of the cosmetics and preening, Kat was still Kat.

She had repeatedly said that they could never be together, and yet they had been. Henry had succumb to her wishes yet couldn't stave off his. He wanted her, always had and likely always would. He wanted this to be one of those times where they did that which had been forbade. He also wanted it to last more than just the one night. Forever had a better ring to it.

Henry made no concealment about his feelings. Never had. As he sat at the cozy table in the fine-dining restaurant across from his unobtainable love, he was lost in her beauty. Lost in her eyes.

The pretense of breaking bread as friends was abandoned, though neither admitted out loud. Thus the volleying continued. Looks. Insinuation. Slight touches. The aching became unbearable.

Hearts palpitated. Endorphins surged. Loins tingled and ached. The yearning grew with intensity as the meal progressed, as the conversation ebbed and flowed.

By the time the molten lava cake came to the table, neither Kat nor Henry were denying what they both were feeling. It wasn't the remnants of the hot July day outside the air-conditioned restaurant, nor the heat of the dessert that made the room boiling-hot. The intensity was too much to bear further.

The hot, sweet liquid remained inside the dessert, each desiring the other over any confection. The cake was left untouched, Henry tossed cash onto the table uncounted. It may have been a prodigious gratuity or it may have been insufficient in covering the bill, he didn't know. He didn't care.

Henry's hotel was practically on the other side of Los Angeles, which seemed like the opposite side of the planet at the time. He chose to bring Kat across the street from the Water Grill to the Hilton Checkers Hotel. He checked them into a room that was as enormous and luxurious as it was expensive. The process at the front desk seemed to take forever.

Use It Up

The hotel room door closed milliseconds before they attacked one another. His body was hers, her slender and slight curves enveloped by him. Buttons popped. Zippers torn.

They tasted one another, each with salty skin tangy with the sweetness of sweat. The perfume of the other's excretions were intoxicating. Nibbles and licks became devouring carnal bites.

Their bodies fit together as if molded. Her nimble body accepted him as he poured into her like casted forged steel. They rolled and writhed and used each other to one pleasure. Neither could get enough. Neither satiated by the wet daubing, session after euphoric session. It was the relentless pursuit in carnal knowledge of the other.

Their sex wasn't about happiness, it was about needs. The oasis amidst a desert. On the verge of death, they found sanctum. They found nourishment in one another.

The lovemaking was familiar yet new. Each were satiating their own wants, simultaneously quenching the other's. It was the kind of love where fulfilling a partner, assuaged their own pent-up desires. Their souls were meant to be paired, their love evergreen.

They partook long at length. Time stood still, yet dawn approached.

As the dawn light breached the crevices of the hotel room curtains, ever so slightly, reality hinted at Katherine as well. She continued to enjoy every forbidden moment.

Kat made love to him like it was the last time she would ever have sex with Henry. It simply had to be, no matter how much she wanted more of him. She knew it would be the last time with Henry, like only a woman could know.

Kat was still interlocked with Henry later that morning. Her head rest on his shoulder, her body turned into his, leg over his thigh, looking at him as he woke. She studied every detail of him, trying to stamp the image of her lover into her mind for future reminiscence.

"Good morning," she whispered.

"Hmmm. Morning. What time is it?"

"It's still early. I have to go to work."

"You should call in sick today. I think we're gonna be busy."

"We got plenty busy last night …. And this morning."

Henry didn't say anything, he just stared back into Kat's deep, beautiful eyes.

"What?"

"You look amazing in the morning. I've never been able to do this with you. You usually leave before I get to look at you."

She lifted off of him.

"Don't. Don't start."

"I'm not starting anything. I was just enjoying it. That is what I was trying to say. That I like being with you."

She got out of bed, padded naked to the other side of the room to collect her clothing.

"Me too," she said. "But it's just physical. We can't be together. Deep down you know that."

Henry sat upright but stayed in the bed they had shared.

"No, I don't know that. Just because you keep saying it, it doesn't make it so. You can't tell me that what we did last night, what we keep doing whenever we get together, means nothing. I know you felt it too. Sex that hot comes from someplace."

"We have some sick kind of chemistry, I'll give you that. But it's not enough to sustain a life. You live on the road—"

"—So I'll get a job in LA," he interrupted.

"Just like that?" She found her torn dress and attempted to wiggle into it.

"Yes. Absolutely. There are recording studios here in LA, I'm sure I can land on my feet. I'm probably out of work with this lawsuit you're defending anyway."

"That's right. I'm one of the lawyers that's putting you out of business. I'm trying to build my career by killing yours."

"You're assuming that your firm and your leviathan client are going to win," Henry said.

"I know we're going to win, Henry. And winning is like timing. It's everything. I work long hours …. I don't need the distraction right now. I don't have a boyfriend for a reason. It's just not the right time, not right now." She felt defeated in trying to piece together her thin designer dress which had been torn from her the night before in the heat of passion. "Look at this. Destroyed. I have to get home and go to work."

"Can we talk about this tonight?"

"No, Henry. No, we cannot. I think you are missing the gist of what I'm trying to get across to you. We can't …. *Be*."

"And for a lawyer you've not made a strong argument supporting your case," he said.

"Well, let me make it more clear for you. You're a great lay. I like you, and you more than obviously like me, but there is no way that we can play house. If you can't be an adult and chalk this up to a casual, physical kind of thing, then we should never do this again."

"Are you listening to yourself, Kat? This isn't you. What are you saying? You keep pushing me away and I cannot for the life of me figure out why. I know you feel what I feel. The way you look at me …. Well …. Not right now. The way you normally look at me."

"It's just an infatuation, Henry."

"Infatuations don't last ten, twelve years."

"I can't love you," she said harshly. "The Tommy thing …. I just can't."

"You're blaming me for something my goddamned father did? How the fuck is that fair?"

"The apple and the tree, Henry. It's just a matter of time before you turn into him. I can't be ten years down the road, pushing forty, with kids and a cheating husband. I refuse."

"Jesus, you've got me pegged. How is it you have any feelings for me at all?"

She was tired of trying to come up with excuses. Tears filled her eyes. She looked at the floor. There was only one way to make him let her go. One way to end this once and for all. It was cruel. It was heartless. But it had to be done. She couldn't look him in the eye, so she didn't.

"I don't, Henry. I don't have any feelings for you at all. I never did. Goodbye."

She clutched the top of her dress to hold it together as she left the room and Henry's life.

30

HENRY'S DAY DIDN'T GET ANY BETTER AFTER THE early morning incident with Kat in the hotel room. He quickly got dressed and raced down to the lobby to catch her, but she was in a cab that was pulling away before he could reason with her. When he got back up to his room for the night, he didn't have his key, so he was forced to go back to the lobby to get a new one. His clothes from the date with Kat were destroyed from the pawing and tearing they had done to one another the night before. He looked like hobo, his ID was with the room key.

Once validating who he was to the concierge back in the room, he took a long, hot shower in the futile hope of forgetting the events of the morning. He stewed in the steam, attempting to wash the dirt and grime that was within. Again it was an exercise in futility. He didn't feel refreshed or unencumbered in any way, made worse by his walk of shame into the hotel room he was originally booked into with Miles.

Because of the traffic, it took over an hour to get across town to the hotel he and Miles were staying in. He went to his room, changed clothes and knocked on the room next door.

Miles opened his room door and looked as bad or worse than Henry.

"Where have you been? I've been knocking and calling all morning," Miles asked.

"I was out with a friend last night."

"The lawyer? Good. Very good. Did you make any progress?"

"No. Why? What do you need?"

"I received a phone call from the firm. Our firm was contacted by Ticketmaster's to inform them that they plan to draw this litigation out for as long as humanly possible. There will be no negotiations. They're digging their heels in."

"I told you coming out here was a long shot, Miles. So now what?"

"The tour is on indefinite hiatus. The label is going to want some sort of compensation for lost revenues …. It's a big fucking mess to put it bluntly."

"And that means that I have some free time," Henry said with a sigh.

"Correct. I haven't heard the official word from management, Curtis hasn't returned my calls, but I would assume that you are out on your ass as well."

"But you get your fees, right Miles?"

"I beg your pardon?"

"A prolonged legal struggle keeps your wallet full. You look like shit but in reality you're probably dancing a jig on the inside, huh?"

"My sole interest is my client. My firm's interest is with our client. Your employer is ultimately mine. With no money coming in, how do we get paid?"

Henry tapped Miles on his back and made his way back out the hotel room door.

"I'm sure you'll think of something," he said.

With time on his hands, he decided to go see his sister. He had no home and no friends other than those that were in the band. The roadies and techs and tour managers and assistants were all going to be out of jobs as well, they just didn't know it yet. Henry decided not to go and commiserate with the fellowship of the miserable, he decided to go back to ground zero. Take a step back and regroup.

It had been a terrible time as of late. His mother passing. Kat. The job he knew and loved and excelled at was in the toilet. All he had left was his sister. So he got on a flight from LAX to San Francisco.

While waiting for the flight, he called Margo who told him that he was welcome at any time.

Again she didn't inform her continued live-in boyfriend, Paul, that Henry was coming.

Margo picked Henry up from the airport in San Francisco at 7:30 p.m., she was seated on a bench by the luggage carousel.

"Henry! Over here," she yelled. The crowd was unfazed and moved about their business, Henry fought through them to get to her.

The pedestrian traffic around baggage claim hid Margo from view, but once Henry was able to see his sister, his eyes couldn't hide what he was thinking.

"I know. I've put on some weight," she said once Henry closed the space between them.

"No, no. You look good."

"Your face said it all, Henry."

"My face is full of shit. It's been a tough couple of days."

"I know. I'm sorry about the way you found out," Margo said.

"That was just the start of it."

"You want to talk about it?"

"Later. Just let me grab my bag." He went to the carousel and found his luggage in short order. It took him longer to fight through the crowd to get to his bag than it had to spot it.

Once he returned to his sister, she didn't offer to take his carry-on. Henry jostled his shoulder-bag and large, heavy checked-bag while trying to keep up with his sister who was leading him presumably to her car.

Henry packed the two bags and himself into Margo's small Honda and they made their way to Sausalito. The conversation resumed on the trip.

"So how are things with you and what's-his-face?"

"It's Paul and things have never been better."

"Oh, good."

"He's a great guy, Henry. You two just need to bond."

"Yeah, sure. So what did he say when you told him I was going to be back in town?"

"I haven't exactly told him yet," she admitted.

"Christ, Margo. I'm going to blind-side him again?"

"He'll be fine with it. Besides, I didn't know what to tell him. Do you know how long you might be staying with us?"

"No. I'm kind of just playing it by ear. I just found out that I don't have a job anymore this morning."

"Oh, Henry. I'm sorry. What happened?"

"Do you know who I worked for or what I do? Read the papers, see MTV news?"

"Well, no. Not really. Geoff said he knew where you were, or at least who you were with. I was depending on your old boss to find your new one."

"Never mind then."

"Don't 'never mind' me, Henry. I hate that. You either want to tell me what happened or you don't, but don't treat me like I'm an idiot. I'm here to help, not be insulted."

"You're right. I'm sorry. I don't feel like explaining it, is all," he said after a few seconds.

"It really has been a rough couple of days," Margo said. "Mom, and now your job."

"And I saw Kat."

"Here we go. Kat again?"

"Don't start with me, Margo. Do you want to hear about it or not?"

"Sorry. Yes. Go ahead."

They crossed the Golden Gate Bridge and had fifteen minutes left of the trip.

Henry told her about Kat. About how he saw her, leaving out the particulars about the lawsuit itself, just that he was there for work on legal business. He told Margo about dinner. About how nice it was and how effortless it was to talk with her in the restaurant. How there was an admitted chemistry between them that transcended time and history. He told Margo about being together, not the coital details, but about how he felt being with the love of his life. And he told her about how Kat had left that very morning.

It took all of the fifteen minutes remaining in the drive.

Margo listened in silence, but put the exclamation mark on the one-sided conversation as she put the car in park when they arrived at her home. She shut off the ignition but made no attempt to leave the small car.

"I tried to tell you, Henry. I know that's the last thing that you want to hear right now, but I did. You're like a nice comfortable blanket for her. A beat up blanket that's familiar, but old and worn and smelly and should be thrown away."

"Nice."

"Not literally, I'm just illustrating my point. You're a smart guy, Henry. You know what I'm telling you is right. You're just too close to it. You can't see the forest for the trees. She's moved on and wants nothing to do with her past. Every time she sees you, she feels things but her brain reminds her of Tommy. Of how a Devlin fucked up her family. You're going to need to let her go. Not for her, but for you. Have a life, Henry. Be good to yourself and let her go. You can't keep pining away for the girl that got away."

"Would that I could."

Paul was indeed unhappy about the unannounced visitor. He didn't say as much outright, but he failed to hide it in his demeanor. They sat at the dining room table for a late supper, where Paul kept trying to pin Henry to a timeframe in which he would be leaving again.

"For the last time, Paul, I don't know. I just sort of came up with this today. I didn't get to see Margo at the funeral, because I didn't know about it."

"Because you never call and we had no way to find you," Paul said.

"Right. I've been properly chastised for that, thanks. Anyway, I also found out that I'm out of work indefinitely, so I'll need to figure out if I'm going back to Seattle or where to go next. I was thinking LA."

"That's a bad idea, Henry. We talked about this in the car," Margo interjected. "You need to let her go."

"And you know I can't do that."

"Let who go? I'm lost," Paul admitted.

197

"Don't worry about it, Paul," Henry said. "Anyway, I should probably go back to Mass and figure out the Carver Pond situation first."

Margo said, "Good luck with that. How are you going to find him?"

"I've no idea. I'll figure it out I guess."

"I can't imagine a father just losing his family. His wife, okay, maybe. But his kids? I'll never do that," Paul said.

Margo gave Paul a look, telling him to shut up without saying it. Henry didn't miss it.

"You're pregnant aren't you, Margo?"

She smiled. "Yes. Ten weeks."

A million thoughts rolled around Henry's mind in a millionth of a second.

"Congrats. To both of you. Are you going to get married?"

Paul said, "We don't have any immediate plans for anything except the spare bedroom."

31

MARGO AND PAUL'S BED AND BREAKFAST OFFICIALLY closed three days into Henry's latest stay, after a rousing contest of *Jeopardy!*.

It was never much of a competition whenever anyone chose to play along side of Henry while watching the television trivia show. More often than not, Henry would answer the trivia in the form of a question before Alex Trebek had a chance to finish reading the clue. The opportunity to consider the answer was nullified as Henry interjected the correct answers, confirmed by either the contestant or Alex himself in his condescending manner.

It was often suggested that Henry apply to appear on the game show, as anyone who witnessed his acumen for obscure intellectual topics marveled at his ability to recall and recite said facts. But he never did. He contended that it would cease to be fun if he were in it for money. It would be more like a job than an entertaining test. The reasoning didn't make sense to anyone but Henry.

On this particular evening, it was Paul who was witnessing this feat from his recliner while Henry was on the couch. The television volume progressively increased as Paul kept insinuating that the reason he wasn't answering the questions correctly or in a timely manner was because he couldn't hear the clues over Henry's vocal outbursts. Paul would inquire as to prospects for employment and permanent housing during the commercials, Henry didn't answer in the form of a question or otherwise.

Use It Up

It was obvious, especially to Henry, that Paul's frustrations were building. It could have been the first round of the game, where Paul hadn't answered one clue correctly, while Henry spouted off correct answer after answer, or it could have been Henry's lack of moving out. Probably a combination of all of the above. In any case, it was simply a matter of time before a fuse snapped. Paul was on the precipice of paroxysm, an additional inconvenience would incite such an explosion.

Paul was an Art History professor at a local college and prided himself on his knowledge in said area. One of the categories during the *Double Jeopardy!* round should have been a lock for the man of the house, unfortunately, as with all of the other categories during the game, Henry was running the board.

"The artist, known by his birthplace in Italy instead of his name which is the 'other' Michelangelo, painted David and Goliath, and Medusa," Alex said over the television. Henry had already read the clue on the blue screen before the television host finished reading it.

"Who is Caravaggio," Henry said less than halfway through Alex's reading.

"For the last time, Henry, can you *please* wait until the question is read in its entirety before you blurt it out?"

"Who is Caravaggio," the middle contestant correctly said.

"Of course," Trebek said before allowing the contestant to pick a category and dollar amount.

"We don't have buzzers, Paul," Henry said. "The only way for us to win is to be the first one to answer correctly."

"I understand how the game works.   Just wait until the goddamned question is read, okay?"

Alex continued with another clue after the middle contestant, who answered the previous question correctly, continued with the same category for $800.

"This Spanish artist is known by the last of his fifteen names and was the founder of the abstract movement with 20th century works such as; Guernica, which represented the bombing of Gernika during the Spanish Civil War."

"Who is Picasso? These are pretty easy, huh?"

"*Henry! Godammit!* Do you know how irritating this is?"

"What? Fifteen names was the giveaway, Paul. Pablo Diego José Francisco de Paula Juan Nepomuceno María de los Remedios Crispín Crispiniano de la Santísima Trinidad Ruiz y Picasso."

"I know! Shut up will you?"

Henry should have let Paul answer the next few, and he tried. But after two clues from other categories went unanswered, he decided to start playing again.

The final clue in the *Poup-Art-Rie* category was requested.

Alex read, "After being injured in a street car accident, this artist painted exclusively 'surrealistic' self portraits depicting the pain and suffering of women."

"Who is Kahlo?"

"*Fuck!*"

"What? Frida Kahlo. Jesus, Paul, isn't art history supposed to be your thing?"

Paul rose from his chair as though he was ejected from it.

"Get out of my house! Now."

"Taking this a little hard, aren't you Paul?"

"Now, you ungrateful asshole. Get your shit and get out or I'll throw it out on the street."

"Why? Because I beat you at *Jeopardy!*?"

Margo entered the living room from the recesses of the house.

"What's going on out here?"

"Honey, I want your brother out of this house. Now," Paul said.

"What happened? Henry? What did you do?"

"I answered one too-many questions for Paul's taste I guess. Beats me."

"Babe?" Margo tried to bring a level of tranquility to the situation, she failed.

"He has no job, no place to live, and he insults me in my own home," Paul said. "I've been patient, but that patience has worn out."

"We can't just kick him out on the street. He is my brother for Pete's sake. He's the only family I have left."

"You're pregnant, Margo. We're making a new family. Yours was no prize, you're not losing much."

"Paul! Take that back! Henry, apologize. Whatever you did, I want you to say that you're sorry for it so we can all move on. This is ridiculous."

"I didn't do anything wrong, Margo. But if that's what you want —"

"—I don't want your fucking apology. I just want you gone," Paul interjected.

"Fine," Henry said as he moved past Paul toward the guest room.

"Aren't you over-reacting a little bit, Dear?"

"You're going to take his side?"

"I'm not taking anyone's side," Margo said. "You've been yelling since you started watching the show. He's smart, so what?"

"It's him or me, Margo."

She began to well-up with tears. "Please don't make me choose between you and my brother. He's all I have. He needs me right now. Us. He needs us right now. Be the bigger man."

Henry exited the guest room with a thrown-together piece of luggage.

"Don't worry about it, Margo. I've put you both out enough. Paul can be the big man of the house if that's what he wants."

She closed the space between them, embracing him as tightly as she could, and whispered into his ear.

"Just give me a couple of days. He'll cool off. You're my brother. This is ridiculous."

"It's okay, Sis. I need to get to Bridgewater anyway. Just take care of my nephew."

She smiled as she held him.

"What if it's a girl?"

"Let's hope."

The flight to Logan Airport from San Francisco was last minute and expensive and long and uncomfortable. Henry had to contend with coach seats on three different planes because of his forced two connecting flights. The term redeye doesn't nearly convey how intolerable the flights were. Between the beverage cart attendant waking him to inquire his desired beverage; to the children screaming at deafening decibels; to the kicking of seats to the bumping of elbows; lack of sleep was a foregone conclusion. Then he would have to deplane, re-board, and start the process anew.

By the time he arrived in Boston, acquired a rental, and drove to the Carver Pond house, Henry was beyond exhausted.

And yet he couldn't sleep as much as he tried. Recent events invaded his thoughts and his ability to rest. The house around him creaked and spoke to him.

The house, once refurbished, had gone into another phase of disrepair. On the outside, no lawn maintenance had taken place in much longer than the nearly four weeks since Faith Devlin had passed. The house looked dirty, run-down, and in need of a bull-dozer.

The inside was as abused as the shell. Of course there was dust on the furnishings and debris on the floors, but the converted fishing cottage had been neglected for even the most modest of maintenance. It stunk of must. It was hot inside the house from being closed up during the summer without ventilation. Cupboard doors had fallen off, sinks leaked, faucets dripped, wallpaper peeled, molding and trim-work missing.

His mother must have been too sick for the upkeep, Henry thought as he lay in his old bed.

It also occurred to Henry that the dwelling was a physical representation of Faith. She had been left to wither, alone, eventually succumbing to cancer which she refused to treat. She too had been closed, a relative shut-in. The house was in an atrophied cancer of its own. It would not take much more sustained decline for the place to perish.

Saddened and in a state of lugubrious contemplation, he turned to what he knew best. Music.

Henry rose from his sagging, creaky bed, padding across the likewise creaky floor to the living-room. A worn armoire sat next to a table which supported his mother's turntable and Hi-Fi stereo. Inside the armoire were shelves filled with upright-filed vinyl records. The albums were each in their own individual plastic sleeves which protected the cardboard cover-art which housed the vinyl record itself. The music collection was the antithesis of the house that sheltered it.

He flipped through album after album, stopping occasionally to reflect upon a time when he had heard it with his mother. These were Faith's prize possessions, cared for and protected in a way that she hadn't

204

for anything else, not even her children in retrospect. There were two facets to the life of Faith Prichard-Devlin; the Catholic church, and her music.

One album forced him to pause for longer than a reflection. The cover artwork was a painting of a woman holding a rose, the yellow and orange sunset reflecting over a body of water behind her. The woman portrayed on the cover was Faith's favorite. It was the Joni Mitchell album, Clouds.

Henry carefully removed the album from the protective sleeve, then the record itself. The cover to the turntable had more than one layer of dust, though underneath the record player was pristine. He placed the album A-side up, then the weight on top of it. Next, he used the soft, velvet brush to removed the nonexistent debris from the black, grooved surface, and placed the diamond needle on the outside edge as it spun.

The sound of Joni strumming her acoustic guitar filled the room. Henry turned up the volume on the receiver and sat back on the beaten up chair in the center of the living room, listening to the first track. Her voice was angelic.

Both Sides Now consumed him. Music is amazing in this way. It was just an acoustic guitar and a slight woman's tender voice, but the sound wasn't anemic in any regard. On the contrary, the sound was rich and powerful and profound.

With eyes closed, he was taken to another place. A place where his mother was still alive. Where she conversed with him. Where she confided in him the secrets and the knowledge she had acquired from a life not fully lived. A time spent, wasted, and now reflected upon. She was privy to all things, before and since.

He had lost a woman that he shared increasingly less with over time. But he loved her despite his lack of demonstration. She was his mother after all.

He had lost a job he loved. There would be others, he supposed. But he was good at it and loved it and already missed it.

He had once again lost his one true love. The woman that loved him and hurt him with the same conviction.

He was overtaken. Tears filled his closed eyes and ran down his cheeks. He felt his mother speaking to him through Joni, and her words were fervent. He remembered listening to the album with his mother and envisioned that in some respect he was again. Henry tasted his tears through quivering lips as he listened. With ears and heart aligned, he listened.

"I've looked at life from both sides now,
From win and lose, and still somehow
It's life's illusions I recall.
I really don't know life at all."

32

MORE THAN A WEEK HAD PASSED SINCE HENRY'S return to Carver Pond. He spent the time going over the dilapidating house, looking for items his mother had left behind. There was nothing of significance. No jewelry. No money or things of value. Just the records. Either Margo had picked it over when she was there making arrangements or there was nothing from the start. In either case, he decided to pack up her only prized possessions while he listened to them. He stopped to only to go out for food.

He didn't dare keep food in the unsanitary refrigerator or cupboards. The surfaces of the appliances weren't fit for cooking. The kitchen, like the rest of the house, was in a prolonged state of neglect. The cottage-to-house-back-to-cottage hadn't happened overnight. It hadn't happened in the last month. His mother had let this happen around her. Henry wondered if it wasn't the house itself that caused her cancer. A cancer that, like the house, she refused to fix.

The same local restaurants existed in Bridgewater. Some big chains had opened, some closed, but the local eateries remained. And so did many of the locals.

When out, he would ask the people within the community that he knew if they had seen Tommy Devlin. There were many families in the town that were fixtures. Roots can sometimes be too deep to transplant, Henry thought. He encountered citizen after citizen that had been born there, raised there, raised their own family, and would likely die in Bridgewater. It was unimaginable to him that so many people would live in a world they hadn't seen, live in a town that they would never leave.

Henry didn't want to see his father, quite the opposite in fact. Henry wasn't even truly curious about Tommy's whereabouts. Whatever rock he was hiding under, Henry was sure it was a place worse for having the man in its occupancy. But he needed to find him to sign over Carver Pond. It began its life as nothing much and seemed to regress to that state more by the day. However, it was all that remained of a woman who was tormented by the man Henry was seeking. Did Faith allow for this to happen to her? Arguably, yes. But did she deserve to be cast aside and left to fend for herself with the offspring that the two of them had produced? Inarguably, no.

Henry felt that if Tommy abandoned them, leaving them with only a house they couldn't afford and a fishing cottage that his father had slapped together, he shouldn't then be able to recollect whatever he had abandoned. The Carver Pond house needed significant repairs, a complete overhaul if not a major reconstruction. It might be more a more appropriate disposition to level the building and start fresh by whomever chose to make it a home, but in any case, it wasn't Tommy's any longer. It was Margo's to do with it was she wished. Henry would see to that.

Nobody confessed to having seen or heard from him. Tommy had vanished.

Trish Bradar, Kat's mom, didn't know. At least she said as much. And she didn't seem very keen on reliving the issue of Tommy Devlin. She and Henry were alike in that regard. He refrained from bringing up Kat, and Mrs. Bradar didn't bring up her daughter either. The conversation was quick and dirty and uncomfortable. Henry wasn't even allowed to cross the threshold of Mrs. Bradar's front door.

With a week of packing and listening and inquiring under his belt, with no progress, Henry decided to enlist the help of a Boston investigator. He went into the city and told the private detective about the man that was to be found, why, and all pertinent information in regard to Tommy's history including last known whereabouts. The young Boston investigator, Cole Renner, informed Henry of his fees and required retainer from behind his desk in his East Boston office.

Henry paid him.

"With all that out of the way, how long do you think it will take to find him?"

"It's hard to say," Renner said. "People go missing for a variety of reasons. You said he didn't show up for his wife's funeral?"

"They were husband and wife in name only. Father too. He had a very liberal approach to fatherhood and marriage. He didn't realize that when you get married, you're supposed to stop dating."

"And this Bradar woman was the last known dalliance?"

"That I know of. I spoke to her, like I said. She wants the whole mess behind her. She finally came to her senses and kicked him to the curb, but not before ruining her marriage and suffering through a divorce. I just want him found so he can sign a piece of paper releasing all rights and ownership to the place on the pond," Henry explained.

"I understand. Do you have the document that you want him to sign?"

"I haven't written it yet. I wanted to find him and see what he has to say for himself first. I reckon he'll sign anything I put in front of him, given the givens."

"Care to enlighten me on the 'givens'?"

"Suffice to say that the last time we met, he left the meeting looking like he went through a meat grinder."

"It got physical I take it."

"He left in an ambulance, I left in the back of a cruiser."

209

"So you're saying that he will probably sign away his claim to the property because he fears a beating?"

"That's the gist."

"Well, that's extortion and it's illegal," Renner said. "I can be found just as guilty as you as an accessory to coercion and assault if I know in advance that you'll do him bodily harm. I propose a different approach."

"I'm listening," Henry said.

"I'll have a lawyer draw up a boilerplate document for him to sign in front of a notary. Once I've found him of course. You can't go anywhere near him, I'll take care of it all with no additional legal fees. That way he can't come back later and say that he signed it under duress. Once it's signed, you'll be good to go."

"That works. I don't really want to see him anyway," Henry confessed. "One more thing though. Have him sign it over to Margo Devlin, my sister. The property probably isn't worth much, the building is falling down and I don't want it. But I *really* don't want *him* to have it."

"Fair enough. Are you going back to San Francisco? I can handle it from here without you."

"I'll be here for a couple more days. If you need me or more money, here's my pager number." He gave the detective his number and Margo's in case he needed it for the paperwork. "I'll get back to you as soon as I can."

The two men stood and shook hands from opposing sides of the desk in Renner's office.

"A guy like that shouldn't be too hard to find, Mr. Devlin."

"Henry. Call me Henry. And it might be tougher than you think. He can't keep a job, he drifts from bed to bed, and generally flies below radar. I've looked around Bridgewater for a week and nobody has seen or heard from him. None of the garages have given him work in years."

"Well, I'll do my best and get on it right away. I'll find him,"
Renner said.

"Thanks. Better you find him than me."

Part Four

"I'll hold the pain, release me."

-Pearl Jam

33

HENRY PIECED TOGETHER A LIVING FREE-LANCING as a sound engineer for a number of bands and albums through the turn of the century. He traveled wherever the work was. He would get a call from this band or that recording studio in need of someone to produce the next big rock album. One project led to another, one success leading to the proposition of another.

Not all of his projects were considered huge successes, but he mixed more great music projects than those that were dubbed either critical or popular failures. Henry wasn't creating the music, of course, the artists were. But he was instrumental in making the music sound the best it could. The Smashing Pumpkins, Incubus, The White Stripes, Foo Fighters, Breaking Benjamin, and The Killers were some of the projects considered to be successes.

The dawn of portable media players like the iPod, and the subsequent emergence and popularity of iTunes, was the beginning of the end of Henry's independent engineering career. Nobody was purchasing vinyl anymore. Nor cassette tapes. CDs were on the decline. Meaning that liner notes were also a thing of the past. In the old days, somebody could look inside the cover art and see who created the images, or look up the names of all band members, and those who collaborated on the various songs within. The name of the recording studio used to be important. The name of the engineer who produced the final version on the album as well.

But no longer.

Big labels were buying up all of the small companies producing the next generation of music, just as large radio stations were buying up all of the small independents. Bands no longer had any control over who helped to create the sound produced on their albums. The large corporations hired and mandated who produced the music. Nobody cared who created this sound or that one, even if they could look it up inside the CD cover, because they were all the same people. Which meant that all the music sounded the same. The 'cookie-cutter' approach to music was simply good business for music executives. Once a sound became popular, other labels would sign a band to imitate it. Live performances often didn't sound anything like what was produced on the artist's album. And talented people like Henry, who tried to collaborate to innovate sound, were out of work.

In 2002, Henry was called back to Los Angeles. He had been given the opportunity to get involved in Hollywood. He wasn't acting. He wasn't directing. But he was sought after to give life to movies through music.

Every movie, once the final shot has been filmed, goes through post-production. Edits take place. Various scenes get deleted. Reshoots sometimes take place to get exactly what the director wants or to add something that was lacking. Sound effects are added to create more authenticity, and music is added to create mood and feel.

Large studios like Paramount and Universal hire sound companies to engineer the orchestration written by magnates within the industry who compose film scores. Directors work with John Williams or Danny Elfman or James Horner or Hans Zimmer or others. The director and the composer will watch a rough cut of the movie to come up with a theme or feel, which the composer will then write music to be performed by an orchestra as a backdrop.

Orchestras like the Hollywood Studio Symphony or the London Symphony Orchestra or a myriad of others, assemble from the most talented musicians for their instrument, will then perform the written pieces. Depending on the score, there could be as many as one hundred musicians distributed into string, bass, woodwind, or percussion sections.

Once the timing and instrumentation has been worked out with a conductor, the 40 to 120 minutes of music is then recorded with the movie running on full screen behind the orchestra. The conductor ensures that the written music syncs with the action on the screen, adding the desired dramatic affect. The critical scenes of the films must be highlighted in the recording.

The sound company hired to record these scores need to microphone and set levels for each instrument in the orchestra. The engineer also needs to account for acoustics and sound bleeding and reverberations on top of the dialogue and the sound effects. It is a daunting task and can be exasperating at times when one of a thousand things doesn't go perfectly.

Henry was hired by one such company, Barking Dog, and was fascinated by all of it.

The machinery mover had seen the sound guy at the sound stage at all hours of the day and night at Big Dog Studios. Anytime he had been in the building to either bring in or remove sound equipment or staging or screens, the sound guy was there. The engineer would be either working or sleeping on a couch and he wondered if the man actually lived there. After two weeks of guessing, he decided to ask him.

"You must live here. Like really live here."

"Excuse me?"

"Sorry," the mover said. "Name is Troy. I'm here at all kinds of odd hours. I like the OT. Anyways, no matter when I'm here lifting shit, I see you. Sometimes just sleeping. So I figured that you live here."

"Yeah. I'm new here. New in town also. I'm Henry." He stuck his hand out and the two men shook hands.

"You don't like hotels?"

"Of course. I just want to get this right. I've never had to deal with so many moving parts. All of the instruments, the precision, it's fascinating but it's brutal. I've done drums and a few guitars, bass and maybe some keyboards over vocals, but this," Henry said as he waved his hand at the enormous room, "this is something different. I've been putting in so many hours that spending money on a hotel for the two or three hours I'd be in it, seems really stupid."

"And because of all that time you spend, you haven't had time to look for an apartment," Troy said acknowledging and nodding.

"Right."

"I thought that might be the case. I've got a friend looking for a roommate. I could introduce you. Save you time and effort in trying to find a place in this city."

"I'm not sure if—"

"—I know, we just met. They don't call LA la-la land for nothin'. There are a ton of crazies, I get it. But she needs help with the expenses and you need a place to live. Just meet her, what can it hurt?"

"A girl? Jeez I—"

"—It's not like that. She's looking for a male roommate anyway. Girls are messier than boys, she says."

"I guess. Can she come by here?"

"Probably," Troy said. "But don't you want to see the apartment? Be best to go over there, right?"

"Oh. Yeah. Duh. I don't know where my head is sometimes. When should I—"

"I'll give you her number. You two can work it out. I don't need a finder's fee, but if you wanna buy me a beer sometime I wouldn't refuse."

"Deal."

Henry's cell phone rang an hour later. He was expecting a female voice, but he wasn't expecting this one.

"Hello?"

"Henry. It's Margo."

"Hey. What's up?"

"I got your message the other day. Congrats on LA. How do you like it?"

"I love it. I'm not sure how good I'm going to be at it," Henry admitted. "It's quite a challenge."

"You're a smart guy, you can handle it."

"Thanks. How's Paul and the little one?"

"They're good. Cloud is growing up so fast. She's starting to look a lot like Mom."

"Seven going on twenty, huh?"

"You know it."

"Only you would name your daughter Cloud. You're such a hippie."

"It was Mom's favorite album right?"

"Yes, but you could have named her Joni, which is a normal name," Henry said as he began to laugh.

217

"Ha-ha Mr. comedian." She let a dozen seconds or so pass. Henry could tell it was because she wanted to change tact and subject.

"Okay, so why are you really calling?"

"They finally found him, Henry."

"Who? Who are *they*, and who did *they* find?"

"He. The private investigator you hired. Well, that's who called me anyway. He tried to call you but after all this time all he had for you was an outdated pager number and—"

"—Margo. Focus. You're rambling."

"Right. Sorry. They found Tommy. They found our father."

"Did he sign over the place? You officially own it after all this time? Frankly at this point I'd just level the fuckin' place and start over."

"He's dead, Henry."

"So what are you going to do? Move back east or sell the place or what?"

"Did you hear me? Tommy is dead. Our father has passed on. Do you get it? Not among the living."

"I heard you. He's been dead to me for a very long time, Margo."

"It doesn't make you sad or angry or anything? You feel nothing?"

"Not a thing. He used up every care I ever had for him, which wasn't much."

"Do you want to know how he died?"

Henry thought for a second.

Margo read the pause as an affirmative answer, interjecting the manner in which Thomas Devlin had passed from this life on to the next. But Henry spoke first and drowned her out.

"No. I really don't give a shit. I kind of hope painfully, but that would mean that I care enough to want him to have suffered. So no, Sis. I really don't care how he went, or when. He's been gone to me and your call just confirms he's gonna stay gone."

"He committed suicide," she repeated.

This time Henry wasn't speaking over her and heard his sister on the other end of the line.

"He must have been so lonely—"

"—Fucking coward. So much for his 'Life is full of punishment, give some back' speech."

"Okay, Henry. I guess. About the Carver place—"

"—Keep it. Or sell it. Do whatever you want."

"You sound pissed off," Margo said. "I'm sorry."

"Nothing to be sorry about. I'm not pissed, I keep telling you. I feel nothing about it. Are you upset?"

Margo also thought for a moment. "I don't know what to feel, Henry. I was hoping to figure it out with you. Isn't it terrible that I don't know what to feel. I was close to him for so much of my childhood. I was daddy's little girl."

"Which is why you have daddy issues."

"Don't start!"

"I'm not. Look, I gotta go. I'm pretty busy," Henry said.

"Okay, okay. Knock 'em dead down there. Come visit soon."

"Sure. When I can."

Ten minutes after the call from his sister ended, Henry received the call he'd been expecting. He set up a time that evening to see his new apartment and his new roommate, Bailey Gaines.

34

BAILEY GAINES WAS NOT WHAT HENRY HAD envisioned when the machinery mover, Troy, mentioned her. When he had said that he had a friend who was in search of a roommate, Henry inferred that she would be of like age and probably a hermit of some sort. Those with a wide social net tend to be able to find a suitable living companion, and those who are comely tend to be able to find someone that will not only share living expenses but their bedroom as well.

Bailey was a stunning, dusky beauty.

Henry rang the buzzer to the red door that sat next to three very wide garage doors. That red door led to an outdoor set of stairs where the stained wooden door was opened slightly at the top. He knocked and announced his presence after ascending the outdoor staircase. He peered into the opening for only a second before the occupant opened it fully.

"You must be Henry." The woman was tall and slender with dark, porcelain skin; chestnut hair that flowed and draped down her back. Her heterochromatic eyes seemed to look through him rather than at him. She was in her mid to late twenties in Henry's estimation, she could not have yet turned thirty. Her jade with brown-flecked eyes seemed to glow, highlighted by her fashionable dress, as she stood in the doorway. Henry stood, stunned and tongue-tied.

"Uh. Yeah. Yes. Bailey?"

She laughed a little. "Obviously."

They shook hands and Bailey broke the pause that was becoming awkward.

"You're not what I was expecting," she said. "When Troy said a sound engineer at Barking Dog, I guess I pictured somebody older. Geekish."

"You've got the geekish part right I guess. When it comes to music I'm a complete nerd. And truthfully, you're not what I expected either."

"No?"

"No. You don't strike me as the type that needs to search high and low for someone to live with. You and Troy—"

"—Troy is just a friend. He's gay and has someone to live with. I'm very particular about who I live with. Neat freak."

"Oh. Still .... "

"Well, this is it anyway. Would you like the tour?"

"Oh. Yes. That's why I'm here, right?"

Bailey walked Henry around the apartment which took up the entire space above the oversized three-car garage below. The kitchen was large with a breakfast bar, a small dining room, a large living room where Henry had entered through the front door, two and a half bathrooms, and two large bedrooms.

Once the tour was completed, she informed Henry of the monthly rent amount, and further shared that all utilities would be split evenly as well. Henry thought the costs more than reasonable, especially for the Silver Lake area of Los Angeles.

"I'll want you to sign an agreement," Bailey said. "It's not that I don't trust you, it's just that I've been burned before."

"Of course. Background check and credit too, I'm sure."

She laughed again. "Not quite that intense. Do you mind if I ask how old you are? My guess is about my age, twenty-six."

"I'm thirty-one."

"Wow. I never would have guessed. You have a Kurt Cobain kind of thing going," she said. "His Doppelgänger."

"He's dead, so not really a true Doppelgänger," Henry said.

"Did I use the work wrong? His twin then?"

"I get your point, though I'm not sure if that's a compliment or not. I haven't showered in a day or two."

More laughter. "I meant it as a compliment."

"Were you a fan?"

"Who wasn't? I still think Courtney had something to do with his death."

"I was lucky enough to work with him. With Nirvana. That band had so much more to offer. Another one gone too soon. I worked with Dave since then with Foo Fighters, and Layne Staley who just died .... " Henry got lost in thought for a few seconds then came back to the here and now. "Sorry. I guess I just name-dropped. Pretty tacky. What do you do?"

"Full-time flight attendant, part-time model. I'm getting too old for modeling."

"You're too old to model at twenty-six?"

"I'm too old to get into it full-time. I've been doing it off and on since I was fourteen. Anyway, I'm in the air for one reason or another so I don't have time to date, no time to deal with finding a roommate, and no desire to have to deal with a messy one. That's not going to be a problem for you is it?"

"Being messy? No. I've been housebroken," Henry said.

She started laughing again. "You're really funny."

"I think you might be the first person to think so. I do listen to music a lot though. I where headphones all day long at work. I can here too, but I prefer not to."

"Music isn't messy. Play it as loud as you want while I'm not here, which is often. I love music too, so if I'm around and like what you have on …. We shouldn't have a problem."

"Cool."

"So what do you think? Do you want to move in?"

"Sounds good. I can go down to my truck and get my stuff now if it's okay."

"You have everything you own in your truck? How big is your truck?" She managed between giggles as she went to the window to look down to the street, his truck was parked in front of the garage doors.

"I've lived most of my adult life on the road. Since Seattle anyway. I don't have anything except my clothes and my music. I'll have to get a bed."

"We will figure something out."

"That's not what I meant," Henry said.

"I know. Me neither. We just met. But since we're on the subject, I do need to ask a favor."

"Shoot."

"Like I said, I know we just met, but I have this wedding I have to go to. I replied plus one, but since then Troy has plans with his boyfriend, so I need a plus one. It's my brother's wedding."

"You need me to go with you to a wedding? That's pretty inten—"

"—I know, I know. As friends. New friends, I suppose. I just don't want to go alone, it would be embarrassing. It's here in LA, no travel…."

Henry scratched his head while he thought. She was gorgeous, he could do worse for a date. But a wedding? There would be relatives, both immediate and distant. He wanted the room at the apartment, would saying no to the invitation be a deal-breaker? Screw it, what harm could it do?

223

"When is it?"

Henry hadn't set foot in a church for as long as he could remember. The wedding was going to be a lavish affair, it was obvious just from the way the church was decorated. By the way the guests were dressed. Very tony.

The church was adorned with large floral arrangements, attendees donning designer formal attire, a full orchestra at the ready. A great deal of money had been spent by all involved for the ceremony alone.

Henry was uncomfortable not only because his relationship with the deity that the church represented had been strained to put it mildly, but also for the fact that he knew no one on either side of the aisle.

Bailey had insisted that he go shopping for a new suit. She further insisted that she go with him. She picked out the style and color to match her designer dress. She had seen it when he had tried it on before being tailored, the day of the wedding was the first time she had seen him in it since it had been altered to fit him.

Henry had sensed the need to make a favorable impression, though Bailey had insisted that the wedding wasn't a date. For this reason he had a drastic haircut and shaved off his perma-stubble. His blonde hair was no longer shoulder length and his face was a smooth as a newborn's.

The phrase, "Wow you really clean up," left Bailey's lips so often that Henry was beginning to wonder how bad he had looked every day prior.

The two arrived at the church, sat on the side of the church designated for the groom when asked by the usher, and sat in a pew near the front. Henry seemed far more uncomfortable than the woman who had invited him there. She was more stunning than the day he had met her two weeks prior. Her jade dress highlighted her already breathtaking heterochromatic eyes—which went with virtually every color because of the multiple hues—and chestnut hair; her exposed shoulders, back, and a hint of her small breasts were tastefully so. Bailey was garnering attention from all sides, which made Henry that much more self-conscious being next to her.

When the time came for the ceremony to begin, the groom and his men stood to the right, at the front of the church, below the altar. Bailey's brother gave his sister a wink.

"Why aren't you a bridesmaid?"

"I think for catty reasons. That's my guess anyway," Bailey whispered back to Henry.

"What do you mean?"

"I don't think the bride likes me, for starters. But more than that, a bride wants to be the center of attention on her day. That's why they always pick out ugly dresses for the other girls that are up there with her. It sounds awful, but I don't think that she wanted me up there. I'm okay with it. Now that you're here, I'm okay with it. I wouldn't need a date if I was at the head table."

Bailey was interrupted by the sound of the strings from the orchestra, playing the beginning of Wagner's Lohengrin, from the balcony above the back of the church. Everyone rose and turned to see the procession of women slowly make way toward the altar.

Henry thought that Bailey's assessment of her not being a bridesmaid was conceited, but once the cortège unfolded and each maid was revealed as she made way toward the front, he began to agree. It was quite obvious, once known to Henry that Bailey was an option for the bride, she had chosen to underwhelm the audience with her current

225

escorts. He then wondered how underwhelming, cosmetically, the bride herself would be.

Each bridesmaid smiled and winked or acknowledged those in the pews that they knew as they slowly made their way toward the altar.

There was a brief pause in the procession as the young girl who was throwing flower pedals had to be coaxed into doing as rehearsed. The audience ooh'ed and aww'ed as the pretty young girl walked down the aisle tossing remnants of de-winged flora.

Another pause as all of the women took their place on the various stairs to the left of the church below the altar opposite the groom and his mates.

The groom smiled as he saw his soon-to-be-bride festoon the doorway on the arm of the man who was giving her away. Henry watched Bailey's brother's eyes take in his fiancée, apparent that he found her the most beautiful person he had ever seen. Henry continued to watch him, and the moment wash over the groom. Henry then turned to see the bride as she made her way down the aisle.

The presumed father of the bride was a white-haired gent of an age Henry guessed to be mid-sixties. He appeared to be in good shape, though a tuxedo can and does often hide a lifetime of sins.

The bride herself was small and fragile looking. She held her flowers in front of her with her left hand, her right held on to her chaperone's forearm. Her white dress was form-fitting, her hair done up, a veil covering her face.

She took her time getting to the front of the church, the strings continuing through the wedding march for as long as was musically needed.

Once she arrived, the chaperone gave her away, stepped around the long train of her dress and took his position standing in front of his seat. The groom lifted the bride's veil to reveal her face. Henry thought that lifting of the veil was the father of the bride's job, but didn't stand on ceremony. He had other things on his mind at present.

She needn't have worried about attractive bridesmaids. The bride was breathtaking, the most beautiful being on the planet. Henry nearly had a heart attack as the lifted veil revealed the face of the most beautiful woman he had ever seen.

Kat was about to be married.

"What the fuck is this, Bailey?" Henry was trying to whisper yet get across his exasperation to the woman who had brought him there.

"Ssssshhhh. Keep your voice down. What are you talking about?"

"Do you know who that is?"

"Who? The bride?"

"Yes, Bailey. The bride. Do you know who that is?"

"Of course I do, Katherine. My brother's very soon-to-be wife. Can this wait? We're causing a scene."

The guests in the pews in front and behind were paying them the attention that was designed for the bride and groom. They weren't happy about the distraction.

"That's my .... She's my ...."

"Who? Who is she, Henry?"

"My ex? .... I don't know. It's complicated."

Bailey could see by Henry's look and tone that the situation was indeed complicated, that he in fact had very strong feelings about her future sister-in-law. His anguish nearly seeped from his eyes.

She whispered back through gritted teeth. "Can we talk about this later?"

"You still want me to stay? Are you nuts?"

"If you leave me at this wedding .... Alone .... Stranded? Don't even think about going back to the apartment. I'll put you out on your ass!"

Henry faced front, contemplating his options. He watched the ceremony continue on but he wasn't focused on it. He was focused on Kat. On a life he had missed out on. About the life that she was about to embark upon.

Time passed in excruciating minutes which felt like hours. Every moment that Henry and Kat had shared flashed through his mind at an equally excruciating pace. Every second was an inhumane torture, each recollection another knife buried deep into Henry's chest.

"If anyone should have a compelling reason why these two children of Christ should not be married, speak now or forever hold your peace."

35

AS PREDICTED, THE RECEPTION WAS A LAVISH affair. More extravagant than the church ceremony, as might be expected. A jazz band played on a secondary stage in the lush courtyard while the guests waited for the arrival of the new bride and groom. Henry had worked with the upright bass player before but he couldn't remember his name. They exchanged nods as the crowd mingled and bellied-up to the open bar.

The sun was warm but not oppressive in the perfect atmosphere for a wedding celebration. The Pacific Ocean lay as the backdrop, the gardens within the courtyard added not only beauty but a lovely fragrance. Tables were set with fine china and crystal, nothing was out of place.

After pictures were taken and the newly formed Mr. & Mrs. Zachary Gaines were announced, arriving through the porte cochère to the event, the jazz band went away and attendees were asked to go to their assigned seats at the correct table. Henry and Bailey were two of six people at a table directly in front of the head table.

Kat had noticed Henry during the ceremony but hadn't made eye contact or acknowledged his presence during the recession or the reception line outside the church. Nor had she so much as glanced in his direction as Henry sat at a table no more than fifteen feet away.

Henry hadn't stopped the wedding, nor had he made any further scene in the church. He had remained quiet, contemplating how to extricate himself from the situation without becoming homeless in the process. He had libations at the reception as his mind continued to run riot. He wasn't much of a drinker, so what he did consume hit him hard and fast. Any number of the many beverages he consumed could have done the trick.

Toasts took place prior to eating. It turned out that the man who gave Kat away was actually the father of the groom. Henry had had enough to drink to gain the nerve to inquire as to how that arrangement came to be, but Bailey begged him to remain seated. He was becoming inebriated with toast after toast prattling on. Food in his stomach to absorb some of the consumed alcohol was still a prospect much too far into the future.

The food was set up in stations. It was less a full-service meal and more a chance to mingle and sample various types of cuisine. There was a kiosk of sorts where they rolled sushi to order. Another served Italian appetizers like fried ravioli and bruschetta. Egg rolls and dumplings in another area. Bacon-wrapped steak tips and pommes frites for the meat and potato guests. Another had samosa and chicken tikka. And still another corner had vegan cuisine. Nobody would go away hungry or without their preferred diet considered.

And of course the open bar remained open. Bottles of various wines were available to bring back to the tables if guests so chose. Henry was getting sloshed.

Since he was making a spectacle of himself, Bailey insisted that he get some substantial food into his stomach. She didn't weigh much, but she was forceful enough to get him over to the steak and fries area. Henry began to eat and as they turned to head back to their table, Henry and Bailey bumped into the mingling bride and groom.

"Oh shit," Bailey said.

"I don't believe I've met your date," the groom said to his sister.

"And you really shouldn't right now," Bailey said as she tried to drag Henry away.

"Nonsense. I'd—"

"—Honey, maybe your sister is right," Kat said. She obviously wanted to avoid any and all confrontation.

"I'm Henry," he said with a mouthful of fries. "Who the fuck are you?"

"What are you drunk?"

"Zach. Please. Believe me when I tell you that you don't want to know and that I had no idea when I asked him to be my date," Bailey said.

"Okay, now I have to know what's going on," Zach, the groom, said.

Kat spoke first. "I know him from a long time ago. We grew up on the same street back east."

"I fucked your wife," Henry added.

Bailey pulled him away. "Okay, that's enough. Congratulations to the both of you."

"White dress my ass," Henry called as he was being dragged toward the parking lot.

"Congratulations to you also. You succeeded in ruining my brother's wedding and made quite the impression," Bailey said once they made an early exit from the reception hall and were inside her car in the parking lot.

"I didn't lie."

"No, but you didn't need to be quite so truthful." She rested her head on the steering wheel. The vehicle hadn't yet been started. She turned her resting head toward the passenger seat. "Seriously, how drunk are you?"

"I'm pretty tanked. I don't usually drink."

"Lucky for us you picked today to start. So tell me, what's going on?"

"She's the one that got away, Bail. She got away over and over and over again. Of all the fucking weddings in all of the world, this is the one I got roped into going to."

"So where does that leave us?"

Henry looked confused. "What do you mean?"

"You've spent the last two weeks in my bed and you haven't bought a bed yet, so I've been assuming that our situation isn't going to change anytime soon. I've changed rotations so we could spend time together. I've passed on modeling gigs, missed flights and time at work, which isn't your responsibility because I wanted to do that. And I wasn't expecting a marriage proposal either, it's only been a couple of weeks, but you obviously have some unresolved feelings for my brother's new wife. So I'll ask again, where does that leave us?"

"I don't know, Kat."

"Bailey. My name is Bailey."

"What did I say?"

"Forget it." She went to start her car, then stopped short. "No. I want you to explain. Go on."

"I was moving on. I had moved on. Then I saw her," Henry said.

"Well, you obviously care enough about her to ruin her wedding reception and my brother in the process. Are you going to be able to get past this? For real?"

"I don't know. It's a lot to process."

"That's not really an answer, Henry."

"No, I guess it's not."

There was a long pause as the two let the information sink in. Bailey sat back in her seat, head tilted up on the headrest.

"But I'm not joining the priesthood either," Henry continued after a time. "I'm going to have to let her go. I just watched her get married to someone else, so I can't live my life like my mother did. She pined away and hoped that my piece of shit father would change. It will take some time though. If you want me to move out, I get it."

She shook her head but didn't lift it off the headrest. "It doesn't mean that I want you to move out. It doesn't mean that I want to stop sleeping with you. I just want to know that at some point, you will look at me the way that you look at her."

"If you want me to say right here and now that I am going to propose to you at some point down the line, I can't say that. We just met in the scheme of things," Henry said.

"That's not what I'm asking. What I'm asking is if we continue to move our relationship forward, even slowly, do I have a shot somewhere down the line or am I wasting my time?"

"I can't answer that, but I'm willing to give it a shot. What I'm saying is that I want to move forward with you, one day at a time."

"That's fair."

"You handled that better than anybody else would have. You really are a beautiful person, inside and out," Henry said.

"You have your moments too. I like you with shorter hair. You look younger with a shave too." She smiled as she looked at him.

"So we're a thing?"

"I think so, Henry. But family get togethers are going to be interesting."

233

"Bail? I'm home," Henry shouted as he entered the apartment in Silver Lake.

"I'm in the bedroom!"

"That sounds promising," he said to himself as he kicked off his shoes and padded toward the bedroom.

Henry made his way down the hall to the master bedroom. He opened the door and found his girlfriend of two years sitting on the love-seat against the far wall.

"Are you okay? You said I should come home as soon as I can," Henry said.

"I'm fine. I didn't mean to worry you. I just know that once you get into a project, it could be days before I see you. What are you working on now?"

"Big budget thing that's coming out next year, early 2005 I think. Medieval war epic about a Scottish rebellion. The music in this thing is complicated, and a ton of it."

"Sorry to pry you from it," Bailey said.

"No problem. What's going on?" He sat down next to her, pulled her legs over his lap and rubbed her thighs.

"That's nice."

"When you said you were in here, I kinda thought you wanted to fool around," he said.

"I quit my job."

"Okay. Good. You hated flying all of the time anyway."

"True. The cities all started to look the same."

"I remember that feeling. When I was touring with—"

"—But that's not why I quit."

"Oh-kaay. Nobody was forcing you to keep that job. You don't think that I'm forcing you to do this job or any job, do you? If you'd rather model full-time, or whatever, do that."

"I quit so I could take some time off."

"Great. So now what?"

"For being so smart, you can be so dumb sometimes," she said.

"Did you come right out and say what the hell is going on and I missed it? I'm lost here."

"Studies have shown that flying in my condition, even early on, can be harmful. I'm pregnant."

"Oh. OH! Congratulations. Who's the father?"

She punched him in the arm. "You're an asshole!"

"I'm just kidding."

"So .... How do you feel about that?"

"You mean how do feel about it in the last ten-seconds that I've known about it? Let's see, since you just said it, I've got the entire situation completely figured out. I think Harvard is the best choice for him. Should I start the application process now or can we give me a second?"

She pushed his hands off of her and slid her legs around and to the floor. She walked across the room and sat on the bed.

"I'm fucking serious, Henry."

"I sense that .... Now ...."

"Raising a child is serious business," she said. "The possibility of destroying another human being scares the shit out of me."

"You mean you're thinking of having an abortion? If that's what you want then I'm O—"

"—No, you imbecile! Your sustained stupidity is starting to piss me off. I mean in raising a child. I'm afraid of doing it wrong. You would be okay with me terminating? Your child is growing in my belly and you would have me kill it? I thought you were Catholic?"

"I'm a lapsed Catholic, number one. And two, I'm pro-choice. It's your body, your call," he said.

"Oh. So this is all on me? Way to be supportive!"

"I don't know what you want me to say here, Bail. Did you *want* to fight about this?"

"I want to know that I'm not going to raise this child alone. I will if I have to, but I want to do it right either way. Abortion is not an option for me. I can't kill it. I won't."

"Okay. Okay. I'm not asking you to. It was just an option."

"An option that you're 'okay' with," she said making quotation marks with her hands.

"I didn't say that. Not exactly. You didn't let me finish."

"I know what you were going to say, so let's not bullshit each other."

"What I was going to say, was that I don't know that I would make a good father, Bail. Mine was no prize. I don't know how to do it. If parenting consists of doing to your kids what your parents did to you, aborting it is the best possible scenario, believe me. You should be very afraid of what I would do the kid."

"You can be such a coward," she said. She shook her head. "So do it different."

"That's what I'm trying to say to you, Bail. I don't know if I'm capable."

"Of course you are. Read a book. Get good at it. We'll make mistakes, I just don't want to make life-altering mistakes. I love you. You say that you love me. This child is the product of our love. You are a smart, sweet, beautiful man. You have the ability to raise a smart, sweet, beautiful child if you want to. My question is, do you want to? Because the alternative is that you walk away. Walk away and never look back. Right here, right now. Those are your options."

"And you have a preference as to one way or the other?"

236

"You know damn well what my preference is. But you can't half-ass this. This is a child. You're either in or out. Right now. Not after the child is born, not one year from now, not two. Now or nothing. I want you, and I want to make a family with you more than anything else in the world. But if not, then pack your shit and go. It's not just about me anymore."

"You're the best thing that's happened to me, Bail. You are my life. My work and you. These have been the happiest two years of my life. It's always just been the work that's tied me over. I lived for it. Most people work to support their life, my work *was* my life. I never knew you could have both. I can't promise that I'll be a great father, I'm not even a good boyfriend half the time. But I promise to try. That's the best that I can do."

"You sell yourself short. I love you. You're a great partner, you'll be a great father too."

He crossed the room toward her. She rose off of the bed and hugged him.

Henry kissed her neck and nibbled on her ear.

"Ooooh, you know how I like that," she said.

"I know you do."

"You really thought we were going to have sex, didn't you?" She sat back down on the bed and pulled Henry on top of her.

"Yes, that's what I thought," he whispered in her ear.

"I like the way you think."

36

THE INSISTENT CELL PHONE VIBRATED DEEP INSIDE of Henry's front pocket. He had just taken a break at the studio, and was forced to break off of the casual conversation he was having with one of the musicians. He reached into his jeans and answered the call on his Blackberry Curve.

"Hello?"

"Hi Henry."

"Margo. How's it going up there in San Fran?"

"Good. I see on MySpace that Kurt is getting so big. He's a spitting image of you, it's such a trip. I remember when you looked like that."

"Bailey is really good about putting pictures up on that damn thing. I got into it for the music and she took it over."

"Everyone is moving to Facebook, you should tell her to open an account," Margo said.

"You can tell her, I can't get into those things."

"Well anyway, what is he? Four now? Five?" Margo said.

"Almost five."

"Time goes so fast."

"It sure does. So what's up?"

"Do you have a minute, or am I keeping you?"

"I've got a few minutes," Henry said.

"I'm calling about the place on Carver Pond."

"You've still got that place?"

"We wanted to keep it and rent it, then we didn't want to keep it, then we wanted to hold on to it because it was built by my grandfather .... Now we have to sell it. We don't have a choice. It's no longer an 'investment opportunity' for us. It needs a ton of work and nobody wants to buy it for what it's worth. The waterfront property without the building is worth money, but between the building and the market .... We'd take a bath on it and we can't keep forking over the property taxes. The place is killing us and we really need the money. College is just around the corner and we can barely keep up, let alone send Cloud to college."

"You're rambling again, Margo. Is there a point coming soon?"

"Paul and I want to know if you would buy it?"

"I don't know, Margo. Why would I want it?"

"The memories?"

"None of them good," Henry said.

"Maybe you could fix it up and sell it. You've got more money than we do."

"How would you take a bath on something that you didn't purchase to begin with? You inherited the damn place."

"The taxes alone over the years have added up to more than we would make after a realtor gets through with us," Margo said. "The place is a half-acre on Carver Pond. It's worth some money, Henry."

"So I'm the sucker now?"

"We'll make you a good price. It's enough to get us out of the hole and set a little aside, but not so much as to take you for a ride. You're in a better spot, financially, than we are. Have it appraised if you want."

"I've got a kid now, too, remember? Bailey hasn't worked since before Kurt was born, how do you suppose I'm better off than you?"

"Will you think about it? Talk it over with your better half."

"I'll talk it over with my *girlfriend*. No promises, Margo, But I'll let you know."

"Thanks. And love to Bailey."

"You've met her twice in the seven years we've been together. You send your love?"

"Don't be an ass …. And it's been more like eight years. Just tell her, okay?"

"Yeah, fine."

"That's an interesting idea," Bailey said as she took some cupcakes for Kurt's school bake-sale out of the oven.

"It's not an interesting idea, Bail, it's just an idea. She takes after my mother when it comes to putting up fronts. She's a hippie but she doesn't like to show her cards. If she's calling to dump the place on me, it's because they are in a real bind. I wouldn't do it because I want the place, I'd do it to help out my sister."

"LA isn't the best place to raise a child," Bailey said.

"Neither is Bridgewater, Mass, I assure you. He's almost five, whatever damage LA has done, it's pretty much done."

"That's bullshit and you know it. Besides, you turned out okay."

"If you say so. I don't want to move back there. Like I said, if I do this, I do it as an investment. Flip the damn place and make a buck or two."

"It's your money, Henry. You don't need my permission."

"I'm not asking your permission, I'm asking what you think?"

"I think we should get married," she said.

"Fuck me, not this again. How did we go from buying the place on the pond to getting married?"

"Don't curse please. He hears you and repeats it. He's been in trouble at school twice for swearing. He hardly ever sees you and when he does, you're cursing."

"I only used colorful language to illustrate my point of frustration with this repeated conversation. A piece of paper is meaningless, I've said this over and over again. Marriage is an antiquated institution. Statistically almost all of them fail."

"It's an insurance policy," she said. "If you love the other person, put it in writing so the other is taken care of if something goes wrong. That's what the piece of paper is for. Women don't age well like men. You'll continue to get better-looking and more distinguished and I'll continue to gain weight and fall apart. What insurance do I have if you dump me when you want something younger?"

"Have I done something to give you any indication that I would trade you in for a younger model? I've got a model."

"I haven't modeled in years. I'm a stay-at-home mom. Very sexy to you I'm sure."

"Your gaslighting is driving me nuts. I've told you that I would be more than happy to sign over whatever you want. You want half? Fine by me. You can take half of the debt too," Henry said.

"And I'm saying that if we got married, we could both be on a mortgage, and we could stop throwing rent money away on this place. Fixing the place up on this pond place sounds like a nice spot to raise a child. Or two."

"Bailey .... "

Henry took a few breaths to calm himself down. It was the same old argument that they have been having since Bailey had started to show a baby bump. She wanted the house with a picket fence and the two-point-five kids. Henry was still trying to be a decent father for one kid, the rest of package was too much. He worked all of the time and didn't spend enough time with the son he had, let alone the probability of not having a relationship with another child. Bailey would often tell him about one of Kurt's milestones days after it occurred, which always made Henry feel bad.

He oscillated between feeling smothered by having his family under-foot and leaving an abundance of room as an absentee father. He feared he was the latter, as he was on the receiving end growing up. He understood both the need for his son to feel nurtured and her need for security. He was failing at all of the above.

"Bailey, I don't want to have this conversation with you right now, if that's okay. I don't want either of us to get upset, or to get into a fight. Let's just take this in baby steps, no pun. The only reason I brought up Carver Pond is because my sister is basically begging me to take it. I'm thinking of doing it just to help them out, well, my sister. I still don't have much use for Paul."

"And my answer to you is that I think you should do it. For the rest of it, we are not done with that conversation. Not by a long shot."

"Fine. Thank you. For what it's worth, my sister sends her love. Oh, and she said you should check out Facebook."

The 3000 mile commute was nearly killing him. When Henry wasn't at Barking Dog Sound in Los Angeles, he was on Carver Pond in Massachusetts. At first he had been dealing with an architect. Then the local planning and zoning commission in order to approve the massive renovation. Then the contractor. He had been traveling roughly 6000 round-trip miles nearly every week for over six months to get the place ready for sale. While his frequent flyer miles were becoming a bonanza, the rest of his coffers were dwindling.

Henry had worked out a Monday through Thursday work schedule when there was a sound project in LA. He would then catch a redeye to Boston Thursday night and return at some point late Saturday or early Sunday morning. His work was suffering.

His relationship with Bailey was suffering as well. While Henry understood her nagging to take some time off, either from work or the Carver Pond renovation, he didn't need the added stress. He needed to work, he told her, in order to pay for the architect and permits and contractor and materials and flights. He also needed to finish the project as quickly as possible, he explained. He now had a mortgage—taken to pay his sister and for renovations—on a place that he couldn't flip until the work was completed.

Bailey was living in a constant state of disappointment. Her boyfriend hadn't proposed marriage nor a plan to invest nearly the amount of time being spent on a house, on their son. Kurt was five and in need of a father, she'd say. She was thirty-two and in need of a husband, she'd say just as often.

Caught between Scylla and Charybdis, Henry felt like he couldn't win. He had never been a complete failure before. He was failing at home, at work, and the cottage wasn't being renovated as quickly as he wanted either.

He'd been talked into taking on the place in Massachusetts that he truly didn't even want at the time. He had been goaded into it by his sister, which was done out of sympathy. Henry had been further urged to move forward on the cottage by the very woman who cursed him daily for neglecting his family.

At the studio, his work suffered because he was so damned tired and unable to concentrate, a necessity for the complexities of movie musical scores. He was making mistakes that he hadn't made in the past. Frustration begat a career trajectory he was no longer enamored with.

He missed the days of collaborating with bands. Music was his passion, not movies.

It was a very long year, made longer by the fact that once the construction was complete in early October, Henry wasn't able to get it sold. The realtor had gotten back to him with offers, everyone that had walked through the open house remarked at how beautiful the place was. But nobody wanted to pay what the new construction was worth. What Henry had put into it in terms of time; flights; money; sweat; tears; sanity; and family; he wasn't being offered in return, not that any compensation would be enough for his investment. The real estate market was in the shitter, and he wasn't alone in suffering for it.

And so the house sat. With electricity and gas turned on. Snow removal. Property taxes. Mortgage payments. Landscapers were hired in the spring of 2010 in order to add further eye appeal to the already gorgeous reconstruction.

What was originally built as a slapdash fishing cottage on a small Massachusetts pond decades before, had become a modestly renovated home in its middle incarnation. That home had been neglected and had wasted away by his mother. The latest manifestation of this structure was an increase in size and a complete remodel with reclaimed wood, stone, steel, large windows, and modernized appliances.

Determined to sell the house, Henry decided to take the summer of 2010 off from the studio in LA to devote his full attention to the Massachusetts, waterfront home. Bailey was livid about the idea at first but eventually relented at Henry's reasoning. Henry was convinced that the place wasn't selling because he was trying to accomplish the difficult task of selling the property from the opposite side of the country. He had been through three realtors who couldn't get the job done. It was time to do it himself. He would take the summer and get rid of it once and for all, which would free him up to make up for lost time with his girlfriend and son.

Bailey eventually agreed on the condition that if the house didn't sell by autumn, the three of them would relocate to Bridgewater and move into it.

A situation that Henry wanted to avoid at all costs.

He hadn't even allowed her to see the house, knowing that once she did, he would be forced to pack his bags and leave his job in Los Angeles. Losing his job wasn't the problem, nor moving out of LA. The issue was the prospect of moving back to Bridgewater. He'd left Massachusetts for a reason. Time may heal wounds, but he still despised the town and area he grew up in. The town refused to change, and Henry continually tried to.

The summer had been dwindling away, open-house after open-house happened without fruition. Weekend after weekend. Henry had been living there exclusively with no trips west. He was losing hope.

The last weekend in August had come to a close, the weekly open-house wrapped up. The signs had been taken down, the balloons by the road popped. The remainder of the finger foods tossed out. Henry stood at the tall windows of the living room overlooking the placid pond.

The sun was closing behind the Berkshires a hundred miles to the west as he stared out at the pond and the horizon, wallowing in his continued failure. He thought of the past. He wondered how he could completely gut and rebuild a structure that held so many memories, so many secrets, so much negativity, and still expect a positive result?

You can't shine shit, he thought.

The building was new and beautiful and yet the negative forces still held onto their stranglehold.

The soul of this place is rotten. Prospective buyers can see it, feel it.

"Wow! This place looks amazing," a voice said from behind him.

Did I leave the front door open?

"The open house is technically over," Henry said as he turned toward the voice. "But if you want a tour …."

"You've done an amazing job. If I didn't know any better, I wouldn't have a clue that it's the same place."

"Kat!"

Henry was stunned as she stood inside his front door. It had been the better part of decade since last he saw her, and yet she looked like it hadn't been a week.

"What, what are you doing here?"

"I'm in town for a funeral. Mom's," she said.

"Oh. I'm so sorry. Where's, uh, Zach is it?"

"You know his name. Zach is in LA. Work. It always comes first even when there's a death in the family."

"Sorry again."

"Stop saying your sorry. I shouldn't paint too bad a picture of him. I wrote off my family a long time ago. They weren't even invited to my wedding."

"Yeah. About that—"

"Don't you dare apologize again. I'm not sure how I would have handled that either. How's Bailey?"

"Come in, will you?" Henry motioned for her to come into the sparsely furnished home. Kat closed the door behind her and made way to the living room. She wasn't in funeral clothes. She was dressed for the late summer heat, the season's last stand known as 'Indian Summer'. She wore a thin, linen blouse and shorts.

"She's good. Pissed at me these days, for a lot of reasons, including this mistake. But we'll manage. We obviously don't come to your gatherings every year, but thanks for the invitations just the same."

"Zach's idea. I don't know what I'd do if you actually showed up. He misses his sister," Kat said, then paused. "You've got a son. Kurt, right?"

"I do. Yes, Kurt." Henry reached for his wallet to produce a picture. It was an old photo from when he was a toddler. "It's an old picture, but there he is."

"After Kurt Cobain?"

"Yes. He's starting to look like him too. At least I think he is, I honestly don't see him very much."

"I could sense that. You're showing baby pictures and he's gotta be five or six by now. I've got more updated pictures, she sends them to Zach."

"Hmmm. It's a sore subject," Henry said with embarrassment.

"Anyway, he looks just like you. Good-looking boy."

"So what brings you by, Kat? Funeral puts you in the area, but why come here?"

"I don't know. You have ads for this place in every paper and on T-stop benches and such. I kept seeing it and was curious. I'm sorry. I should probably go."

Henry grabbed her hand. Her hand felt like it always had. Soft yet strong. It fit perfectly in his.

"You should definitely go," he said.

"This was a big mistake." She moved closer to him, her lips millimeters from his. "You have Bailey .... And Kurt .... "

"And you have Zach." He tucked a wisp of her hair behind her ear.

She pulled the back of his head toward her and they kissed. They pressed their bodies together and tasted each other. The sun had fallen behind the distant mountains, the oranges and yellows were waning into dark blues and purples.

247

If they had spectators on the pond, an angler getting one last cast in before full-dark, they didn't care. They melded into one another, petting and caressing. Kissing and embracing. Time stood still. They savored every moment as if it was the last.

They made love without thought, without care of consequence. It was familiar yet new. Again it was everything that they needed. They satiated every carnal need of the other. Another state of evergreen.

Again it was rapture.

THE EARLY MORNING SUN CREATED A SPARKLE from the surface of Carver Pond. The reflected light peered into the master bedroom. It was an indirect, soft light as the windows to the room on the back of the house faced west. The late summer heat had not yet begun to drop its heavy, humid blanket on the day. The two had been up late, or early depending on how one looked at things. They began to stir, still interlocked.

"Thanks for helping me christen the place," Henry whispered.

"I don't think what we did was very Christ-like, but it sure was fun. You and Bailey have never ….?"

"She's never been here. If she saw the place, she'd want to move here."

"It *is* gorgeous. You wouldn't want to live here?"

"Never even a consideration until now."

"Ah. Don't go there," Kat said.

"So where will you be running off to?"

"I'm here for the next couple of weeks. I have to take care of Mom's final affairs," Kat said.

"Here as in *HERE,* or here as in town?"

"I guess that depends on you. What we did was wrong."

"But it felt so right," Henry said.

"Often the case. I'm married."

"Happily?"

"That's not the point, Henry, and you know it."

"And you always thought that I would be the cheating one," he said with a chuckle. Neither of them made an effort to get up out of bed or disentangle.

"You're cheating too, don't kid yourself. You have a child with the woman. My sister-in-law. What is it with us?"

"You can't fight chemistry, Kat. We just fit. I'm not going to try and convince you to stay, we'll just get into another fight. I'll just say that you're more than welcome to stay here for as long as you'd like."

"What about Bailey? When are you going back? When are they coming here?"

"The fall. I've got a couple of months before I have to jump off of that bridge," Henry said.

"And if I stay here, we're just going to continue to do irreparable damage to both of our relationships. I'll have no hope of salvaging mine."

Henry rolled on top of her.

"But the damage is done. One time or ten times won't really make much of a difference," he said.

"We've already done it tens times," she laughed and bit his lip.

"So why stop now?"

She reached under the sheet and grabbed him. He was ready for the task at hand, she was all-too ready to receive him.

Henry entered her, Kat pushed back against him, wanting all of him.

"Mmmmmm," she moaned. "I love the way your mind works."

Use It Up

Two weeks went by in a blink of an eye. They didn't spend the entire time in bed, though sex was a big part of their lives.

They walked and biked around the pond. Henry borrowed a neighbor's rowboat for a late-night jaunt on the water. They tried to have sex in the boat but as careful as they were, it capsized. Rather than submit to defeat, they continued their lovemaking in the water.

The two spent every hour together, waking or sleeping. It was the first time in their lives that they had shared so much of one another for as long an interval.

The conversation was just as it had been when they had gone on the date a decade prior in LA. They talked and laughed and reminisced and fantasized about a life spent together. The pauses were spent visually taking in the other, if not physically.

Open-houses were put on hold. Phone calls went unanswered. Kat's obligations toward her mother were abandoned. The couple was locked away in a heaven of their own design. Neither ventured far from home when a resupply of provisions was necessary. There wasn't a TV or other distractions. Cell phones were turned off. Music added to the ambiance. Henry chose various albums from his collection while they spent time together, enjoying them while enjoying each other without fetter.

The morning of Kat's return to Los Angeles was a somber morning indeed. Henry put on a vinyl record, as usual, though she picked it. Kat marveled almost daily at how many records Henry had brought with him from LA, though knowing full-well that he never went very far without them. This particular record that she chose was a compilation of various artists.

He made breakfast for the two of them while she packed. They ate Henry's egg-white omelettes in silence, other than the music in the background. Diana Ross's *Love Hangover* came on after a time.

"Ah, if there's a cure for this
I don't want it
Don't want it
If there's a remedy,
I'll run from it.

Think about it all the time
Never let it out of my mind
'Cause I love you

I've got the sweetest hangover
I don't wanna get over
Sweetest hangover …."

"She's right, you know," Henry said, finally breaking the lull in their conversation.

"Hm?"

"The record. 'If there's a cure for this, I don't want it.'"

"Me neither. But we live in the real world, Henry. The really, real world where the sky is blue and there are consequences for things. We don't always get what we want."

"I've never cared for the way that works," Henry said.

"There's probably a club you can join," she replied with a chuckle. "But it wouldn't change anything."

"Why can't we change it? Why can't you stay here? We can figure out how to make this work."

"You don't think I want that too? The past two weeks have made this the hardest thing I've ever done. There are a hundred reasons to go back and face the music, and only one reason to stay," she said.

"But that one reason is pretty fucking huge."

"Zach, Bailey, Kurt, my job, your job," she said starting the list. "Those are just the most important ones, should I keep going?"

"And yet?"

She nodded, then pushed her plate away from her.

"And yet."

They didn't speak for some time. They both tried to find another, more compelling reason to stay in that moment. In that house. In that refuge. Neither were successful.

"If you're packed I'll drive you to the airport," Henry finally said.

"Thanks, but I've got to bring the rental car back anyway."

"Who did you get the car from? There's probably a branch in town where we can drop it off, I'll drive you the rest of the way. We probably should have done that two weeks ago. You've been paying for that thing and it hasn't moved since you drove it here."

"Funny."

"Funny but true," Henry said.

They dropped the car off at the local rental branch, Henry drove the rest of the way on Route 24 North and Interstate 93 to Logan Airport. The forty-five minute ride was done in silence, neither of them had anything to say that would lighten the mood. Both hoped for heavy traffic. A detour. Anything to prolong the inevitable.

But none presented itself.

Henry pulled up to the drop-off area outside Terminal B at Logan and put the car in park.

"Last chance to miss your flight," he said.

"I would just have to book another one. I can't. Henry .... We can't."

"I feel like my entire life has been spent begging you to stay."

"I know. I'm so sorry, Henry. This isn't the first time that I've wanted to do just that. But one of us has to be strong, to do the right thing. Even if the right thing doesn't feel right at all,"

There was a knock on the passenger window. Kat jumped in her seat.

"You can't park here. Unload or move along," the man in the uniform yelled to them.

Tears filled Kat's eyes. She kissed him. A long kiss that wasn't nearly long enough.

"I love you," she said.

"I love you more."

She got out of the car, collected her bags from the trunk, and was gone.

Henry watched her walk into the terminal for as long as he could, but the persistent State Policeman told him to move his car or he was going to be ticketed. He lost her in the crowd of people anyway, so a ticket was senseless.

The drive back to Carver Pond ate at him. Tears formed, the lump in his throat throbbed as fervently as the ache in his heart. But the tears wouldn't come. He had been down this road before. Each time a new assault, each time a new callous.

It began to rain on the drive home. The miasmic weather did nothing to lift his spirits. In fact, it made things worse. It was as if the universe was sad as well. Nothing was right. Not in Henry's life, not in the cosmos. The earth wept.

Depression kicked in when he pulled into the driveway at Carver Pond. He entered the barren home, further adding to his misery. It wasn't fully furnished because it was a property for sale, nothing on the walls. It wasn't a home, not yet. It was made a home because Kat was there. It was once again empty. Devoid of anything that made the dwelling worthy of living in.

Henry shouted at no one.

"No wonder this fucking place won't sell!"

All Henry wanted to do was sleep. Depressed and despondent, he laid down to shut out everyone and everything. But rest wouldn't come. His mind wouldn't turn off.

After tossing, turning, dwelling, and aching, he decided to put on some music. Music always helped, always made him feel better. Music would again soothe the turmoil within.

Pearl Jam's Ten was the first vinyl Henry touched and instinctively put onto the turntable.

The first track on the A-side, *Once*, began. Henry slowly padded back to his room and bed. He'd heard the album countless times while recording it, perfecting it, and since it was released. His copy was one of the first ten pressed, which made it extremely valuable. He listened to the staple album, reminiscing about working on the project.

But thoughts of Kat returned and ran riot. Fantasies of what could have been invaded and set root.

He had been so close. *They* had been so close.

The beach on Cape Cod. Their time together in the previous incarnation of the house after she came to his job at AIW. That night in Los Angeles.

Then the years of disappointments and rejection entered into his thoughts. Their very first date and the embarrassment at the movie theatre. Her visit to him when he was incarcerated. Kat's rejection of

255

him at Stanford. His being forced to watch her get married to someone else.

The album continued to spin on the turntable in the living room. The fifth track on the A-side played. The somber song, *Black,* sent Henry further into the depths of Hell.

".... All the love gone bad,
Turned my world to black
Tattooed all I see
All that I am,
All that I will be ....

.... I know someday you'll have a beautiful life,
I know you'll be a sun
In somebody else's sky
But why,
Why,
Why can't it be mine .... "

Tears soaked his cheeks and pillow; the complete, utter sadness washed over him, slowly setting him adrift on a sea of despair, floating into a slumber at long last. Wave after wave of thought began to languidly dissipate.

And yet in that sorrow, he felt her embrace. He felt her near him. He could smell her. Hear her whisper to him.

"I can't believe you left me at the airport."

Henry's eyes burst open. He rolled over to see her looking at him in bed. Was she real or was she a dream?

She kissed him.   Her mouth felt like bliss, her taste was perfection. She was real.

"You're back," he whispered.

She nodded.

"I don't wanna do the right thing."

38

HENRY WAS IN THE MIDDLE OF SPEAKING TO THE band, Horus, when his cell phone vibrated in his pocket. He never took calls while he was in a recording session, but he had been expecting the call from Kat.

The Boston rock band was in the process of producing their third album, *Drug Fueled Sky*, at the relatively new recording studio on Carver Pond, Little Leviathan, in Bridgewater, Massachusetts. The band could have chosen to follow up their smash second album, *God of Vengeance*, in Miami or Los Angeles or anywhere else for that matter. Their star was on the rise, they had toured with Metallica, Disturbed, and most recently opened up for Five Finger Death Punch. They would be headlining their own shows, their own arenas on the next tour, once the new album was finished. That album needed to have a punch. That album had to be the next great hard-rock album. Horus needed a great producer. Horus needed and wanted Henry Devlin.

Henry had converted the house on Carver Pond into a recording studio shortly after officially quitting his job at Barking Dog in Los Angeles. The house wasn't selling, and with Kat deciding to live with Henry in Bridgewater, they decided to live in the new home for a short time.

Kat had relocated east, never returning to her husband and loveless marriage. She was hired by the largest law firm in Boston;

Taylor, Higgs & Pratt. She loved her work, loved her life, and would love her new husband once her divorce finally went through.

Henry and Kat had lived on Carver Pond for nearly a year, but the commute into Boston was killing her. What normally would take forty-five minutes, often took two hours. Traffic was a nightmare, the Big Dig construction process made it worse. Her twelve to fourteen hour days at her new job, the hot-shot law firm downtown, became sixteen to eighteen hours with traffic. So they purchased a condo in a new high-rise building on the Seaport. Kat's office was only three T-stops from their new place in the city overlooking the Atlantic, which freed up the house on the pond.

Converting the expansive renovation—which began its tumultuous life as a fishing cottage that his grandfather had thrown together—into a state-of-the-art recording studio, was the most ambitious undertaking Henry had ever embarked upon. It was also the most financially risky. Little Leviathan studios was up and running within a few weeks of moving out of the renovated house, bands large and small sought out the new enterprise on the name of Henry Devlin. The same Henry Devlin that produced some of the greats.

"I want to punch up the drums and bass-line," Henry was saying to Horus when the pocket of his jeans beckoned. "I want it to thunder, rock should be felt in your bones. John Bonham and Dave Grohl didn't love-tap, they thumped …. Hold on guys. Take five or so, I have to take this call."

Henry left the sound booth and answered his insistent cell phone.

"What's up, Honey?"

"The paperwork finally came through," Kat said.

"Finally. I would think that with you being a lawyer, it wouldn't have taken a year to get unhitched."

"Good things come to those who wait."

"So it's final? You are officially a hot, incredibly sexy, single woman?"

"Hot and sexy, maybe. But not quite single. I have to go back to LA for one fast court appearance. But barring any last minute nonsense that Zach would have up his sleeve, I'll be free to marry this well-hung music producer I've been seeing."

"Beautiful. Where are you? We need to celebrate."

"At the office, naturally. I have a deposition and then I'm free. Couple of hours?"

"Perfect. I'll finish up here for the day and head home before the after-work traffic rush. We can go to that new restaurant you like."

"Yay. I can't wait. I'll want to go home first so I can change, will you be there or at the restaurant?"

"Restaurant. If we meet up at the condo, we'll be having sex and never eat."

"That sounds like a good idea too," Kat said.

"Fine by me. Eating is overrated anyway."

"Very funny. So I'll meet you there then?"

"Absolutely. I'll be the horny guy in the back wearing something clingy."

"Wait 'til you see what I'll be wearing. I Love you."

"I love you more, Kat."

Henry went back into the booth where the four members of Horus were waiting for him.

"Okay! So where were we?"

"You haven't touched your wine, is everything okay?"

260

Henry and Kat sat next to each other in a corner booth in the new, small, boutique restaurant that made up for lack of seating with exorbitantly high prices. The room was dimly lit, the music low but loud enough so that the next table, which was very close, couldn't eavesdrop. Henry and Kat had been there once before, she found the food to be almost as good as sex.

"Of course everything is fine," she said. "Everything is more than fine. I'll fly to LA next week and be back the next day. I'll return to you a single woman."

"I kinda like the idea of sleeping with a married woman."

"You're a funny guy. How's your foie gras?"

"There's not enough of it. For this kind of money, I would think the portions would be bigger."

"You can afford it, your studio is doing really well," Kat said. "You should be very proud of yourself. I'm so proud of you."

"The music industry is cyclical, babe. One minute I'm king of the studio, the next I'm begging to record Zamfir on his pan flute so I don't starve. Grunge is dead and Rock is on the downward trend right now," Henry explained as he pushed his cleaned plate toward the center of the table.

"You'll be fine." She pushed her plate toward the center of the small table with Henry's. The server removed both plates immediately after Kat was finished. He was about to suggestively sell another course of food, but Kat waived him off temporarily.

"Can we talk about Kurt again?"

"Really Kat? We're gonna do this again? Why spoil a great night?"

"Because he's your son, Henry."

"A son that Bailey won't let me see. How many times have we been over this? I'd love him to come here and visit. I'd go there and visit

261

if need be. The woman hates my guts and won't let me see him. I've tried to explain to her that you and I …. It's force majeure. How could I possibly stay in that relationship when all I've ever wanted was you? I couldn't stay even if I wanted to just suppress my feelings and live a life of torment. I would have resented her, fought with her, and that wouldn't be good for Kurt."

"I agree, but not having any relationship with your son isn't right either, Henry. You know what that's like and it sucks."

"I'm not sure how much he would want to see me anyway, he's almost eight years old and the only thing he knows about me is the stuff his mother tells him. I'm guessing it's not complimentary."

"And I've told you that I would help you fight for a joint custody arrangement. He only has a few years before he can legally make his own decisions about where he wants to live. You have a right to see him. You send her over $2,000 a month for his care even though you aren't forced to. Don't you at least want to see him?"

"Of course I do. He's my son. Even though I've been an absentee father up to this point, I'd like to make up for that. But Bailey is beyond angry and it's all about punishing me." Henry took a few breaths and a sip of his wine before continuing.

"Maybe when this is all over in a couple of weeks, your divorce, maybe we can start paperwork on the custody issue."

Kat smiled, to Henry her smile defined radiance. Every problem was solved with her smile.

"I'll get right on the paperwork. And by the way, I'd take payment for my expert legal services in trade," she said.

"Oh really? What did you have in mind?"

Kat took his hand and brought it under the corner of the table between them. She put his hand under her short skirt, between her thighs, as she looked around the restaurant to make sure that they weren't being watched, then looked into Henry's eyes.

"You're not wearing any—"

Kat shook her head and gave a not-so-sheepish grin.

"You're a dirty girl."

"Mmm.Hmm." She seductively bit her lip.

"I should get the check," Henry said loudly.

"You should definitely get the check."

39

THE FACT THAT KAT WASN'T ANSWERING HER CELL, in singularity, mightn't have been enough to cause Henry panic. But added to the remainder of the facts, he was beyond panic. Well beyond.

Two weeks had passed since their celebratory dinner, and she'd flown out to Los Angeles very early on Monday to finalize her divorce. Henry had dropped her off at the airport personally, though the Silver line would have taken her to Logan Airport rather quickly. Kat had given Henry a long kiss on the mouth as she left the vehicle and told him that she would call him from LA when her divorce was finalized.

She didn't.

Nor did she call that night. Nor did she answer her cell phone when Henry repeatedly called.

The excuses started to fester in his mind. The time difference. It probably took longer with the judge or whatever than she originally intended. No news is good news. She'll call when she has something to report. Time just got away from her.

But time was getting away from everyone.

Henry spoke to representatives from the airline on Tuesday. Twice. He spoke to a gentleman in Boston and a woman in Los Angeles. She boarded the plane and it arrived safely. The return flight arrived back Logan the following day, Tuesday. The plane was thirty-minutes late, but it too had arrived safely. Kat wasn't on it.

The hotel concierge where she was to spend the night in Los Angeles said that she checked in, but hadn't been back since. The hotel staff took her single bag up to her room, at her request. The bellman left it just inside the door while Katherine re-exited the hotel without going up to the room. Upon Henry's phone call, the concierge purportedly checked the room again, personally. The bag hadn't been moved, nor did it look like the bed had been slept in.

Nobody at her former LA law firm had heard from her either, not that they had expected to. She was handling her divorce herself to save on attorney's fees. She was a phenomenal lawyer, she could certainly handle her own divorce.

Wednesday came and went. Still no word. Still no answer.

Henry decided to do the unthinkable on Thursday. He called Zach. He wasn't thrilled to hear from Henry, but once he heard that the woman he'd still loved was missing, he was more willing to hold a conversation.

According to Zach, she hadn't shown up to the scheduled court hearing. He found it odd, but chalked it up to a missed or late flight. He was legally separated from her, though still married to Katherine Bradar-Gaines, in the eyes of the law. A status he was comfortable with as he clung to any hold on her, no matter the futility.

The LA hospitals and police were of no help. He either wasn't taken seriously or was forced to leave messages. One policeman told him that they had their own missing persons to deal with, they certainly didn't need to solve Boston's.

On Friday, Henry flew to LA.

"Who is your girlfriend again?"

Detective Strayer of the LAPD Missing Persons Unit looked worn out as he sat at his desk across from Henry at 100 West 1st Street in downtown Los Angeles.

Henry would have been sympathetic to the plight of the unappreciated had he himself not been so tired and near hysteria. He had been told time and again that people go missing all of the time, for lots of different reasons, sometimes on purpose. He wanted to break the jaw of the detective that told him that missing women were like sand on the beach.

Detective Strayer felt as though he was as accommodating as possible, considering he had been moving that beach with merely a spoon for over fifteen years.

"Katherine Bradar," Henry said for seemingly the hundredth time. "Technically, still Katherine Bradar-Gaines."

"And how long has she been gone?"

"Like I said, since Monday."

"Address?"

Henry gave them their address on Seaport Boulevard in Boston, Massachusetts.

"Wait," the detective said. "Massachusetts? And you think she's missing here in LA?"

Exasperated, Henry tried to keep calm but was losing the battle. "Yes! We've been over this a hundred times, are you even listening to me? She flew into LAX on Monday afternoon."

"I'm trying to help you, mister. You getting an attitude with me isn't making me want to bend over backwards," Strayer said.

"Aren't you supposed to 'Protect and Serve'?"

"For the people of Los Angeles, sure. Where you from again?"

"Can I get somebody else to help me? You don't seem like you're trying to be helpful," Henry said.

"Maybe she was trying to get away from you. Have you thought of that?"

"Rejected. Not possible. Listen to the facts *ONE* more time, then tell me if that makes any sense at all." Henry went through the timeline and facts as he knew them with the detective one more time. For the first time, Strayer was actually taking notes. Henry thought that a good sign. He again showed the detective a recent picture of Kat, explaining that she was in the detective's city to finalize a divorce to be with him.

"Why would she be getting a divorce to be with me, just to fly back to LA to get away from me? She'd be moving back to the very place she was initially trying to get away from. She was finalizing the divorce to make it permanent. How does that make sense?"

It didn't make sense.

The detective seemed to agree.

"Pretty girl," Strayer said as he looked at the photo. Henry again slid her picture on the desk closer to Strayer.

"Yes, she is. I love her very much and I am losing my grip on sanity. I'm worried and I want some help. I'm begging for help, actually."

"I understand. You have no idea where she is? Just here in Los Angeles? LA is a big place."

"I have no idea. I've given you everything that I know, which isn't much. And not knowing if she's okay is my portion of suffering."

Strayer was still staring at the photo, tapping a pen on his chin in silence.

"I know she was supposed to have a quick hearing in divorce court on Monday, but she never showed up. At all, late or otherwise. Zachary Gaines is definitely someone that you should talk to," Henry added to the uncomfortable silence. But the reticence continued.

"Wait here a sec, will ya?"

Henry said, "Where am I gonna go?"

Strayer was gone for nearly an hour. When he came back, he was different. Softer. Less callous. Prevarication obviously absent.

"I'm sorry to have kept you waiting.   Will you come with me please?"

Henry followed the detective to a parking structure. Strayer told him to get into the unmarked vehicle.

"What's going on?"

"We need to take a ride, Mr. Devlin," Strayer said.

"Where?"

"We think we've located your girlfriend. She used to be a lawyer out here, correct?"

Henry got into the Ford sedan and closed the passenger door. "Yeah, that's right. Where is she?"

Strayer started the car and began to drive out of the parking structure.

"We'll get to that. You get fingerprinted before you take the bar exam. We got a hit on her fingerprint," the detective explained.

Henry didn't like the way Strayer made his last statement.

"What do you mean? Where is she?"

"Like I said, I'm bringing you to her. It's not far," Strayer said.

The detective was right. It wasn't far. Kat was only nine minutes away from the Missing Persons Unit on West 1st Street, in fact.

The detective's unmarked vehicle pulled to the curb on the street in front of a large, brick, municipal-looking building. Strayer put the car in park while Henry tried to ascertain the meaning.

Use It Up

He was dumb-founded and Strayer wasn't making any explanations. The detective thought the signage on the building spoke for itself.

Kat was on North Mission Road.
Katherine Bradar-Gaines was at the Los Angeles County Department of Coroner.

THE THIRTY-NINE YEAR OLD BODY OF KATHERINE Bradar-Gaines lay on a slab in the belly of the morgue in downtown Los Angeles, along with an unborn fetus in hers. Strayer had known that a picture wasn't going to satisfy Henry Devlin, though seeing her cold body and the body of the three-month embryo she was carrying wasn't going to be satisfying either. Quite the opposite, in point of fact. But it was necessary to bring some sense of closure.

The bereaved boyfriend had traveled 3,000 miles to find the woman he loved. He may have known what the result was going to be deep down, but nobody could be fully prepared. Especially not in the way that Katherine Bradar had died.

Henry Devlin tried to keep his emotions in-check while seated in the passenger seat, as the detective's sedan pulled in front of the Coroner's building. Strayer could see it. The detective watched as the look of confusion manifested into a realization. Devlin was refusing to believe what science had already determined, hoping against hope that the fingerprint analysis was a mistake. Strayer watched as the man tried to keep dry eyes. But he could not.

Once inside, there was no denial to cling to. The woman he loved and the child he hadn't known existed were dead. Taken from him.

This was the part of the job that Strayer hated but an unfortunate reality. His job was to bring closure to those with missing loved ones, bring peace to those who had none. He lived for the days when there was a happy ending, when a victim was reunited with their loved ones. For the missing person to be alive and well. But those days were rare, and they almost didn't make up for days like these.

Strayer introduced Henry Devlin to the other detectives involved in the case, from Robbery-Homicide Division, after the body of Katherine Bradar-Gaines was identified.

The boyfriend continually blamed her would-be ex-husband. He shouted the name over and over again. ZACH. ZACHARY GAINES.

But he had it all wrong.

Once Mr. Devlin was able to hear, able to understand, the small group of involved detectives took turns explaining what had ended the life of Katherine Bradar, far too soon. Strayer, along with the two other detectives, sat him down, offered him a terrible cup of coffee, and explained the facts.

CHP conducted a routine traffic stop near the 110, in the dark, early morning hours on Tuesday. The driver was operating the vehicle erratically, and well under the posted speed-limit. There was no reason for the vehicle to drive so slowly, traffic was not yet congested.

California Highway Patrolmen are taught to look for suspicious driving. Paranoid driving. Driving a vehicle thirty miles per hour in a forty-five in Los Angeles, when there's no traffic, either means that the operator is lost, is paranoid about getting pulled over, under the influence, or some combination of the three.

In the words of the CHP officer who wrote the report, "The operator was driving the vehicle like it was stolen, and was attempting to go undetected."

There could have been all sorts of reasons why the driver wouldn't want to be stopped, all of them were reasons to do just that. The operator could have been texting while driving. But experience suggested that the driver was operating illegally in some capacity or another.

The cruiser lights were turned on, the car pulled over to the side of the freeway without incident. Once the pair of California Highway Patrol officers ran the tag, they identified the probable owner of the late-model Nissan. The car hadn't been reported stolen.

As one of the officers approached the driver side of the vehicle, he could see that the female driving was distraught. She looked a mess and insisted that she hadn't done anything wrong. When she handed over her driver's license and registration, the officer noticed blood on the woman's hands. The tags matched the registration, which matched the female's valid driver's license.

He asked the driver if she had cut herself, she answered that she hadn't. He asked if that is why she appeared to have been crying, because she had been injured. The driver insisted that there was nothing wrong. He further inquired if the woman had been drinking, she said that she had not. The operator of the vehicle further tried to exculpate herself from any wrongdoing, saying that she was simply having a tough day. The officer finally asked if she knew why she had been pulled her over. She said that she had no idea, and again insisted that she had done nothing wrong.

When he asked her to step out of the vehicle, the driver attempted to start her vehicle and drive away, but by that time the other officer, who was on the passenger side of the vehicle per regulations, had opened the passenger door. The secondary officer held the gear lever in the center console, between the bucket seats, into park.

The female driver was subsequently removed from the vehicle, put into cuffs and seated on the side of the road. Inspection of the interior of the vehicle produced nothing of value other than dried blood on the steering wheel and center console, likely transferred from the driver's hands.

The dried blood, however, did provide probable cause for the officers to legally search the remainder of the vehicle, including the trunk. It was there that the CHP found the proceeds of a horrible crime.

The opening of the trunk had produced the body of a deceased female.

A team was then brought onto the scene to run it down by the numbers. CHP closed off the closest lane, rerouting traffic, CSU worked the scene for evidence, the body was taken to the morgue for identification, and the female suspect was taken in for questioning.

The female operator, Bailey Gaines, was interrogated for three hours before she confessed to stabbing and killing Katherine Bradar-Gaines. The body of the victim was examined and was determined to have been stabbed more than twenty times, some of her wounds were defensive, though most of the damage was concentrated on the torso.

Ms. Gaines, the accused, further confessed without the presence of counsel, that she had heard of Katherine Bradar's planned trip to Los Angeles from her brother, who was in the final stages of divorcing the victim.

When asked why she planned and executed the murder, Bailey Gaines stated a number of reasons and indicated that she had been planning it for some time. The impetus for timing, being the legal papers she'd recently received from the victim on behalf of her previous boyfriend, Henry Devlin, seeking custody of their mutual seven year old child.

Zachary Gaines was later found and taken into custody, subsequently produced at the Robbery-Homicide Division for questioning. Both Zachary and Bailey Gaines stated separately that the husband of the victim had nothing to do with the murder, that he had no knowledge of what his sister was planning.

The victim was abducted outside of her hotel and forced into the trunk of the Nissan at knifepoint. The car was then driven to Elysian Park several hours later, where the victim was murdered in the trunk. Gaines had planned to dump the body in Elysian Park, under the cover of night, but thought that she had been seen from a distance by the joggers or pedestrians that she'd seen approaching.

She was pulled over and apprehended in the early morning hours searching for an alternate place to dispose of the body.

"Take as much time as you need, Henry. We'll be here takin' care of business for you while you're away," Steven, one of Henry's protégés at Little Leviathan studios, said.

"I can't even imagine," he continued.

"Neither can I, truth be told," Henry said over the phone in the hotel room Kat had checked into a week prior. "I can't even process it." Henry stayed there for the remainder of the week to give statements, make arrangements, and to get his head together. He requested that specific room. It was torture and yet somehow comforting at the same time, though she supposedly hadn't spent any time in the room.

Added to his torment, Zach was fighting him tooth and nail at every turn. About her belongings, about her final wishes, about his son.

"Do you want to talk about it?"

"I don't really know what to say," Henry admitted to his employee.

"Do you know why she did it?"

"I guess she snapped. I cared a lot about Bailey, but not like I loved Kat. She knew that, she always knew that. She wanted to get back at me? Maybe somewhere in her sick mind, she thought that if Kat was gone? That if Kat went away, that all of her and her brother's problems would go away with her? For my son, Kurt? A fucked-up amalgam of all of it? Who knows? Whatever was going on in her head, I can't find in mine."

"So what now, Henry? Gonna stay in LA for a while?"

"I'm gonna be a father for once in my life. I'm not sure where that takes me, but my son needs me. I need him. Zach is going to fight me on custody, though I don't know how an uncle would have parental rights over an actual parent, but he's already said he's going to try. I need to do this for both of us. I need to hold onto Kurt and he needs a father, now more than ever. It's one of the last things Kat said to me. She was going to help me with it."

"Good luck with that. If you need anything, let us know. We'll all be here holding down the fort."

"Thanks. Hey Steve?"

"Yeah Boss?"

"Can I give you a piece of advice?" Henry spoke through the lump in his throat. Tears rolled down his cheeks. Henry fought through the pain in his chest, he needed to impart his knowledge. His feelings.

Henry spoke to his employee and friend 3000 miles east as if it were life and death. Because he felt like it was. His tears dripped down his chin and he spoke from his broken heart, through quivering lips.

"Never leave anything on the table, Steve. This life is so damn short. It just flies by and all of the things that you say, and that you want to do …. Those things that you keep putting off? The important shit? Do it. Find someone to do it with and experience it. Use it up. Every last bit of it. Every minute. Don't save anything for later, because there may not be a later. You don't want to look back on your life and wish you had loved more, or wish you'd *been* loved more. Don't just *look* happy …. *Be* happy.

"The time that I spent with Kat was the best of my life. I gave her my whole heart, and she gave me hers. After years of fighting it, she decided to give me her love. No small thing.

"And it was worth the wait. I felt loved like there was a new meaning to the word. And I gave her all I had. If someone gives that to you, Steve …. Give it back. All of it."

"It's not over, Boss. Maybe your best years are still to come. Another love might just be around the corner."

"Then I didn't give her everything I had, did I?"

AUTHOR'S NOTES AND ACKNOWLEDGEMENTS

The previous work is one of fiction, any resemblance to specific and true incidents is purely coincidental. The names of real places, people, music, etc. are either coincidental or simply to give the story an authentic feel. None of the events that took place in this novel are real to my knowledge.

The bands mentioned in this novel are some of my favorites, true artists who changed rock music forever. Very few are making music such as this today, thus the apparent slow death of the genre. Nirvana was inducted into the Rock and Roll Hall of Fame last year, 2014, the first year of eligibility, and for good reason. Alice in Chains will absolutely be inducted, this year is their first of eligibility. Pearl Jam will be as well, eligible in 2016. Soundgarden has been snubbed up to the writing of this novel, but will absolutely be inducted, in my humble estimation. STP will have to wait until 2017. Why do I mention these dates? Because these artists, among others, were mentioned in this work and changed music — period. Rock music listener or no, these bands, and others like them, changed whatever music you do listen to.

I would first like to state for the record that I took liberties with regard to the rock bands mentioned in the novel. Only those who are serious about alternative rock slash grunge would likely recognize those liberties, but facts are facts and I used them all willy-nilly.

For those the serious Alice in Chains fans, as I am, you will likely scratch your head when looking at the dates where Henry fictitiously worked on the recording of the album Facelift. The album was released in August of 1990, so certainly my main character couldn't have been still engineering it later in that year. It is one of the many liberties I took in order to make my novel correlate between my imagination and what actually occurred in real life.

I concentrated on the use of the history of Pearl Jam with regard to Henry's fictitious career for a variety of reasons, primarily because I am an enormous fan. If ever there was a band to use their fame as a platform for change, and to give back to their fans, Pearl Jam is certainly one. To those band members and their representatives, I sincerely thank you.

The Seattle studio, London Bridge, is real. Some of the recordings that I mentioned in this book were produced there, some not. Again, I was quite liberal with my imagination. Many of the records I listen to were perfected in that building, I have nothing but admiration for the work that they do there.

I would like to take the time to thank those that took the time to speak with me, give me tours, and provide their invaluable expertise. If you enjoyed this book, it is largely because of them. A character or two may have been named in lieu of payment.

Finally, thanks to you, the reader for your time. I hope you enjoyed the story.

-sw-

ABOUT THE AUTHOR

Photo ©2014 WWPGroup

Scott Wellinger is a well-traveled writer and novelist. He has written many articles, scripts, lyrics, and essays under pseudo-names. His more popular novels feature, among others, the fictitious private investigations of Warren Dennihan. A native of New England, he was born in Vermont and was educated in Boston, Massachusetts. He holds a Master's Degree in Applied Economics and when he is not traveling, writing, playing music, cooking or painting, he is on a golf course.

Also by scott wellinger:

Warren Dennihan crime-fiction series:

CRASH

A Warren Dennihan Novel (first of series)

Venom

A Warren Dennihan Novel (book 2)

Sinn

A Warren Dennihan Prequel (book 3)

Ebb

A Warren Dennihan Prequel (book 4)

These novels can be purchased in Ebook and print wherever books are sold.

Thank You for Reading!

If you enjoyed reading this novel, please help others appreciate it as well.

Recommend it.   Please help other readers find it by recommending it to friends, reader groups, discussion boards, or wherever you purchased the book.

Review it.   You can add your thoughts to Amazon, Google, iBooks, at the publisher website (WWPGroup.webs.com), reader clubs like goodreads or LibraryThing, etc.   If you do write a review, please share it with me at scottwellinger@gmail.com so that I can thank you personally.

Follow me on twitter and Instagram for updates and special offers.   @wellinger_scott , and @SCOTT_WELLINGER , respectively.

Best Wishes,

~SW~

www.ingramcontent.com/pod-product-compliance
Lightning Source LLC
Chambersburg PA
CBHW020610260626
47157CB00003B/940